A smile spread across Eric's face

"There's something inside you that warms me." Eric stroked Emma's hand, and a faint shock snapped between them. "You see? Electricity."

Emma laughed, trying not to show the confusion tumbling through her mind. "Static, actually."

"My domesticated Emma," he murmured. "Full of household wisdom and common sense. Except that underneath—who are you really?"

At the moment, she honestly didn't know. A new and unfamiliar Emma was struggling to break free. An Emma who could respond to Eric not with words but with actions, unafraid of his masculine strength or of the demands he might make on her, an Emma eager to please him and herself at the same time.

Where had she come from, this passionate woman? Had she lain buried beneath the surface all these years? And how had Eric managed to awaken her?

ABOUT THE AUTHOR

An incurable dreamer, Jacqueline Diamond has at various times wanted, in vain, to be a librarian, an actress and a playwright. On the other hand, she has succeeded in becoming a news reporter, a novelist and a mother.

Books by Jacqueline Diamond
HARLEQUIN AMERICAN ROMANCE
218–UNLIKELY PARTNERS
239–THE CINDERELLA DARE
270–CAPERS AND RAINBOWS
279–A GHOST OF A CHANCE
315–FLIGHT OF MAGIC
351–BY LEAPS AND BOUNDS

Don't miss any of our special offers. Write to us at the following address for information on our newest releases.

Harlequin Reader Service
P.O. Box 1397, Buffalo, NY 14240
Canadian address: P.O. Box 603,
Fort Erie, Ont. L2A 5X3

JACQUELINE DIAMOND

OLD DREAMS, NEW DREAMS

Harlequin Books

TORONTO • NEW YORK • LONDON
AMSTERDAM • PARIS • SYDNEY • HAMBURG
STOCKHOLM • ATHENS • TOKYO • MILAN

For Pear Wilson
with special thanks to Kelly Oropeza

Published September 1991

ISBN 0-373-16406-8

OLD DREAMS, NEW DREAMS

Printed in U.S.A.

Chapter One

When Genevieve Loos walked into the beauty shop, Emma noted, the mauve-and-silver decor suddenly glistened and a hint of some mysterious perfume breezed through the usual chemical smell.

Hurriedly, Emma swept wisps of hair from around her workstation. She did not want to keep Genevieve Loos waiting.

Eighteen months ago, when a new stylist joined Marta's Beauty Center and brought the retired movie star with her, Emma had recognized her big chance. She'd introduced herself, offered a few tactful suggestions and boldly stepped in six months ago when the other stylist moved back East.

With Genevieve, Emma had achieved the empathy that came with her best clients—the ability to see through the other woman's eyes. The result had been a superb working relationship which, she hoped, would lead to important referrals.

"Emma!" Genevieve advanced through the salon like Queen Elizabeth at the races. "Something simply extraordinary has happened."

The voice had lost none of its rich texture, familiar from musicals of the late fifties and early sixties. Heads swiveled beneath the blow dryers and curling irons.

"Well, don't keep me in suspense!" Emma escorted her client to the shampoo bowl.

"Ah." Genevieve leaned her head back with a dramatic sigh. "You must give me the truth, Emma. You're the only one I can trust. Do you think my hair, well, dates me a little?"

Emma hesitated. The former actress clung to her dramatic upsweep, a look popular several decades before. She'd only allowed Emma to modernize it a little.

The last thing Emma wanted was to antagonize her. But she'd always been honest with Genevieve.

"I think we could make some improvements," she said as she shampooed that famous head. "Is there some special occasion coming up?"

"Indeed." And then, maddeningly, Genevieve closed her eyes and fell silent to enjoy the scalp massage.

Emma tried not to wince at the twinges in her back as she bent to her work. It was already four o'clock, and it didn't help to remember that tonight she worked until nine.

Still, she loved styling hair and always had. In some ways, she supposed, she felt about it as an artist must feel about clay, seeing forms and possibilities where others saw only shapelessness. Finding the techniques—inventing them if necessary—to make the most of a woman's potential challenged and intrigued her.

Ten years before, just out of school, Emma had aimed high. After volunteering to style hair for the school's drama productions and at a community theater, she'd dreamed of becoming a hairdresser for movie stars. After all, Hollywood was just an hour's drive up the freeway from La Habra, California.

She'd never really given up hope, but events seemed to get in her way. No, that wasn't true, Emma told herself firmly as she wrapped a towel around Genevieve's hair and helped her to the workstation.

In truth, Emma's choices had led her in another direction. Accustomed to taking care of her widowed father, she'd felt cast adrift when he'd remarried. Maybe that was why, at nineteen, she'd married Bill; he'd needed her. And then she'd gotten sidetracked trying to have children, suffering several miscarriages before she finally succeeded. Only now...

"What sort of improvements, precisely?" Genevieve wrenched Emma's attention back to the present.

"It would help if you told me what the occasion is," Emma said. "A cruise? A charity ball? Dinner at the White House?"

"Oh, that." Genevieve, having dined with presidents many times, waved a dismissive hand. "No, no."

"Genevieve—you aren't going to be mother of the bride!"

"Oh, heavens, no." Her client's mouth twisted wryly. "Alyssa, get married? To one of those long-haired hooligans in her band? Spare me!"

Genevieve's daughter, the child whom she'd retired from show business to raise, had become America's top female rock singer. Famous for her brassy shock of red hair and her belting contralto voice, Alyssa was also known for her on-again-off-again feuds with her mother.

"Well?" Emma said lightly. "I give up."

Genevieve smiled. "My dear, I'm going to stage a come-back."

Emma didn't have to feign delight. "That's wonderful!"

"Alyssa is broadening her career," Genevieve went on. "She's going to host a music special on TV. She's hoping to get some acting jobs, she says. And since she and I are currently on good terms, she's asked me to guest star."

Emma fluffed her client's hair and examined it in the mirror. "Might I suggest—a little shorter on top, and a touch more curl? Dignified, but more youthful. What do you think?"

"I can never visualize these things," Genevieve said. "But you always come through. You will do my hair for the show, won't you? We'll be taping week after next."

"There's nothing I'd love more." Emma went to work with comb and scissors. "I'll clear my calendar."

Inside, her heart thumped in what felt like a tango. Here it was, her first break. She would have to do such a terrific job that Genevieve would never even consider switching to a more famous stylist.

A short time later, Genevieve examined her new hairstyle in the mirror. To Emma's critical eye, the actress's cheekbones looked more pronounced and the determined squareness of her jaw had softened.

Genevieve turned her head and examined her hair from a different angle. "You know, it does make me look younger. How clever you are, Emma."

"It was fun." She whisked the protective cover from her client's clothes and dusted away leftover bits of fuzz. "I like a challenge."

That was when the idea came to her, full-blown. The step that might, if she were lucky, make a big impression on Hollywood with one fell swoop.

Emma took a deep breath as her client left a generous tip on the table. "Genevieve, thank you. And—well, this may seem a bit presumptuous—"

"My dear." The actress laid a hand on her wrist. "I do realize that you're ambitious. You ought to be, with your skill. You're wasted here. Go ahead and ask."

"I wondered if Alyssa might consider a new look, as well," Emma said. "Since she's broadening her scope."

"You don't have to convince me." Genevieve chuckled. "Do you think I like that hideous red mop? I'll tell you what. Alyssa is coming for dinner Sunday night. Why don't you drop by for coffee afterward? Around seven, perhaps. Then it's up to you.''

Emma kept her tone crisp and professional, while inside she wanted to shout. "Thank you so much.''

"Here's the address.'' Genevieve handed her a card. "I'll see you then.'' And she strode away through the salon, momentarily silencing conversations as, again, everyone turned to look.

"Who did her hair?'' someone asked when Genevieve was gone. "It looks great.''

A shiver ran through Emma as she cleaned up her station and got ready for the next client. Good luck had come calling at last, and she wasn't going to let it get away.

"MOMMY! I CAN'T GET the seat belt off!''

Emma paused on the sidewalk in front of her California bungalow-style home, balancing her oversize purse, Otto's bag of toys and the gallon of milk she'd picked up at the drive-through dairy. "Could you try again, honey? I don't have any extra hands.''

"I can't do it!'' Otto declared with three-year-old fervor. He wasn't even trying to unhook the belt from around his booster seat.

"Honey—''

"Why's it so dark?'' Otto asked.

"Because it's nine-thirty at night.'' Emma sighed.

"Why is it?''

"Otto!'' Emma set her purse on top of the car to help him out. "You know I work till nine on Fridays.''

"I know,'' he said sadly. "I miss you.''

"Did you have a good time at Roy's house?'' she countered as she helped him out, slammed the car door and scooped up her purse with the dexterity of a circus contortionist, or an experienced mother.

"He's got all the Transformers and a fire truck," said Otto, to whom his four-year-old friend's house was almost as exciting as Disneyland. "Why does he?"

"Because his daddy buys them for him." Emma unlocked the door and switched on the light with her elbow as she staggered inside. Her feet hurt, and right now not even the prospect of redesigning Alyssa's hair could raise much excitement.

She needed a cup of coffee and a bath. And lots of hugs and cuddles from her little boy.

That first year, when she'd only worked a few days a week to supplement Bill's earnings, she and Otto had spent joyful mornings at Mommy and Me classes and blissful afternoons at the park.

Since Bill's death and her return to full-time work, their moments together had become even more precious. Otto attended preschool during the day, and her two best friends helped out with baby-sitting the evenings she worked.

"Can I watch *Bambi?*" Otto padded along like an eager puppy as Emma made her way into the kitchen. "Can I have some pudding? Can I have juice in a bottle?"

"You're too old for a bottle," she said automatically as she put the milk away.

"But I'm thirsty," Otto protested. "Please, Mommy?"

In the full glare of the track lighting, Emma got a good look at her son for the first time that night.

His large dark eyes, so like her own, were surrounded by black smudges. The curly blond hair, just like his father's, clumped together at the top where Roy must have poured something over it.

"What did you two do, roll in the mud?" Emma closed her eyes for a moment. When she opened them, he was still there, and still dirty. "Bath time, fella."

"I don't wanna take a bath!" Even as he spoke, Otto began pulling off his Big Bird sweatshirt. It got stuck around the upper arms. "Help me, Mommy!"

Emma knelt and gave him a hug, then eased the shirt off. "You poor baby! I've hardly seen you all day and I just want to hold you."

"Can I have my milk?" Otto asked.

"In a cup." Emma glanced wistfully at the empty coffeemaker. "And one bath, coming right up."

Fifteen minutes later she felt much calmer. Otto had been scrubbed and was blowing soap bubbles through a pipe, giggling as they landed on the water. She'd given herself a pedicure while Otto bathed, and the house was warming up against the February coldness.

"Mommy!" Otto said. "My hands are all wrinkled!"

He kept up a running chatter as she dried him and helped put on his pajamas. Only then did she notice that the water hadn't drained out of the tub.

"Did you open the drain?" He nodded earnestly. Emma checked. Sure enough, the drain was open.

"Is it backed up again?" Otto said.

"Looks like it." Hoping against hope that it would gradually clear out, Emma steered her sleepy son into his bedroom. Sitting on the edge of the bed, she read him two books and then went over the events of his day, first at preschool and then at her friend Betsy's house. Finally she kissed him good-night and turned off the lights.

Please, she prayed silently, let the tub be empty. I won't even try to take a bath myself, I promise.

But the brownish water just sat there, not an inch lower than when she'd last checked.

Emma leaned against the door frame, feeling exhausted. She and Bill had talked about the dangers of his being a firefighter, but La Habra was such a quiet town, she hadn't expected anything to happen. A lousy cigarette, a roof that collapsed unexpectedly—none of it seemed significant enough to have taken Bill away.

She hadn't been ready to lose him. Not just because she and Otto needed him, but because there was so much unfinished business between them. And especially between him and Otto.

Why was it, Emma wondered as she called and left a message with the plumbing service, that such a good man could resent his own infant son? Not that Bill hadn't tried to be a good father, but he'd lacked patience. And he'd missed having Emma's undivided attention.

All those years, after her miscarriages, he'd been unfailingly kind and understanding. Each time, they'd taken a vacation together, had played on the beach and enjoyed long luxurious dinners.

Of course she'd missed that, after Otto came, but the baby had been so perfect, so tiny and amazing. She could still smell his slightly soapy innocence, feel the exploratory grasp of little fingers on her hair and see the toothless grin as Otto propped himself up on chubby arms and welcomed her to his crib in the morning.

It had hurt and puzzled her, seeing the irritable look on Bill's face when she left his arms to answer Otto's call. She didn't like the fact that their last year together had been so difficult. Surely he would have changed, as the boy grew old enough to talk and play games with Daddy.

"Mommy!" Otto called from the bedroom. "Come give me 'nother kiss!"

Emma hurried in. Gathering the boy in her arms, she kissed his sweet little face and cuddled his body as he relaxed into sleep. She sat on in the dark for a while, holding him, wishing that fate had given Bill time to fall in love with the miracle that was his son.

THE WATER WAS still sitting in the tub the next morning as Emma wandered into the bathroom at seven o'clock, awakened by an unsympathetic internal clock.

She glanced blearily into the mirror and then quickly away. Her brown hair, short and curly on top and hanging straight to her shoulders, lay limp and dull against her neck.

Emma made her way to the kitchen, musing that it was a good thing Alyssa Loos couldn't see her looking like this; she certainly wasn't much of a walking advertisement for her own services.

On the other hand, she didn't suppose even Alyssa looked all that terrific first thing in the morning.

What *was* she going to do about Alyssa's hair, anyway? Emma wondered as she measured coffee into the filter. Would the singer go for a dramatic change? A client's personality was as important as her hair type in determining what style to choose. Maybe Emma should work up some drawings, except that her pictorial talents were confined to the stick figures she drew for Otto.

As she was dropping her bread into the toaster, a familiar voice began chattering from the bedroom.

"Mommy!" Otto called. "I want my Breakfast Bears!"

Mentally, Emma weighed whether to fight him over the cereal, which wasn't much better than eating graham crackers. She decided to cook oatmeal and hope for the best.

A short time later, Otto was drinking his juice and eyeing the oatmeal. "Is this good?" he said.

"Delicious." Emma poured out a cup of coffee.

After a moment's internal debate, Otto began eating.

As she ate, Emma contemplated the chores she had lined up. Grocery shopping, and checking beneath the hood of her car. If she was careful, she could postpone a tune-up for another month or two.

She earned a decent income, but it never stretched quite far enough. And she'd be taking a big chance, postponing other appointments to work exclusively on Genevieve for however long the taping lasted. It was a risk worth taking, but Emma had more than herself to consider.

Still, it looked like the weather was going to be beautiful, one of those special days that brighten up Southern California even in February. She and Otto could pack a picnic lunch and go to Oeste Park this afternoon. Otto loved swooping down the slide and clambering up the play rocketship.

"Did I eat enough?" asked the subject of her thoughts, pushing away his bowl. "Can I have bears now?"

The doorbell rang. Otto started to get up.

"Stay there," Emma said. "It's probably some kid selling chocolate."

The doorbell rang again, loudly and merrily. "Plumber!" came a masculine announcement.

"Don't leave!" Emma hurried into the living room. Only as she opened the door did she remember that she was still wearing her bathrobe and looking like a refugee from an all-night horror film festival.

"Hi," said the last man she'd ever expected to see, leaning in the doorway.

Chapter Two

Eric Jameson. Even in overalls and a plumber's cap, there was something commanding about his presence.

His light blue eyes examined Emma with friendly but impersonal curiosity. There was no reason why he should remember her, and yet Emma felt oddly disappointed. They'd spent only one afternoon together, many years ago, but in those few hours they'd touched each other in a special way. Or at least, so it seemed to her.

Eric's high-cheekboned face had matured in the ten years since high school, although an unruly shock of sandy hair still curled like a question mark across his forehead. But what was the La Habra High School class president, the son of the city's former mayor, doing in a plumber's uniform?

"Mrs. Lindt?" He studied her reaction curiously. "Is something wrong?"

"No—I'm sorry." She stood back, wiping her hands on her bathrobe. "You're from J&J Plumbing?"

"Your message said something about a plugged drain." He stepped inside, tool kit in hand, and looked at her again. She thought for a moment he had recognized her, but he gave no sign of it. Still, he was studying her with an intensity that sent a warm rush across her cheeks.

"Actually—" she began.

"I'm sorry. I don't know why—" he said at the same time, and then Otto appeared in the kitchen doorway, still wearing his bib and clutching a box of Breakfast Bears.

"Is this the plumber?" he asked. "Is he gonna fix the tub?"

"I sure am." Eric squatted down so he and the boy met at eye level. "What's your name?"

"Otto. I'm three."

"I'm Eric and I'm twenty-eight. Those look good."

"You want some?" Otto asked.

"Honey!" Emma shot him what was meant to be a quelling look, but her son ignored it. He knew she wasn't going to escort him back to the table right now and force him to eat oatmeal, so he thrust a hand into the cereal box and held some out to Eric.

"We can share," Otto explained.

"Sounds like a good idea." Solemnly, Eric helped himself to a few sticky bears, then straightened. "Now, where's that tub?"

"Through here." Emma led the way down the hall, wondering if he would notice the photographs that lined it, especially the one from Emma's high school graduation.

But Eric's attention was focused on the job. "If it's just some hair, we'll have it cleaned out in no time."

"I hope so." Emma caught Otto as he tried to follow Eric into the bathroom. "It's time to finish that cereal and get dressed."

Ignoring his protests, she steered her son back to the kitchen, listening with half her attention to the clinking as Eric tried to clear out the drain.

Eric Jameson. She'd thought of him in momentary flashes, wondering about what might have been. By now, he should have finished architecture school and begun changing the way homes would be designed in the twenty-first century.

Mostly out of curiosity about Eric, she'd regretted not being able to go to their class reunion last summer, but she and Otto had both come down with the flu.

She'd imagined Eric strolling into the reunion with a beautiful and accomplished wife on his arm, and pictured him quietly dominating his fellow alumni. There had always been a sense of coiled tension about him, as if he were merely pausing on his way to some vital destination. It had made everyone listen carefully to whatever he'd said.

What was he doing working for J&J Plumbing?

In the back of her mind, Emma recalled that Eric's father had died years ago. Harlan Jameson, a prominent physician and former mayor, had made the front page of the *La Habra-Brea Star-Progress* when he collapsed of a heart attack right after performing a kidney transplant. But surely he'd left enough money to see his children through college.

"Mom?" Otto said. "Can I wear my Mickey Mouse T-shirt?"

"In February?" Emma shook her head. "How about your Magic Bees sweatshirt?"

Getting his consent, she escorted her son to his bedroom. While he went ahead, she glanced in to see Eric retrieving his plumber's snake from the drain.

"Bad news, I'm afraid." He rinsed black muck off his equipment. "The problem is outside. I don't know how serious it is, but I'll have to do some digging."

"Oh, dear." It sounded expensive, but Emma couldn't very well leave her plumbing permanently plugged. "That's the trouble with having pipes that are older than you are."

Eric gave her a sideways grin that lit up his face, triggering an unexpected warmth in her chest. "I like these older homes, though. They seem so sure of themselves, so solid."

"Yes, but you don't have to pay somebody else to unclog your bathtub," she pointed out.

His eyes never left hers. "I suppose that is a disadvantage. Your husband isn't the handyman type?"

"My husband died two years ago." Seeing that he was about to apologize, Emma said, "He was a fireman. And he was pretty handy around the house."

"A lot of women are taking do-it-yourself classes these days." Eric packed up his equipment. "Not that I recommend you try something like this yourself." As he moved toward the doorway, he paused a few feet from Emma. There was plenty of room for him to pass, but he didn't seem in a hurry.

She pulled her bathrobe tighter, but she wasn't eager to move, either. Seeing Eric in her home redefined all the spaces and infused the air with an unfamiliar energy. "Do you—want some coffee?"

"No, thanks." He hesitated as if about to ask a question, then turned and strode toward the back door.

He couldn't place her, Emma decided. She'd have to refresh his memory—but not while she looked like a specimen from *Fright Night*.

It took only a few minutes to dress Otto and turn him loose in the backyard to watch Eric. Then she went to her closet and selected a pair of trendy jeans and a new yoked shirt that gathered around the hips with a buckle.

This was silly, Emma scolded herself as she fluffed her hair and attacked it with the stiffest hair spray she could find. It didn't really matter how she looked, did it? She wasn't some adolescent still in high school.

High school. She felt as if it had been ten decades ago instead of ten years.

Everyone at La Habra High had been aware of Eric. Not just because he was senior class president, but because of the indefinable sparkle that filled the air whenever he came near. No one had doubted that he would be someone special when he grew up.

He'd gone steady with Sally Monroe, the captain of the girls' basketball team. Their friends had been the school leaders, mostly well-to-do kids who went on to top-rank colleges. Sally, Emma recalled, had headed back East to Wellesley.

Emma's boyfriend in those days, Jerry Ramis, was a camera freak who now owned a photography studio in nearby Fullerton. Their relationship had never been more than casual, the result of being thrown together in the same circle of friends.

Emma had hung out with a slightly rowdy group from blue-collar backgrounds. Looking back, she could see that although she'd enjoyed their company, she hadn't been intimate with any of her group. Even her old girlfriends had drifted away after their marriages.

She'd rarely mentioned her ambitions. It had seemed preposterous to imagine that she might actually make a career for herself in Hollywood. Yet she'd had an undeniable flair for hairstyling, even then, and Emma had volunteered to fix actors' hair at the local community theater and for the school plays.

That was when she discovered the change that took place in her while she worked. She became a different person: more confident, more alive. The prospect of pleasing an audience filled her with excitement.

Emma would never forget one community theater performance of the romantic comedy *Cactus Flower* for a senior citizen audience. Afterward she'd watched an elderly couple emerge arm in arm, their eyes twinkling, their step light. For one dizzying moment, she'd looked past their wrinkled faces to witness the two young lovers who still lived inside. The realization that she had played a part, however small, in their enjoyment had buoyed Emma all the way home.

So when some brave soul chose *Romeo and Juliet* for the
senior play, Emma had volunteered as hairdresser. She
couldn't remember now who'd played the title roles, but
Eric had been cast as Mercutio.

Their brief encounter had occurred one rainy afternoon
in March when they both showed up for a dress rehearsal,
only to find it had been canceled. Faced with a solid sheet
of rain outside, they'd decided to wait rather than get
soaked.

Emma could still smell the mustiness of the auditorium
and hear the hazy thrum of rain on the roof. They'd sat side
by side, their feet propped on the back of the next row of
seats, sharing an orange Emma had brought with her.

She hadn't known what to say at first, so she'd made
small talk. Where was he going to college? When he said
California State Polytechnic University, Pomona, she'd
wondered aloud why he hadn't chosen the more prestigious
University of California.

"Because I'm going to be an architect and I like their
program," Eric had said. "We're going to need a whole new
approach to housing in the twenty-first century. All the rules
will be different, Emma. Not many people understand
that."

Fascinated, she'd listened as he explained that shortages
of land and energy were going to change the way houses had
to be designed. "We could end up with ugly, cramped places
like those apartments in the Soviet Union," he warned.
"But it doesn't have to be that way."

His dream, Eric said, involved using airy, eye-tricking
lines to make smaller units seem spacious. Moreover, clustering houses around joint recreational facilities would encourage community spirit, a return to small-town
neighborliness.

"Architects help determine what societies are like," Eric
had declared. "We need a vision."

Enthralled, Emma had listened for a long time before she hesitantly confided her own dreams. She hadn't expected Eric to take much interest, but he understood instinctively that she wasn't some star-struck airhead. Nor did he dismiss hairstyling as a matter of vanity.

"The world is shrinking," he'd said. "What we see on TV and in the movies brings us together, helps us understand each other. And images help to shape how we think."

Looking back, she supposed his words might have sounded overly grandiose to an adult, but they suited her eighteen-year-old idealism perfectly, and Eric's encouragement had stuck in Emma's mind. When she got sidetracked over the years, she'd allowed herself to keep on dreaming, and had gradually steered herself back on course partly because once, long ago, someone who mattered had thought that her goals mattered, too.

"Mrs. Lindt?" Calling from the back door, Eric's deep voice echoed through the house. "Could you come here for a minute?"

"Right away." Emma finished putting on her lipstick and hurried out.

She emerged to see Otto sitting astride his tricycle, studying the plumber's tools with fascination.

Eric gestured ruefully toward the hole he'd punched in the ground. "I've been trying to clean this thing out but I'm not having much luck." He indicated the metal coil called a snake, to which fresh earth still clung. "I'm afraid your problem is tree roots. We're going to have to dig up a section of pipe and replace it."

The fenced yard was one of Emma's favorite features of the house, especially since a huge tree shaded most of the area in summer. Unfortunately, as Eric pointed to the line beneath which lay her drainage pipe, she could see that it ran dangerously close to the trunk. "Is—is this going to be expensive?" she asked.

"I could help," Otto said. "I'm a good digger."

"I'll bet you are." Eric turned to Emma. "I'm afraid this is going to take a couple of guys with strong backs...." He stopped and stared at her with an expression she couldn't read.

He'd recognized her, all right. But what on earth was he thinking?

ERIC JAMESON had awakened that morning with the sense that he'd missed a turn somewhere.

Maybe he owed it to having celebrated his twenty-eighth birthday yesterday, this nagging sense that thirty was sneaking up on him and he still lived in his parents' ranch-style house, far from achieving what he'd intended.

Restlessly, Eric climbed out of bed and headed for the bathroom. On the way, he passed his computer, beside which lay a graphics printout of a futuristic city. It wasn't complete—he hadn't yet considered all the transportation needs and the effects of a changing climate—and, as always, he had to fight the temptation to sit down and lose himself in the program. He had real work to do and, for the present, that meant plumbing.

In the bathroom, Eric paused to listen to his twenty-year-old brother, Peter, snoring in the adjacent bedroom. It was hard to believe Peter had grown up so quickly.

Eight years ago, as a sophomore at Cal Poly, Pomona, Eric had walked dreamily through a landscape of overlays, of buildings that faded when he looked at them, remodeled by his imagination. He could almost touch the future, not too far away, when his youthful visions would be translated into stunning reality.

And then, on an April day that basked in sunshine, he received a halting call from his mother: Dad had collapsed at the hospital and been rushed to intensive care.

Eric arrived to learn that his father had died half an hour earlier.

More bad news came a few days later. Dad had let the premium lapse on his life insurance, and had lost much of the family's savings in a bad business investment. There wasn't enough money left to support their mother and Peter, let alone finance Eric's education.

So he'd had to find a job. Fortunately Dad's brother, Irwin, owned a plumbing business and had no children of his own. He took Eric in and taught him the trade.

When Uncle Irwin died three years later, he left the business to his nephew. Working twelve hours a day, seven days a week, Eric had helped support his family and had begun saving a nest egg. He enjoyed the work, liked using his hands and helping solve people's problems, but always he looked forward to moving on to something more intellectually stimulating.

At first, the savings had been intended for Peter's education, but Peter hated school and loved working. Reluctantly, Eric and their mother agreed that Peter didn't have to go to college.

And so, after eight years, the wheel had turned again. By this fall, Peter would be able to take over the business and Eric could return to college.

He faced a long haul: three more years of studies, followed by a lengthy internship before he could even take the state exam. By then, he'd be in his mid-thirties.

But he couldn't wait. This fall, his life would begin in earnest.

Restlessly, Eric finished washing and went into the kitchen. Stella Jameson looked up as he came in. "You could have sent Peter out on that call," she said.

"Let him sleep. He'll be working his tail off soon enough." The familiar sight of his mother puttering about in the kitchen filled Eric with an unexpected sense of peace.

Stella Jameson loved everything about being a mother and a homemaker. Although she'd worked for the past eight years as a salesclerk at the Brea Mall, she always cooked a hearty breakfast for her sons.

Eric regarded his mother lovingly, scarcely noticing how gray her hair had become. Any sacrifice he'd made for her these past few years was worth it.

As she set a plate of pancakes and a cup of coffee in front of him, Stella said, "Did you hear Mary Winston is getting married?"

"No. Who's the lucky guy?" Eric had dated Mary a few times, but nothing serious had developed.

"I don't know." Stella sighed and sat across from him, sipping her tea.

Eric regarded her with a twist of amusement. "Mom, you're getting that 'I-want-grandchildren' glint in your eyes again."

His mother blushed. "I'm in no hurry."

"The heck you're not." Ever since his mother's best friend had become grandmother to twin girls, Stella had developed a fascination with little children. And eligible women.

"It never hurts to plant an idea," she said. "In case you run into the right person and are too thickheaded to realize it."

"She'd have to be awfully patient," Eric said. "I've got a long stretch ahead of me."

Stella reached over with a fork and stole a bite of pancake from his plate. "I know, but—Eric, you push yourself so hard. I'm proud of you, and I admire your persistence. But you need to enjoy your life, too."

"I do." He smiled reassuringly. "Mom, for heaven's sake, I do date once in a while. And I've got you guys, and my computer."

"A well-rounded life." His mother's tone verged on irony, which surprised him.

"What's going on with you?"

"Oh, nothing." Stella waved her hand. "Your birthday yesterday just stirred up some memories. Like how your dad was always postponing the day when he could relax and spend time with us."

"I'm not Dad," Eric said automatically.

He knew his mother was right, though. Eric didn't doubt that his father had loved him, but Harlan never made it a priority to spend time together. The only time he'd paid much attention was when Eric won some honor.

Well, Eric wouldn't be that way when he had children, but that was a long time off, thank goodness.

Eric was still mulling all the ways he wasn't like his father when he arrived at the Lindt home. And then the door opened, chasing away his thoughts and leaving him unaccountably tongue-tied.

It was the inquisitive brown eyes that did him in, Eric decided. Emma Lindt had a small, intelligent face and a curious gaze that pierced the wall he kept between himself and most people.

He found himself strikingly aware of her quick, graceful movements and of the delicate shoulders briefly visible under her oversize bathrobe. Most of all, Eric kept feeling that he knew her from somewhere, that he had lost her and shouldn't take the chance of losing her again.

But it wasn't until now, when he saw her with her hair tumbling free and her eyebrows darkened to quizzical peaks, that he placed her at last. Emma Conrad!

He'd thought about her occasionally these past ten years, wishing he hadn't let the opportunity pass to get to know her better. At the time, though, he'd been so focused on heading off to college that he hadn't been about to start a new relationship.

And then, after his father's death, something else had held Eric back. He didn't want to be the old schoolmate who never made it. Yet he realized now that inside, he'd been hoping to see her again.

Only apparently life hadn't worked out the way she'd expected, either. Running into her was a pleasure, but he couldn't help wishing she'd achieved more of her own ambitions.

"Hi." She gave an embarrassed shrug. "Sorry I didn't identify myself earlier, but I wasn't expecting you."

"I wasn't exactly expecting you, either." Since their high school days, her pixyish quality had mellowed, Eric realized. She held herself with the confidence of a woman—and he found himself yearning to explore all the ways in which she'd become a woman.

Climbing off his trike, Otto moved protectively alongside his mother. "This is my mommy," he announced, as if the fact weren't obvious.

"And she belongs to you, right?" Eric's eyes met Emma's. "Your little man knows how to protect his territory. I don't blame him."

He wasn't sure why he'd said that. Eric didn't usually flirt, but with Emma, he didn't feel as if he were indulging in anything as superficial as flirting. More as if he wanted to get close to her, to watch the sunlight reflect off her expressive eyes and find out what she was thinking and where she had been all these years.

"Otto." Emma knelt beside her son and gave him a hug. "Eric and I are old friends. We went to high school together."

"When is he gonna fix the tub?" Otto said, unappeased.

Emma regarded Eric apologetically. "I'm sorry. You were saying something about men with strong backs."

"I'm afraid so." Reluctantly, he pulled out his calculator and worked out the sum.

When he named it, Emma flinched, then quickly disguised her reaction with a shrug. "I guess that's the price we pay for having a tree."

She's a widow with a little boy—money must be tight, he thought. Darn it, he didn't want to be the cause of her distress. "I'll tell you what," Eric said. "I have to charge for my out-of-pocket expenses, but that should knock it down to..." The figure he named was half his previous amount.

"I don't want charity." Emma lifted her chin.

"Why not?" Otto piped in.

"Because we pay for what we get," she told him sternly.

Eric tucked his calculator into his pocket. "I wouldn't feel right, charging you full price."

"It's not as if—I mean, we didn't know each other *that* well," Emma pointed out. "You certainly don't owe me anything."

"No, I don't," Eric agreed. "But put yourself in my position. Wouldn't you want to give an old friend a break? Listen, you've got to have this work done. Why don't I go ahead and get some guys to dig up your pipe, and we'll worry about the price later?"

"Okay," Emma said slowly.

He wanted to reassure her further, but Eric sensed that might simply get her back up. He didn't often feel like rescuing damsels in distress—anyway these days most damsels were plenty capable of rescuing themselves. But with Emma, he felt a boyish urge to make a grand gesture.

"I'll be back in a couple of hours." Eric collected his tools before she could change her mind. "See you later, Otto."

"See ya."

Eric swung around the side of the house and exited through the gate, noticing that the hinges squeaked and the latch was coming loose. She needed a man around here.

Not that he was in the market for anything serious. Neither was she, most likely; Emma had plenty to keep her busy, with that little imp of a son.

But he wanted to find out what had happened to her dreams. And he missed having a friend to listen to his ideas and get excited about his plans.

He needed a friend, the way Emma could have been in high school, if they'd found each other earlier. And he suspected she could use a friend, too.

Eric chuckled to himself as he climbed into his van. He'd have to be careful not to let his mother get the wrong idea.

"I'M A PLUMBER, TOO," Otto informed his mother, and trotted over to the sandbox he'd been ignoring for weeks. A few minutes later, he was happily digging his own little trench.

Why, Emma wondered as she retreated into the house, had she let Eric go ahead? He'd never let her pay the full price, and she hated to take advantage.

Yet he'd made a good point; in his place, she'd act the same way. Emma liked being able to do others a favor, and she supposed it was only fair to allow him the same satisfaction.

Only she hadn't felt as if Eric were merely being kind. Not that he seemed to expect anything in return, either. In fact, she wasn't sure exactly what she had sensed about him; several times, she'd caught him staring at her, and yet his manner had never been more than politely friendly.

For one moment, as she hauled out the vacuum cleaner to begin her Saturday housecleaning, Emma indulged in a flight of fancy. She visualized Eric, stunning in a dark suit, arriving to spirit her away to an exquisite restaurant where they'd lean across the table and whisper to each other by candlelight.

She shook her head and headed for the living room. Romantic musings were all very well, but in reality the prospect of being courted by Eric Jameson would scare the heck out of her.

He might be working as a plumber, but he hadn't lost any of that taut energy. Whatever he applied himself to, he was going to succeed at it.

That was a good trait, of course. But Emma knew she had a natural instinct to take care of other people, to put their interests first. She'd given up most after-school activities to keep house for her father, when he could just as easily have taken his clothes to the cleaners and eaten frozen dinners. And then when Bill came along, she'd scaled down her career and kept her schedule flexible to suit his.

With a man as forceful as Eric, Emma knew, she'd have to fight like crazy not to lose herself. Of course, she was older and more confident now, but she was also, finally, on the verge of a breakthrough in her career.

Well, the issue would probably never come up. After her plumbing got fixed, it might be another ten years before she saw Eric again. Or they could maybe have coffee once in a while, maintain a light friendship. . . .

Resolutely, Emma turned to her cleaning.

The rest of the day went by quickly. Otto didn't require much entertaining, not with a couple of laborers digging through their backyard and Eric dropping by from time to time to check on the work. She hoped to get a chance to talk with him about how his plan to become an architect had gotten sidetracked, but the occasion didn't arise. The pipe was laid, the laborers left and the dinner hour came and went. Somehow Eric had managed to get the tub to drain and depart without Emma realizing it.

Trying not to feel disappointed, she fed and bathed Otto, shared his favorite Winnie-the-Pooh story with him for the fiftieth time, and put him to bed.

A few minutes later, reading in the living room, she heard a tap at the door. Surprised, Emma set her book aside and answered it.

"You weren't sleeping, were you?" Eric had changed out of his plumber's uniform into a blue pullover sweater. His slicked-back hair bespoke a shower.

"No, I—" Seeing him here at night, with the house quiet around them, made Emma's breath come quickly. "The—the tub drains great."

"I'm so glad." His mouth quirked into a smile. "I'd hate to dig up half your yard and not solve the problem."

"You're good at your work, which is exactly what I would have expected." She stepped back to let him in.

Emma tried to picture how the house looked to Eric, wanting him to like it. The architecture wasn't exactly Frank Lloyd Wright, but the California bungalow had a 1920's charm and she'd decorated in colorful Art Deco.

"You've nested." His voice sounded gentle. "A person could get comfortable here."

"I've made coffee." She led the way into the kitchen, where a Tiffany hanging lamp cast colored reflections around the room.

As she fetched cups, Emma tried in vain to fluff up hair that had gone limp during a sweaty stint with the vacuum cleaner. "You'd never guess I was a hairdresser," she muttered.

Eric turned a chair backward and sat down. "So you are a stylist, after all."

She poured their coffee. "Yes, but Bill didn't like me to work long hours. And then it took us a long time to have children. It's only now that I'm starting to make things happen."

"Good for you." Amber light swayed across Eric's strong features, giving his eyes a mysterious cast. "Tell me about Bill the fireman."

"We had fun together," Emma said. "And he needed taking care of. If nobody fed him, he'd forget to eat. And the laundry could never do his shirts right…." She stopped, hearing her own words as if through a stranger's ears. "I suppose that's why he seemed to resent Otto. But he would have gotten over it. How about you? Are you married?"

Eric shook his head. "No time. I've been supporting my mom and my brother and saving up. I'll be going back to Cal Poly this fall."

So his father's death had left them strapped, after all. "Looks like we've both had to wait awhile, but we're back on track."

"I don't think I could have waited any longer," Eric admitted.

They both fell silent, swept by memories. Watching emotions flicker across his face, Emma felt a momentary dizziness. Was Eric Jameson really sitting in her kitchen?

From time to time this past decade, she'd imagined him here, phrased what she would say, even told herself that he would understand why she hadn't reached her goals yet. Then she'd laughed at her own fancies, supposing Eric by now to be well established in Los Angeles or New York.

"Our tenth high school reunion," he said. "Did you go?"

"Otto and I had the flu. How was it?"

A shadow fell across his eyes, or maybe it was a trick of the light. "I didn't go, either, and I don't have an excuse. I'm a coward."

"Because you're a plumber?" Without thinking, Emma leaned forward and touched his arm. The contact felt more intimate than she'd expected, and yet she didn't want to overreact, so she left her hand in place for a moment. "Eric,

I can't believe anyone would look down on you. It's a good, honest job."

"And it pays well." He twisted the coffee cup around in his hands. "Sally's an assistant prosecutor in Boston. My friend Ted's doing his residency in surgery at Stanford. I'm pleased for them, and I like the work I'm doing. But I always thought I'd still be the leader of the pack."

Part of Emma wanted to reassure him that in his own way he'd accomplished much more, taking on responsibility for his family, but she knew more than pride was at stake. Eric's self-image was bound up in his accomplishments.

Instead, she said, "You'll get there. This is life, not some half-hour sitcom. Nobody expects us to work out all our problems and come up a winner by the next commercial break."

The look Eric gave her was full of appreciation and something more, a connection that reached right inside Emma and made her quiver. "I've missed you," he said.

"Me, too." Then, since she couldn't think of anything to add, she said, "More coffee?"

"No, I— Oh, before I forget." Eric pulled a windowed envelope from his pocket and laid it on the table. "I talked to my brother, who's my partner, and he wouldn't hear of charging you full price. And there's no hurry."

"I don't feel right about this," Emma said.

"There is something I'd like." Eric stood up and carried his cup to the sink. "A home-cooked meal. And a chance to talk some more. Are you free tomorrow night?"

On the point of consenting, Emma remembered her commitment. "I can't. I'm meeting with a client—Genevieve Loos—about a possibility that might help my career. Could we make it next weekend?"

"Saturday at six? I'll bring the wine."

"I hope you like lasagne." Emma stood up reluctantly, not wanting him to leave yet. "I'm glad we've met again. It makes me feel as if not so much time has gone by, after all."

"I haven't felt like a kid in a long while," he agreed. "And I'd kill for lasagne."

She saw him to the door, then sat in the living room, bits and pieces of memory bubbling up—silly incidents, long-forgotten faces, a whole teenage world that had faded unnoticed.

Through the center of it walked the youthful Eric Jameson, his boyishness overlaid now with the multifaceted man he had become. A man Emma was only beginning to know.

Chapter Three

Genevieve Loos lived in nearby La Habra Heights, an area that retained its rural character with multi-acre lots, meandering roads, horse stables and individualized homes that ranged from cottages to mansions.

In the February darkness, Emma had to backtrack several times along narrow streets, looking for signs half-hidden among oleander hedges, before she found the winding driveway that led to Genevieve's estate.

The house turned out to be an impressive mock-Tudor structure with a view over the lights of La Habra. Emma circled to the back, where she parked her compact next to a fiery Maserati that must belong to Alyssa.

From here, she could see steam rising from the lighted pool, but there was no one outdoors in the chilly night. Emma sat in her car for a moment, trying to steel her nerve.

Did everyone have a little voice within that muttered, at times like these, "Who do you think you are?" Emma didn't suppose so; some people, like Alyssa Loos, appeared to possess endless self-confidence.

At twenty-three, Alyssa was already the veteran of five years on the hit charts. She'd won Grammy Awards for her vocals and songwriting, and had already stayed on top far longer than most singers. Five years, in pop music, was like two decades in any other field, Emma reflected.

And now she had the nerve to try to tell Alyssa that she needed to remake herself in order to tackle an acting career. Surely Alyssa already employed enough managers and agents to fashion whatever image suited her best.

Except that Emma could do something they couldn't, something entirely instinctive. She could, if she and Alyssa struck the right note, if she could get inside her client's mind. She had a gift for taking account of the whole person and tailoring a style for her.

More than that, Emma really wanted Alyssa to succeed. Maybe, as her friends sometimes teased, it was her mothering instinct, but she cared whether a client made a hit at her dinner party, or impressed a new suitor, or simply felt better about herself.

Although Alyssa's music was a bit strident for Emma's taste, she admired the young woman's originality and panache. Furthermore, she couldn't help seeing Alyssa as Genevieve's fiercely loved daughter.

She's *got* to hire me, Emma decided as she emerged from the car and took a deep breath of cold air. For her sake as much as mine.

At the front door, Emma rang the bell. She wasn't sure what she expected to find, although rumor had it that Genevieve and Alyssa occasionally had screaming, plate-throwing fights. It was hard for Emma to imagine her gracious client ever behaving that way, and certainly tonight there was no sound but the crisp rustle of a chill wind in the trees.

The door opened and a maid in a black dress and white apron admitted her. The entrance hall arched upward for two stories, framing a gleaming circular staircase that could have come from a movie set. Emma's pumps clicked loudly as she crossed the marble floor.

She followed the maid through an octagonal living room graced with an oversize sofa and fireplace, and passed into

the dining room. There, at opposite ends of a mahogany
table, sat the regal Genevieve and her daughter, relaxing as
a manservant removed their plates.

Emma had only an instant to appraise Alyssa. In the clear
white light of a chandelier, the singer's hair appeared even
brassier than on television. The thick, untamed mop made
her face look thin and her mouth seem tight and ungener-
ous, but the expressive green eyes saved her. Right now, they
blinked warily.

"Emma!" There was nothing reserved about Genevieve
as she rose to welcome her guest. If anything, she seemed
relieved at the distracting presence of a third party. "We
were about to have dessert."

"Dessert? You know I'm on a diet, Mother." Annoy-
ance edged Alyssa's throaty voice.

"Aren't we all?" Genevieve indicated for the maid to
serve coffee. "Alyssa, my dear, this is Emma, the most
wonderful hairdresser."

Alyssa nodded in acknowledgment. "Yes, well, I'm sure
she is, but we have Robert. He does the whole band."

"Only you aren't going to be just a part of the band anymore," Genevieve reminded her, seating Emma halfway
between the two of them.

"I suppose you feel the way my mother does," Alyssa
addressed Emma directly for the first time. "That my hair
'is simply awful. Most unsuitable.' " She mimicked her
mother's phrasing.

Before Emma could respond, the manservant entered with
a large, cut-glass bowl filled with out-of-season fruits—
grapes and kiwi, mangoes and strawberries—cut up with
apples, bananas, nuts and cherries. Behind him, the maid
brought a smaller bowl of whipped cream.

Genevieve favored her daughter with a nod that said,
"You-see-I-do-know-what-I'm-doing."   Alyssa's   lips

quirked, as if she weren't entirely pleased at having her complaints anticipated.

Warning bells rang in Emma's mind. The tension between these two was palpable. What was she letting herself in for?

Finally dessert had been served and the servants departed. Both of the Loos women turned to Emma, waiting for her answer to Alyssa's challenge.

"Actually, I think your hair is terrific," she said.

Alyssa tilted her head in surprise. Genevieve didn't move, not even a blink, but Emma could feel her disapproval.

"You have exactly the look you need as a rock singer," Emma went on. "The question is, how do you want people in Hollywood to see you?"

"I'll tell you what I don't want." Alyssa speared a cherry with her fork. "I don't want to look like a clone of my mother."

"That's hardly likely," Genevieve joked.

Alyssa's afraid. The thought pierced Emma's mind as if the singer had shot it there on purpose.

She desperately wants to succeed on her mother's turf, but she's afraid of losing her identity and of being laughed at. For all her success, she still doesn't feel secure.

Emma studied the singer carefully. "I'll tell you what I'd recommend, if you like."

Alyssa shrugged.

"I wouldn't change it, not drastically," Emma said. "The color is too harsh, so I'd tone it down. And your hair looks like it's been overdyed and permed. It needs a lot of conditioning. As for the cut, maybe a bit shorter to get rid of those split ends. We could soften your whole image without really changing it."

She took a deep breath and waited. If Alyssa rejected her advice, there was nothing more Emma could do.

"I'd think you'd want to do something really different,"
Alyssa said after a moment. "So people would notice that
I've got a new hairdresser."

The woman didn't miss a trick. "Sure, I'd like that,"
Emma agreed. "But it wouldn't be the best thing for you.
And I'm not the one who has to get up on stage and face
your fans."

Alyssa leaned forward, elbows on the table. "Let's get
one thing straight. When you do my hair, you work for me,
not my mother. I don't want to hear her opinions come out
of your mouth, and I don't want anything I say to get back
to her."

In spite of Alyssa's rudeness, Emma's spirits soared. She
was hired! "Absolutely," she answered in her calmest tones.
"Alyssa—may I call you that?— I take my professionalism
seriously. Discretion is a big part of it."

At the head of the table, Genevieve beamed, but wisely
refrained from pointing out that it was she who'd seen Emma's potential. "Now, let's talk of other things, shall we?"

Emma listened silently for the next hour as mother and
daughter compared their ideas for the TV special, in which
they and guest stars would enact scenes from famous musicals. Genevieve preferred scores by Rodgers and Ham-
merstein and Lerner & Loewe, while her daughter tended
toward Andrew Lloyd Webber and Stephen Sondheim, but
both of them quivered with enthusiasm.

When she finally excused herself and stepped out into the
clear night, Emma noticed that the sky was cloudless and
pricked with stars. She smelled the perfume of some unidentified flower, mixed with the odors of pine and freshly
spaded earth.

After ten years of detours, her career was finally back on
track.

ERIC WORKED until nearly eight o'clock on Sunday. He should have been exhausted, but instead he felt on edge.

Meeting Emma again had stirred up a need he hadn't realized he had. He wanted to sit down with her and talk for hours, the way they had that afternoon in high school.

More than that, he wanted to make laughter touch her eyes, to watch the appealing way she ducked her head in sudden shyness. He missed the scent of her herbal shampoo and the clarity of her voice.

What on earth was the matter with him?

The last house where Eric worked was empty, a rental being remodeled. After he finished, he used one of the bathrooms to shower, then changed into the clean clothes he always carried in the truck.

Later, as he walked into the doughnut shop, Eric asked himself what he was doing. Usually, he maintained tight control over every aspect of his life, and tonight he should be heading home to get in an hour of computer work—good training for the courses that lay ahead—then watch the news with his mother and Peter, and turn in early.

Instead, he bought a dozen doughnuts, taking a ridiculous amount of time to make his selection. Suppose Emma was allergic to chocolate? Would cream fillings be too rich for Otto? Only when he heard the man behind him jingling his keys impatiently did Eric settle on his choices.

Then he drove to Emma's house, sat in the truck for a minute feeling like a teenage boy about to ask a girl to the prom, and finally rang the doorbell.

The girl who answered it looked about fifteen. "Yes?" She eyed him suspiciously.

"Emma's not back yet?" His voice stuck in his throat and came out hoarse.

"No." Her expression softened a little as she sniffed the doughnuts. Otto's small face poked into view beside her.

"Who's that?" The little boy frowned. "Oh. The tub works fine."

"Maybe I should wait for Emma out here." Eric didn't want the baby-sitter to get in the habit of admitting strangers.

"Okay," the girl said, and, shooing Otto inside, closed the door. Eric went back to his truck, turned on the radio and put his feet up on the dashboard.

What was he doing here? Usually his hours were packed together like sardines. Even now, he could feel restless energy thrumming inside as if he'd left an engine on idle.

But he couldn't leave without seeing Emma.

She arrived half an hour later. When she emerged from the car, he saw that she wore a soft white sweater belted over a tweed skirt. Her hair, silhouetted against the house lights, curled generously around her head.

The way she moved was graceful but intense. He liked her smallness and the way she managed to look self-sufficient yet vulnerable.

"Eric?" She approached the truck. "Did you forget something?"

He opened the driver's door and swung out. "I just happened to be in the neighborhood—" which was a bald-faced lie "—and thought you might need someone to help you celebrate. Or to console you. Whatever."

She gave a happy little hop on the sidewalk, appearing at that moment not one day over seventeen. "She liked my idea! Eric, Alyssa Loos wants me to do her hair for a TV special! I'm still not sure I believe it."

Together they walked up to the house, his long stride tempered to her shorter one. "You must have impressed her."

"I could see what she was thinking, that she was afraid of making some enormous change and being ridiculed." Emma fitted her key into the lock. "I knew exactly what she needed— Oh, hello, Jennifer."

The teenager, who was on the floor helping Otto scoot toy trucks in and out of a plastic garage, rose to her feet. "Hi."

"I see everything went all right." Emma counted out some money and handed it to the girl. "Thanks a million."

"Have a doughnut." Eric held out the box and, with only a split second of hesitation, Jennifer selected a cream-filled one.

"Thanks," she said, and headed out the door.

When they were alone, he asked, "Does she ever use words of more than one syllable?"

"Rarely. She's very pithy." Emma gave her son a big hug.

"Why'd that man bring doughnuts?" Otto stared dubiously up at Eric. "Can I have one? Can I have two?"

"With milk," Emma said, and led them both to the dining room table.

They sat there for a quarter of an hour, eating, consuming their coffee and milk, while Emma described her encounter with the Loos women. As she talked, Emma glowed brightly enough to light up the room all by herself.

Eric was fascinated by the way her mouth moved. She had full, clearly defined lips that stretched expressively. She drank her coffee in tidy sips, and once in a while the tip of her tongue would lick at the corner of her mouth, giving her an impish demeanor.

He didn't hear half of what she said, but he wouldn't have stopped listening for anything.

Finally Otto began to yawn.

"Bedtime." Emma glanced at Eric apologetically. "You don't have to stick around if you don't want to."

It was after nine o'clock and he should be heading home; he'd be up before six and out on call by seven in the morning. But at the moment Eric couldn't remember why sleep seemed so important.

"I'm in no hurry," he said.

They ushered the boy down the hall. Eric waited in the child's bedroom while Otto's mother brushed his teeth and changed his clothes.

Sitting on a child-size chair, Eric gazed at the hammock full of teddy bears stretched diagonally across one corner. On the far wall hung framed portraits of Mickey and Minnie Mouse, whose faces also dotted the curtains, while bins of toys lay stacked precariously underneath.

To his surprise, an unfamiliar yearning filled Eric. It was for his own long-vanished childhood, for the happy days when he'd built castles out of blocks and never worried about the future.

What was it like to be a parent? Did you relive the innocence and wonder, or did you shut it out the way his father had? He supposed that what you experienced as a parent had a lot to do with what kind of person you'd become, and knew instinctively that Emma shared the magic with her child.

When mother and son returned, Eric sat on the side of the bed with them and read a delightful picture book called *If You Give a Mouse a Cookie*.

Finally Otto had been tucked in, given a glass of water and kissed good-night. He even unbent enough to give Eric a hug.

"I like doughnuts better than cookies," Otto mumbled. He smelled of bubble-gum toothpaste and he clung to Eric for a minute before letting go.

"Then I'll have to bring them again," he said.

Emma clicked off the lamp and they retreated to the living room. The old-fashioned decor, with Art Deco sofa and gold-toned draperies, wouldn't normally have suited Eric's taste, but in this old house it created an aura of hominess.

"You're good with kids," Emma said.

"I am?" He sat across from her in an armchair. "I'm not used to them."

He wondered if someone had spiked the doughnuts. A fuzzy imprecision had settled over his thoughts, as if he were viewing the world slightly out of focus. Except for Emma; he could see her face quite clearly.

"What's it like?" he asked. "Having a child?"

"Scary." She ran one hand along the arm of the sofa, her fingers seeking out the velvety texture. "Every time you lose your temper, you wonder if you've scarred his little psyche for life. Whenever you see some undesirable trait—he chews his lips, or he uses a scissors two-handed—you envision him still doing it at twenty-one."

"But it must be exciting, too," Eric pressed. "Watching him grow."

"It's the most fascinating thing in the world." She leaned back. "I don't think we can really understand ourselves unless we've watched the process from day one."

"Someday," Eric said.

"Why didn't you get married?" she asked. "I thought you would be, by now."

Bold as the question was, it didn't disturb him. "Maybe I never fell in love."

"Sometimes you have to give love a chance." She closed her eyes for a moment, then reopened them. "I'm sorry. Listen to Auntie Emma, the expert on life."

"No." Eric shook his head. "You're right. I've dated, but I never let anybody get close. Although I'm not sure any of them would have been the right woman, even if I had. You were luckier."

"What Bill and I had wasn't the kind of romance you read about in storybooks," she said thoughtfully. "We felt—comfortable. Solid. He could be very supportive—I had a couple of miscarriages before Otto, and I don't know what I would have done if Bill hadn't buoyed me up. And yet I hardly ever opened up to him. I used to censor the things I said.''

''Why?'' Eric suppressed an impulse to lean across and cradle her heart-shaped face in his hands. He didn't understand this urge to feel the way her jaw moved, to touch the words as they came out of her mouth. It must be those damn spiked doughnuts.

''Bill had strong ideas about things.'' Emma curled her feet up beside her; she was small enough to be able to do it easily. ''I didn't like to set him off by expressing an opinion he disagreed with. Unless it was something important, of course. I deferred to him the way I'd always done to my father, without realizing how pervasive it became.''

''Didn't he notice?'' Eric asked. ''Didn't he miss having heart-to-heart talks?''

''He wouldn't have been comfortable.'' Emma's lips parted, as if she'd suddenly realized something. ''How come—you and I hardly know each other—and yet we talk so openly? It wasn't a fluke, all those years ago.''

The irony was that, right now, Eric didn't want to talk anymore. He wanted to slip onto the sofa next to her and sit there barely touching, hip against hip and knee brushing knee. He wanted to listen to noises he ordinarily would ignore—to her breath sighing out, to the hum of the refrigerator from the kitchen, to the gentle rumble of Otto's snoring down the hall.

He felt more alive in this house than he had in years. It must be, Eric realized, because for once he could forget about the future and simply exist right now, here with Emma. It made all his senses come alert, and his skin prickle.

He wanted to stay and explore these unexpected sensations. To touch her cheek, her earlobe, the pulse of her throat. To taste them with his lips....

Abruptly he realized she was watching him with dawning understanding. And with alarm written on her face.

"I'm sorry," he said. "I feel as if I've been thinking out loud."

"It's late." Emma swallowed hard.

"I should go."

"Yes, I—think you should."

They walked to the door together. "Are we still on for next Saturday?" Eric asked.

"Otto won't be here," she warned. "He has a play date."

"We could eat and then go somewhere." Damn it, he *did* want to be alone with her, but the idea obviously frightened her. "A long walk, maybe. Or a movie."

"Sure." Emma hung back as he stepped onto the porch. "Something like that."

"Next weekend, then." Suppressing a gnawing sense of incompletion, Eric headed for his truck.

The evening should have ended in a kiss. He let himself imagine, for one tantalizing instant, how it would have felt to encircle her with his arms and taste her mouth.

They were both grown-ups. They could handle it—the physical contact, the attraction—without letting themselves get out of hand. After all, he just wanted to hold her.

Well, maybe by next Saturday she wouldn't feel so awkward with him.

EMMA GOT OUT ONE of her old records, a recording of *West Side Story,* to listen to a duet Genevieve and Alyssa had agreed to sing. But instead of playing it, she sat on the carpet holding the album and wondering why her heart was beating so rapidly.

Eric Jameson. What did he want from her? And how much did she want to give?

There was no denying the feminine response that surged up whenever he came close. All the needs that had been denied these past two years had sprung back to life with very little prompting.

Yes, she wanted him, and not just physically. But her own instincts could betray her, the way they'd done with Bill. Gradually, if she weren't careful, she would find herself reshaping her schedule to suit him. Making sure she was always around when he needed her, battling guilt whenever her career interfered with their relationship.

Emma disliked her own weakness, and yet it was the flip side of a strong maternal instinct. How could you have one without the other?

She could still see Eric as he'd looked tonight, his eyes fixed on her face, his body angled toward her, no matter where they sat or stood. The memory sent warmth tingling down her spine.

She was a big girl now. She could handle a man like Eric.

Chapter Four

"If you need a good lasagne recipe, I've got one." Emma's friend Betsy Bellago stretched her long, coffee-colored legs in the sunshine.

"Thanks, but I've got one that was Bill's mother's." Emma took the opportunity to check Otto's whereabouts. He was bouncing across a bridge between two slides, matching paces with Betsy's four-year-old son, Roy. "You don't think that's too, well incestuous, do you? Using my mother-in-law's recipe?"

"I thought you and this guy were just old friends." Josie Frye turned at the table and spooned another glop of baby food into Greggie's open mouth. The seven-month-old wiggled happily in his stroller and sprayed a fine mist of applesauce across his mother's arm. "Great. Thank you, baby."

"He's so cute." Betsy reached over and touched a blond wisp of baby-fine hair. "I know you guys don't need to hear it again, but I want another baby so bad."

"Matt will come around," Emma said.

It was a typical conversation for the three friends, Ping-Ponging from one subject to another. They met every Saturday, usually at a park or, like today, at the Burger King playground. Fortunately, the Southern California weather made such meetings feasible; in the rare event of rain or cold, they opted for a pizza place that sported video games and coin-operated cartoons.

Betsy, a former fashion designer in Los Angeles, was married to a workaholic lawyer. She and Emma had met three years earlier in an elevator at Nordstrom department store, drawn together by the similar ages of their sons.

Their casual friendship had intensified during the months after Bill died, when Betsy had become a day-in, day-out source of counsel and companionship.

Josie, a beautiful blonde still in her twenties, had given Emma an inferiority complex when they first met in a Mommy and Me class. The fact that she lived in a luxurious home in La Habra Heights had also left Emma feeling distinctly out of her league.

But she'd learned that looks and money, those icons of the eighties, wore thin rather quickly. At least, they had for Josie.

Her husband Sam, ten years her senior, worked for a computer company with ties to Japan. He and Josie had decided they didn't want to bring up their children in a foreign culture, so she stayed home with three-year-old Kiki and the baby while he traveled for months at a time.

He'd missed Greggie's birth; it was Emma who'd coached Josie through her twelve-hour labor, and Betsy who'd taken care of Kiki for the next few days. Sam hadn't seen his son until the baby was three months old, although Emma knew he doted on his children.

Josie was plain old-fashioned lonely in her big house with her big bank account. But then, Emma reflected, at least Josie's husband was alive. And when he was around, he played horsey with Kiki on the carpet and took Josie out for romantic evenings of theater and dining.

Her thoughts broke off as Otto and Kiki ran up.

"I'm thirsty, Mommy. Can I—" Otto grabbed the nearest cup on the table.

"That's Roy's!" Emma handed him the right one. "Honey, you guys get enough colds as it is."

Otto peered at her skeptically over the rim of the cup, then thwacked it down on the table and raced to a coiled-spring horsey. Kiki mounted its mate, bouncing and giggling.

The last to arrive, Roy found himself without a horse. He stood staring unhappily at the others until, to Emma's satisfaction, Otto hopped down. "Your turn," he said, and wandered cheerfully away.

"Back to this guy," Betsy said. "Is he marriage material? Does your heart pound? Does he like kids?"

Emma laughed. "'Does he like kids?'" she repeated. "I take it that's the number one question in your book right now. Well, he seems to like Otto but he's about to head back to school for a degree in architecture. I don't think marriage or children are in the near future."

"As long as the architecture school isn't a few thousand miles away," Josie said wistfully.

They chatted for a while longer over cold French fries and the dregs of their soft drinks. There was nothing said of any great intellectual depth, and today nobody came up with any vital tips for preventing ear infections or persuading garden snails to stop eating the flowers, but by the time they collected their kids at three o'clock, Emma felt centered.

Having a small child was more all-absorbing than she could have imagined. It helped to compare notes with two women who understood why she was agonizing over which type of preschool to choose, women who cared deeply about whether it was safe for kids to watch the commercials on TV, women who could debate for half an hour whether to let a child eat cartoon-character cereal or insist on serving oatmeal.

The old Emma might stand back and shake her head, wondering if her brain was turning to mush. But she knew it wasn't. Raising kids was the most important job she would ever undertake, even though the details might sometimes seem trivial.

"Next week—the park?" Josie called as she belted Greggie into his car seat.

"Sounds good." Emma helped Otto into his booster seat. Watching him click the ends of the seat belt together all by himself, she felt a surge of pride.

And a twinge of regret, too. How quickly the time had gone. Where was her baby, her tiny new Otto who wriggled with joy when she picked him up? At forty-two pounds, Otto was barely liftable any more.

"What time do you want to bring him tonight?" Betsy called from her car. "Five-ish?"

"Perfect." Emma regarded her friend gratefully. "I can't tell you—"

Betsy waved a hand. "Forget it. He and Roy will keep each other out from under my feet. Besides, Matt's working on a big case. He'll probably be reading briefs all evening."

Roy peered out the car window, his Afro-styled hair framing a pixieish face. "I got a new robot arm! Otto! I'm gonna get you!"

"I'm gonna get you first!" Otto squealed back in delight.

Emma waved goodbye to her friends and slipped behind the wheel.

As she backed out, she couldn't help hoping Matt would change his mind about not wanting another child. He had a good point—that a new baby would cramp their freedom just as Roy was getting old enough not to need constant care—but Betsy wanted a baby so much, and she was a terrific mother. It wouldn't hurt Roy to have a kid sister or brother, either.

And Otto? Making a left turn onto Whittier Boulevard, Emma reflected that she'd never intended for him to grow up as an only child.

She'd always expected to have another baby someday, to delight in the similarities and differences to her firstborn, to watch the magic happen one more time. But her chances were even more remote than Betsy's.

THE LAVENDER DRESS had a flattering effect on her complexion, Emma decided as she sat at her dressing table, combing her hair. Tonight, she could have sworn her skin glowed as if she were seventeen.

For one sharp moment, she could smell again the bubble gum hidden inside a school desk, hear the clang of lockers, taste the stale cigarette smoke wafting out of the girls' rest room. Emma smiled at herself in the mirror. Well, here they were, ten years later, not terribly much wiser.

The sound of the doorbell jolted through her. He was ten minutes early. Smoothing down her skirt, Emma went to answer it.

Maybe it was that momentary slip into the past, but she felt like a teenage girl on a date as she looked up at Eric. His blue eyes widened at the sight of her and his mouth parted as if in anticipation, making him look young and vulnerable himself.

"I—" Her voice caught, and she swallowed.

"You're amazing." He stepped inside and fingered the soft fabric that covered her shoulder. The movement was light, but she felt it all the way to her bones. "Not nearly old enough to be a mother."

She knew she should try to keep things casual. "The lasagne's nearly ready. I had to promise Otto to save him some."

As they walked into the dining room, Eric reached around and blocked her path. "Emma, you're nervous."

"I'm sorry." His arm was only inches from her breasts. Emma couldn't be sure exactly how she felt about that or why it seemed important. Her brain was floating somewhere over her head, connected by the merest tendril of thought.

"I want you to feel comfortable," Eric said. "I'm not going to pounce on you." He took a deep breath. "At least, I don't think so."

Emma struggled for a rational, practical thought. "You could help me set the table."

"Good idea."

Together, they placed the china dishes and silverware on the dining room table. Laying out napkins and filling water glasses seemed like an erotic ritual, performed side by side with Eric.

It didn't make sense. She and Eric weren't going to be lovers. He didn't have time for anything serious, and she didn't want to get all tangled up with a man. It had been a long time since she lost Bill, but she couldn't let her needs cloud her judgment.

"That dress," Eric said, "I like the way it moves. It's loose and yet I get a sense that underneath..." He caught himself.

"Would you like to toss the salad?" Emma hurried into the kitchen. "I haven't added the avocado yet. I didn't know if you like it."

"I love it."

As she diced the green fruit, Eric moved through the kitchen restlessly, examining Otto's painting taped to the refrigerator, picking up an unusual napkin holder Emma had found in an antique shop, straightening spice bottles on their rack where Otto had spun them around.

Emma felt as if she were the one being inspected, held turned this way and that in the light. As if he were seeing right into her mind, pulling out thoughts she never shared with anyone.

"Why didn't you go after your dream?" he asked unexpectedly. "I figured you'd be coiffing movie stars by now."

Emma retrieved a bottle of Italian dressing from the refrigerator. "I think there's a chameleon in my ancestry. I change colors to suit the terrain."

"Meaning what?"

She carried the salad and dressing to the dining room. "It's not exactly that I reshaped myself to suit Bill. But—I adapted."

"And you found you were happy as a mom and a small-town hairdresser?"

She glanced up at the sharpness of his tone. "Does that bother you?"

"Bother? No, actually, I'm envious." Eric took the salad bowl, which Emma realized had been tilting dangerously from her inattention, and set it in the center of the table. "I wish I had your knack for adjusting."

"No, you don't." Back in the kitchen, she removed the lasagne from the oven and set it on the stove. "Because it could happen again. I could lose my way. And I don't want to."

"You shouldn't," he agreed. "Losing your way twice— that would be really dangerous."

She wondered if he knew she was talking about the perils of getting involved with him. And then she wondered why he was worried about such a thing, anyway. She wasn't going to lose her way with Eric or any other man in the foreseeable future.

They sat down at the table, he at the head and she at right angles to him. Emma debated the merits of sitting at the other end but decided that would be carrying things too far.

They were only talking, after all.

Fortunately the food provided its own diversion, and they discussed favorite restaurants and mishaps with menus written in foreign languages. The lasagne had turned out perfectly, and Emma could see Eric was impressed.

"So what happens now in your career?" he asked as they cleared away the dishes and settled down to coffee and ice cream. "What's the next step?"

"Taping on the special starts next week," Emma said. "I don't know how they're going to put it together so fast. They were still arguing which songs to include when I saw them."

"Things happen quickly in television, or so I hear." Eric tapped thoughtfully on the rim of his cup. "I can't believe we're so close to making it. Finally. You know, all along, I believed we'd get there, and yet it seemed impossibly far away. My dream still is, I guess."

"This fall," Emma said. "That's not so far."

"I don't just want to be good enough." He leaned forward earnestly. "I want to be the best, Emma. The best in the class—maybe the best student my professors ever had. Is that egotistical?"

"No, but you sure place a burden on yourself." She could feel the stress in his muscles as if he were wired to her. "Eric is this realistic? You don't have to be tops all the time."

"Second best isn't good enough," he said. "I know I sound like my father. But it's what I feel. Don't you want to be the best, too?"

"I want to do *my* best," she admitted. "And I hope that puts me near the top. But I learned something from having a kid, Eric. Life isn't a competition. We can all win. We can all have the things that matter."

A smile spread across his face. "There's something inside you that warms me." Eric stroked her hand, and a faint shock snapped between them. "You see? Electricity?"

Emma laughed, trying not to show the confusion tumbling through her mind. "Static, actually."

"My domesticated Emma," he murmured. "Full of household wisdom and motherly common sense. Except that underneath—who are you really?"

At the moment, she honestly didn't know. A new and unfamiliar Emma was struggling to break free. An Emma who could respond to Eric not with words but with actions, unafraid of his masculine strength or of the demands he might make on her, an Emma eager to please him and herself at the same time.

Where had she come from, this passionate woman? Had she lain buried beneath the surface all these years? And how had Eric managed to awaken her?

"You frighten me sometimes." She busied herself stacking empty dishes. "Or maybe I scare myself."

"Why?" He reached out and laid a hand on her wrist, halting her attempt to rise. "Emma, we're friends."

They stared at each other across the corner of the table, only inches apart. She could smell the spiciness of his shampoo. His cheeks looked clean and a little rough; his lips were pressed together. He was waiting.

"I don't think we can be friends." Emma forced the words out. "There'll always be this—tension between us. This sexual—curiosity."

"Curiosity?"

"I don't know what to call it," she said. "This—wondering."

"I have a suggestion." He drew her toward him. Emma couldn't find the strength to resist as he pulled her onto his lap. "I think we should indulge ourselves a little. We'll probably both feel foolish, and that will be the end of it."

"I question your motives." She tried to make her tone light but failed miserably.

"I don't know what they are, myself." His hands ran gently up her sides, touching the edges of her breasts, caressing her shoulders. "Taste me, Emma."

She leaned into the kiss, knowing she shouldn't.

His mouth felt every bit as wonderful as she'd imagined it would. Better, even. The hint of coffee on his breath carried her away somewhere, maybe Italy, maybe the stars. Without any directions from Emma, her fingers caressed Eric's muscular shoulders, discovering the soft skin of his neck, the tickling edge of his hair.

Somehow they were kissing again and exploring each other with their hands. Emma knew they ought to stop. I took at least five minutes to manage to speak, and then she'd forgotten what she wanted to say.

Because inside Emma, a young girl was springing to life, a girl who'd taken on the responsibilities of adulthood much too young. A girl who discovered, all at once, that she didn' know her own body, hadn't guessed she possessed a wan tonness that would have been shocking except that it felt so good.

This girl, this other Emma, responded to Eric's em braces with delight and spontaneity. She tingled and yearned, she invited and she teased. Before she knew it, they had abandoned the dining room and were lying on the living room rug, opening themselves to the ferocity of their need.

Making love with him felt deliciously naughty and deeply satisfying. Most of all, it felt right.

Why didn't we do this ten years ago? Emma wondered a they lay together afterward. But it was impossible to imag ine what their lives would have been like if they had.

She dozed off. When she awoke, Eric had covered he with a comforter from the sofa.

"What time is it?" she asked sleepily.

"Not late. Eight-thirty." He sat up beside her, drawing on his shirt.

Her whole body ached to possess him again. Now, and tomorrow, and next week. Damn, this was more than friendship, maybe more than an affair. Almost certainly more than Emma could handle.

"Where do we go with this, Eric? I don't think I'm ready for it," she said.

He ruffled her hair tenderly. "Emma, I'm the last person you should turn to for advice."

"But you're my friend."

"You really think we can go back to being just friends?" He hugged his knees, his expression troubled. "Emma, that's not possible. I want to be around you. I want as much of you as I can get."

"Until fall?" she reminded him. "Until you get all tied up being the best of the best? That's not going to be easy, Eric."

"I wish there were some way I could break all this down mathematically," he admitted. "I'm much better with my intellect than with my emotions."

"Put it into your computer?" Emma said. "Maybe print it out on labels?"

They both chuckled, but an uneasiness remained. "I guess we'll have to take it one day at a time," she said finally.

"That sounds so darn sensible." He drew her closer. "Don't you think we've both been a little too sensible in our lives?"

"You have a better suggestion?"

"No," he conceded. "Just promise that you won't shut me out, Emma."

"The only thing I can promise is honesty."

"I'll settle for that." He kissed her shoulder. "But you know, I like to be the best at everything. The best lover. The best friend."

"You are." She relaxed into his embrace and let him tantalize her again, his mouth on hers, his body edging away the comforter until her breasts pressed against his shirt.

Abruptly, she stiffened. "Otto!" Emma said. "It's his bedtime—he'll be exhausted."

Eric released her reluctantly. "I don't know how I'm going to get used to this children business."

"It comes as a shock to the love life, let me tell you." Her mind already drawing back into its accustomed routine, Emma dressed quickly. "You understand—when he's around—we'll have to be careful."

"This is all new to me." Eric slipped into his clothes. "Everything feels different. Even the air. Did you spray something in the air, Emma? I swear, it's sparkling."

She tapped him playfully on the arm. "You romantic lug. You expect me to buy that?"

He wrapped her into a hug. "I'm not much of a poet. I didn't think it was half bad, for a mechanically oriented guy like me."

"Not half bad," Emma repeated. "Actually, I liked it."

They walked out of the house together, the heat of their lovemaking gradually dissipating into the crisp night air.

Chapter Five

The guard at the studio gate checked Emma's name against a list, then let her through with directions to Building D.

An early-morning mist muffled the mostly empty lot as she circled around to the correct area. Emma stifled a yawn, grateful that Otto's preschool opened at seven.

The TV studio occupied a sprawling one-story structure that looked as if it had been built during World War II, with the wings tacked on later. There was nothing grand or imposing about it, Emma reflected as she swerved around two men unloading lighting equipment from a truck.

Nevertheless, her pulse ran fast and her breath came short, as if she'd run instead of driven for thirty miles on the freeway.

I'm really here. Me, Emma Lindt, at a television studio.

She half expected someone to challenge her as she parked and got out, but no one paid the least attention. In fact, the only people in sight were a man in a business suit, climbing into a Mercedes, and a young woman in jeans and a sweatshirt, carrying a parcel.

From her trunk, Emma retrieved the blow dryer and a kit of supplies. Yesterday, she'd visited Alyssa's airy westside home and spent a good part of the day conditioning and dying her hair.

Afterward, she'd watched anxiously as Alyssa examined herself in the mirror, then called in her lead guitarist and her personal assistant, Corinne.

They'd scrutinized in silence for several agonizing minutes before the guitarist said simply, "Yeah."

"I like it," Corinne agreed. "It's not that different. You just look more—real."

"It *was* kind of overdone before," Alyssa said, still studying herself in the oversize mirror that dominated one wall of her bedroom suite. "Okay. We'll see you tomorrow, Emma."

Corinne had arranged payment as they walked out. Emma wasn't crazy about the way Alyssa dismissed her as some kind of servant, but she supposed humility wasn't a strong point with rock stars. On the other hand, Genevieve had never been anything but gracious.

I mustn't take sides, Emma reminded herself as she carted her supplies to the wing marked D.

Angling her way through a narrow door, she found herself in a long corridor. Emma poked her head into the first office and asked the secretary for directions to Genevieve's dressing room.

"Go down the hall, turn left, turn right at the water fountain, then go left...."

Emma nodded her thanks and proceeded to get thoroughly lost. A polite executive so young he looked fresh out of college put her back on track, and she still had time to spare when she staggered into Genevieve's room.

It was just as plain as the rest of the building. A lighted mirror lined one wall, fronted by a stained counter and two worn chairs. The room also boasted a costume rack, a frayed couch and its own bathroom, from which Genevieve emerged a moment later.

"Well, good!" She smiled at Emma and then gestured at the room with distaste. "Isn't this awful? It has all the elegance of a barracks. Thank goodness I only have to use it for a week."

"I can't imagine Alyssa putting up with this," Emma said, placing her equipment on the counter.

"She isn't." Genevieve grimaced. "She made them rent her a trailer. It's right outside—but I supposed you parked around the corner like the rest of us. Look."

She guided Emma to the room's one small window. Through it, Emma had a clear view of the largest trailer she'd ever seen, dominating a secluded corner of the lot. As they watched, workmen installed an awning, its green-and-white stripes creating a carnival effect against the asphalt.

Both women turned at a tap on the door. Corinne stuck her face through.

"Excuse me." Corinne, an attractive woman in her early twenties, looked uncomfortable. "Alyssa asked me to see if you were here yet, Emma."

"I just arrived." Emma checked her watch. "I'm early, but I thought I'd go ahead and get Genevieve ready."

"Well..." Corinne gazed at them apologetically. "She really would like you to do her first."

Genevieve shrugged. "She *is* the star, after all."

"I suppose she's considering that, after our long all-day session yesterday, it won't take as long to get her ready," Emma offered. "Let me get my stuff."

Actually, it took longer than it should have to curl and fluff Alyssa's hair, because she kept breaking away to take last-minute costume fittings, consult with the director and the conductor, and answer phone calls from her agent.

Emma was left with barely half an hour to get Genevieve styled, a fact that made the older woman furious.

"That isn't the way people acted in the old days." Genevieve managed to sigh without moving her head, so as not to disrupt Emma's work. "Do I sound positively ancient? This light is merciless. Look at those wrinkles."

Actually, in makeup, Genevieve didn't appear much older than thirty-five. "I think you look terrific. I—I hope you don't mind my saying how much I appreciate your help. I'm thrilled to be a part of all this."

"Oh, dear Emma." Her client's eyes met hers in the mirror. "Don't let this glamour business fool you. You must know, in Hollywood, fame passes so quickly. The years are cruel, especially to women. Alyssa thinks she's immortal. She thinks she'll be on top forever. She's my daughter and I wish her well, but none of us is immune. Don't start believing all this fakery."

Emma finished her job and stood back to admire the actress. "There. With five minutes to spare."

"Thank you." Standing up, Genevieve patted her hand. "It's good to have someone I can count on. Someone who doesn't make me feel like a has-been. Bless you." The actress moved past her, ready for work.

The production was to be taped on a sound stage down the hall. Emma entered to find the tiers of seats rustling and buzzing as the audience settled in.

Two sets dominated the open space. One represented a city alley with tenement balconies, to be used for the *West Side Story* and *Cats* numbers. The other, an abstract blue-on-blue space, would be dressed up in various ways for songs from *South Pacific* and *The Phantom of the Opera*, as Genevieve's private secretary, Amalie, explained.

Despite her romantic name, Amalie was a down-to-earth, heavyset woman in her late fifties. She watched her employer with a proprietary air, as if ready to swoop down should any problem arise.

"Can we watch?" Emma asked eagerly.

"Oh, sure." Amalie accompanied her to some seats at the side. "Believe me, this audience is going to thin out in a few hours. The producers will be happy to find bodies wherever they can."

Emma couldn't imagine why people wouldn't love the opportunity to watch, for free, two brilliant singers performing wonderful songs.

By the lunch break four hours later, she understood.

Taping a TV production must be something like watching bread rise, she mused as she and Amalie waited in line in the studio lunchroom. It seemed to take forever to get lighting set and to coordinate the orchestra with the singers.

Complicating matters was Alyssa's extreme nervousness. She fluffed her lines repeatedly, each time blaming someone else for distracting her. She called for frequent makeup and hair touch-ups, blew cues and argued with the director.

Genevieve sailed through it all like the veteran she was. The fact that the crew and backup singers were beginning to smile at her mother and cast exasperated looks in her direction wasn't lost on Alyssa. By lunchtime, she teetered on the edge of hysteria.

She didn't appear in the lunchroom, Emma noticed, and assumed the star was being served in her trailer.

"Is Alyssa going to be all right?" Emma asked Amalie. "She seems edgy."

The older woman shrugged. "You have to remember, she's running a terrible risk. If the show fails, it's on her shoulders. Her career could be ruined."

"But she has a tremendous following," Emma pointed out. "Surely her rock fans won't care."

Amalie slathered butter on a roll. "The way she tortures her voice, it won't last long. Then what?"

Annoyed as she had become with Alyssa's posturing and rudeness, Emma couldn't help feeling sympathy for the young woman. "I hadn't thought about it. I suppose it would be hard to hit your peak so early in life."

"Now Genevieve, she's another story." Amalie nodded fondly toward her employer, who was nibbling at a salad and chatting with the director and choreographer. "A gracious lady. Always knows her lines and gets to the set early."

Emma finished eating and headed for Alyssa's trailer, although she wasn't sure what she could do to help. She knocked lightly, and Corinne peered out.

"I thought she might need a touch-up," Emma said.

The personal assistant chewed on her lip as she opened the door. Inside, Alyssa lay on a couch with a cold cloth draped over her forehead. Hearing footsteps, she sat upright, her features tensing.

"Oh, it's just you," she said, and leaned back. "Those lights gave me a headache."

"I can see why," Emma sympathized.

She didn't want to offer empty flattery like some sycophant. On the other hand, it was in everyone's best interest that Alyssa feel her best.

"I thought you'd like to know," Emma said. "I was sitting in the audience and people were commenting how natural you look in front of the camera."

"Really?" Torn between her usual haughty posture and a desperate need for approval, Alyssa drummed her fingers against the couch arm. "I mean, what did they say?"

Emma tried to remember the one comment she'd overheard. "One man said you reminded him of—now let's see—was it a young Julie Andrews? Or Barbra Streisand?"

"I don't know," Alyssa said. "I felt a little nervous."

Emma couldn't bring herself to say it didn't show; that would be a lie. "I think the audience found it endearing."

"I miss my band," Alyssa went on. "Getting used to that big orchestra—and then all those singers and dancers. I'm not really a dancer. It makes me feel clumsy."

Recognizing a plea for compliments when she heard one, Emma said, "But you're so graceful. No one expects you to hang upside down and do splits—" that brought a smile "—but you move well."

"Of course, this is a snap after my last tour. You wouldn't believe some of the facilities. They were positively medieval." Alyssa tossed aside the washcloth. "Corinne, where's that makeup girl? Stick around, Emma. She always makes a mess of my bangs."

Later, after taping had resumed and was proceeding smoothly, Corinne bought Emma a Coke and saluted her.

"You have the touch," Corinne said. "She was a basket case before you walked in."

Emma clicked her tongue. "I don't know. I wouldn't want people to think I'm trying to butter her up."

"I frankly don't care why you did it," Corinne said. "You're making my life easier. You have the knack of saying exactly what she wants to hear, in a way she finds believable. If I try it, she just waves me aside."

"I hope everything goes well," Emma said. "For all our sakes."

They wandered back toward the sound stage, two ladies in waiting dancing attendance on their queens.

"DO YOU THINK I did the right thing?" Emma asked Eric the next night, after he appeared unexpectedly and whisked her and Otto to a Chinese restaurant. "I feel as if I manipulated Alyssa. There's a fine line between being diplomatic and—"

"You did what you had to do." The waitress approached with their orders of aromatic chicken, *kung pao* beef and egg rolls for Otto. "That looks terrific. I'm glad we came here."

"So am I. It's good to see you." Emma couldn't say anymore, not with Otto right there beside them, but Eric's nearness was stirring a very feminine response. It made the ongoing drama at the studio that had monopolized her thoughts suddenly seem small and far away.

They kept touching each other without intending it—their hands brushing in the car, their knees bumping under the table. Her clothes felt tight, and hungry as she was, she didn't really want to eat. She wanted to take Eric someplace where they could be alone....

"Mom! This is hot!" Otto wailed.

Guiltily, Emma broke his egg rolls into pieces and blew on them. "I'm sorry. Did you burn your tongue?"

"It hurts!"

"Drink some water."

As the little boy sipped, tears welled from his eyes.

"Look." From his pocket, Eric retrieved a pad of paper and a pen. "Why don't you draw some pictures until your food cools off?"

"Okay!" Otto seized the pen, a beautiful gold-toned implement, and began clicking the button on the end. "Is this your pencil? Can I keep it?" As he spoke, the pen flew out of his hand and landed under the table.

"No, you can't keep it." Emma bent down and fished around until her fingers met the metallic tube. "It's a beautiful pen and Eric was kind to lend it to you."

Eric switched chairs to sit beside Otto. "Would you like me to draw a picture of you?"

"Yes, please." Otto sat still as Eric's hand moved rapidly over the pad. "Can I see? Is it done yet?"

"There." Eric turned the pad. The cartoonlike sketch actually did capture something of Otto's bright-eyed restlessness.

"I'm impressed," Emma said.

"I'd like to sketch you sometime." Eric handed the pen back to Otto, and his eyes met Emma's. "There's something about you I'm not sure I could capture, but— There, hold your head just like that. You look so delicate but so determined."

"I've missed you." She didn't want to talk so personally in front of her son, but she couldn't help it.

"I keep thinking about it, replaying every detail...." He turned sharply as Otto, waving the pen, brought it in contact with Eric's shirt. "Hey!"

"Otto! Look at that mark!" Emma snatched the pen from her son, dipped her napkin in water and handed it to Eric, who rubbed futilely at his shirt. "I'm sorry. I'll be glad to wash it for you."

"I'm sorry," Otto echoed. "I could wash it, too."

"I hope it comes out." Eric was trying to be a good sport, but she could see he had taken pains to dress for the occasion and wasn't used to the casual destruction children wrought.

"Mommy! Can I have more tea?" The shirt already half-forgotten, Otto clanked his spoon against his cup until she refilled it.

He kept up a running list of demands as the two adults tried to eat. He wanted to taste the chicken, then he pronounced it yucky and pushed it off his plate. He needed more water, more tea—and a trip to the bathroom. Then, before Emma had hardly tasted her food, Otto announced that he was done.

"Your mother needs to eat," Eric said with barely disguised exasperation.

"It's okay." Emma waved to the waitress. "We can take it with us."

"But he shouldn't act like this." Eric glanced around in embarrassment, although the other diners seemed absorbed in their conversations. "Should he?"

"Little boys tend to be active," Emma said as the waitress produced white paper cartons.

"Are you sure you aren't too easy on him?" Eric pressed, and she realized he hadn't eaten much, either. "I can understand, being a single mom, that you'd be tempted to indulge him, but he ought to be able to sit through a meal without making you jump up and down all the time.''

Emma wondered if he was right. She knew Bill would have said the same thing, and yet Roy and Kiki weren't much better.

"Maybe I am a little soft," she said as they rose to leave. "But he's a good kid."

"Of course he is." Eric looked down at the pen mark on his sleeve. "I guess."

They rode home in uncomfortable silence.

It was seven-thirty by the time they arrived, and Emma steered Otto off to bed. This time, Eric slipped naturally into the ritual, picking out a book to read and providing distinctive voices for each of the characters.

"Read it again!" Otto begged when he finished.

"Don't be silly. You just heard it." Eric set the book aside.

"But it's my favorite story!" Worn out from the long day, Otto was losing control. "Please, please!"

"It's okay, honey," Emma soothed. "We'll read the book tomorrow. Do you want a glass of water?"

"But I'm not tired." Otto stood up in the middle of the bed. Emma cringed inside, seeing him headed for a full-fledged tantrum. "I'm not going to sleep!"

"You lie down right now, young man!" Eric's voice boomed through the small room. "Do you hear me?"

Startled out of his pique, Otto stared at him blankly for a minute and then dove under the covers, buried his face in the pillow and began to cry.

"Hey." Eric put an arm around the boy. "I didn't mean to yell."

"Go away!" came the muffled response.

"Oh, baby," Emma said.

"You, too, Mommy." Otto lifted a tear-streaked face. "I want to go to sleep now."

As Emma hesitated, Eric took her hand and led her out. Half of her wanted to resist, but she knew Otto was simply exhausted and would be sound asleep in thirty seconds.

"I'm sorry," Eric said when they reached the living room. "I don't have the right to interfere between you and your son. But I felt he was taking advantage of you, and you're too warmhearted."

"I know." Emma collapsed onto the sofa, and was pleased when Eric took a place beside her. "But he's had such a rough time, losing his father."

"It won't do him any good to be spoiled." He eased her shoes off and began massaging her feet. "Now tell me more about what happened today."

She ran over the events, focusing on how she had coaxed Alyssa out of her fit of insecurity. "I don't want to toady up to her. I hate people like that."

"It's your maternal instinct." Eric did something wonderful to the arch of her foot that sent tantalizing sensations all the way to Emma's fingertips. "I wish I had some. With Otto, I feel as if I'm always doing the wrong thing."

"You'll get used to him," Emma said. "After all, I've known him for three years longer than you have."

They sat together for a while, her feet resting in his lap. It amazed Emma that they had come to feel this close in so short a time.

She hadn't really let herself think about the consequences of their impulsiveness, about the link they'd forged by making love. Maybe to some people intimacy didn't have to mean anything serious, but it had changed their relationship.

Tonight, she supposed, was how things ought to be. Neither made demands on the other, or expected much. If they could go on this way, the relationship would suit them both.

Why did she have the nagging sense it wouldn't be that easy?

"A penny for your thoughts," Eric said.

She told him.

He stared down at her ankle, which he was flexing between his palms. "You store a lot of tension in your feet."

"That's all you have to say?"

He looked up in surprise. "No, of course not. I was just musing out loud."

"But what do you think?" she asked. "About our relationship? How it ought to go."

"Emma, let's not worry this to death," he said. "The future is unpredictable enough."

She wondered why his answer failed to satisfy her, and then, all at once, understanding dawned.

She'd been trying to fit Eric into Bill's place. How convenient it would be—or so she imagined—if he simply slipped into their lives as if he'd always been there.

But Eric wasn't Bill. He didn't want to be, at least not now, and she shouldn't want him to. Not when her career was just beginning to be more than wishful thinking.

Eric set her foot down and wandered over to the bookcase, where he busied himself examining her small collection of CDs. His body language, with his back turned toward her, told Emma all she wanted to know.

"It felt like pressure, didn't it?" She waited until he turned toward her. "Well, didn't it?"

A slow nod. "You fascinate me, Emma. I want you, in a lot of ways I don't understand yet."

"But..." she said.

"But."

They smiled at each other, understanding the unspoken. Dreams lingered in the air between them, too precious to shatter.

Wasn't there room for a new dream, too? Emma supposed she'd have to wait to find out. Maybe a long time. But then, what was her hurry?

"There's a good movie on tonight," she said. "We could make popcorn."

He looked as if he wanted to agree, but shook his head. "I've got to be up early."

He didn't move, though, standing a few feet away, gazing down at her. Emma could feel his eyes tracing the collar of her blouse, the soft fold of fabric across her breasts.

She wanted to feel his lips on her throat and to move into the unique rhythms they created together. She knew she could keep him here another few minutes, another few hours.

Her body gave Emma a certain power over Eric, but it wasn't right to use it to control him. Not any more than it would be right if he tried to steer her life into patterns that suited him.

You can't domesticate him, Emma. Both of you need to be free.

She remembered one of those high-flown slogans of a past era, that if you loved something you should let it go, and if it really belonged to you, it would come back.

On the other hand, she'd seen a bumper sticker that said if you loved something you should let it go, and if it didn't come back you should hunt it down and kill it.

Emma started to chuckle. At Eric's startled look she explained the joke.

After a brief laugh, he said, "This could get complicated."

"Life is complicated," Emma said. "Go away, Eric. Go sleep, and plumb and I'll see you when I see you."

She stood up and they embraced, she on tiptoe, her skin tingling wherever his body touched her. When Eric's breathing grew ragged, she caught his shoulders and steered him toward the door.

"You have more self-control than I do," he said.

"That's what you think."

She stood in the doorway watching him drive away until his car was just a tiny blur of red taillights.

Chapter Six

Emma had just finished a comb-out at the salon and was about to break for lunch the following Monday when she was called to the telephone.

"It sounds very official," teased Denise, the nail specialist, who had answered the phone. "Miss Loos is calling for Miss Lindt."

"Are you sure that wasn't *Mrs.* Loos?" Emma hurried to the front desk and picked it up. She hadn't expected to hear from Alyssa so soon. "Hello?"

The voice belonged to Corinne. "Can you hold for Alyssa?"

She sounded excited. "Yes, of course," Emma said.

The special had finished taping Friday on schedule, to everyone's relief. After the first day, Emma had taken a book along to read between touch-ups, but didn't make it past the first chapter.

That was because, even when she watched a scene over and over, there was no mistaking the chemistry between mother and daughter. Songs crackled to life between them.

She hoped the magic would come across on the small screen when the program aired. The special was tentatively scheduled for March.

Alyssa came on the phone a moment later, her voice tinny as if talking over a speakerphone, which she probably was. "Emma? Is that you?"

"What can I do for you?" Around her, Emma realized, the salon had grown quiet. A phone call from America's top female rock star wasn't exactly a commonplace occurrence at Marta's Beauty Center.

"You won't believe this!" Glee pulsed through Alyssa's voice. "I've been offered a regular role on *Hotel Marango!*"

"That's fantastic." Emma didn't watch much TV, but she'd caught the nighttime soap opera a few times, mostly because Josie was a devotee.

The plot line, replete with passion and betrayal, focused on the wealthy Hoover Collins and his tropical luxury hotel. Hoover had so far survived four marriages, three mistresses, two murder attempts and a plane crash.

"I didn't even have to audition!" Alyssa went on. "I'm going to play Hoover's daughter, Janelle."

"He has a daughter?" Emma wasn't sure how a full-grown child could suddenly appear, even on a soap opera.

"He was madly in love with my mother but she ran away because he was still married at the time, and then she died," Alyssa recited earnestly, as if she were telling her own life story. "He never knew I was born."

Emma smiled apologetically at the other women clustering around her. There was no way she could explain the situation to them yet. "Who raised you?"

"I was brought up in a convent." Alyssa hooted. "Can you believe that? And see, I'm in this period of rebellion, but underneath I'm really an innocent. And I fall in love with this totally gorgeous, sophisticated man who works for my father, and Dad just hates it. I get to do love scenes and everything!"

"I'm so glad," Emma said. "A role like this will give you a chance to grow as an actress. It's perfect."

"That's what I think," Alyssa said. "You will do my hair, won't you? I'm going to have lots of opportunities to change my look—Janelle, my character, is kind of in transition—and I need someone I can trust."

"Of course," Emma said without daring to give herself time to think. "When do you start?"

"In two weeks." Alyssa handed the phone to Corinne, who provided the details and arranged a generous salary.

Hanging up a moment later, Emma felt dazed.

Everything looked familiar and yet strange, as if she were returning after a long absence. The spacing between the styling stations seemed to have changed; she'd never noticed how scuffed the linoleum was getting; and had that decorative stripe on the wall always been periwinkle blue?

"Well?" Denise demanded.

"I think..." Emma swallowed hard. "I just accepted a job as Alyssa's hairdresser. She got a continuing part on *Hotel Marango*."

Leanne Dorrance, the young stylist who worked next to Emma, let out a shriek, and several clients began congratulating her.

Marta Green, the shop's owner, pressed her lips together. "I'm happy for you, Emma. I know it's what you've wanted, but we'll be sorry to see you go."

"I may be making a big mistake," Emma said. "If this doesn't work out..."

"We'll always have room for you here," Marta said, but Emma knew that clients' loyalty shifted easily. Well, it was a risk she had to take.

She worked through the rest of the day in a haze of disbelief. Her dream was taking shape so quickly that she wasn't ready for it.

She wished her new boss was someone less volatile than Alyssa. With Alyssa's inexperience and insecurity, who knew how well she'd adapt to the pressures of a weekly TV series?

In the middle of shampooing a client's hair, Emma stopped and took a deep breath. The future had arrived and, ready or not, there was no turning back. She'd just have to take it, like her relationship with Eric, one day at a time.

WHEN EMMA CALLED to tell him the good news, Eric insisted on treating her and Otto to dinner. He'd already promised to meet his brother and their mother at the Brea Mall for a quick bite after she got off work, so Emma agreed to join them.

Eric pulled up in the next row as she was parking outside the May Company. He strode over and caught Emma around the waist as she reached to open the door for Otto.

Pressing his face against her hair, he inhaled deeply. "It's happening. Finally. Congratulations."

"I'm a little scared," Emma admitted. "And I'll be driving to Hollywood every day. That's so far from Otto."

"You have to do it," Eric said. "Emma, you can't let anything come before your dream. Not even Otto."

For reasons she didn't want to examine, his words sent a chill up her spine. Emma busied herself escorting Otto safely across the parking lot.

Stella Jameson turned out to be a warm lady in her fifties who wore an air of calm even amid the bustling food area. When Otto requested ice cream and cake for dinner, Stella enticed him away with visions of hamburgers. Emma and Eric selected crisp fresh salads and sandwiches from one of the minirestaurants.

Peter, a lanky, good-natured young man, opted for a baked potato piled high with bacon, cheese and chives.

They all met at a table in the middle, and Emma explained the day's developments as she helped Otto shovel food into his mouth. As a result, he finished before she'd even started.

"I'm excited for you," Stella said.

"I feel a little off balance," Emma admitted, and Peter nodded sympathetically.

"You'll do well." The older lady regarded Otto with mock sternness. "Well, young man, what do you say we go check out the toy store while your mother enjoys her meal?"

"Will you buy me something?"

"Otto!"

Stella smiled. "A coloring book wouldn't strain my budget."

"Could I have an electric train instead?" Otto asked, and everybody laughed.

"He doesn't understand about money yet," Emma said.

"How refreshing." Stella took the little boy's hand and stood up. "We'll meet you folks in an hour—first floor by the glass elevator."

"Thanks." Emma watched the two of them go.

"Look out." Peter regarded her between bites of potato. "Mom's dying to be a grandmother."

"Otto could use a grandparent," Emma said wistfully. "My parents are both dead, my stepmother moved to Miami and Bill's parents live in Michigan."

"Well, if you'll excuse me, I'm going to cruise the bookstores." Peter stood up. "See what new science fiction they've got."

"Peter's a real Trekkie," Eric teased.

His brother grimaced. "I am *not* a Trekkie. You ever been to a science-fiction convention, Emma?"

"I'm afraid not."

"There are people who parade around in costumes. Especially from *Star Trek,* but anything weird will do. I'm interested in the scientific and futuristic aspects of the conventions, though, not the costumes. Eric likes it, too. He

won't admit it because he doesn't think science fiction is serious stuff.''

"It's good escapism.'' After his brother left, Eric said,
"He's always trying to get me to go to conventions with
him. Who has time?''

They were surrounded by hundreds of diners, but suddenly Emma realized they were alone.

"Tell me I'm making a mistake,'' she said. "No, forget
that. Tell me the next two weeks will zip by, and I'll be
walking onto the set before I know it. How will I sleep? How
will I eat?''

"You've done okay tonight.'' Pushing their empty plates
aside, Eric leaned across the table and caught her hands.

"Thank goodness,'' Emma said. "If you hadn't done
that, I might have bounced right up to the ceiling.''

"You're glowing.'' Admiration shone in Eric's blue eyes.
"You've earned this. But I can't say I'm not envious. It's
magic, isn't it? When you finally break through . . . all that
sacrifice, it's worth it.''

His thumbs caressed the backs of her hands. Emma shivered deliciously.

"I wish we had more than an hour,'' Eric said. "And I
wish we were somewhere other than the middle of a shopping mall.''

Her body was saying the same thing. Reluctantly, Emma
withdrew her hands.

"Are we—Eric, are we going to get together again? Or
just eat, talk. . . . We kind of left things up in the air.''

"What do *you* want?'' he said.

"That isn't an answer.''

He looked away from her, across the room. "I could tell
you want what I want, but— Emma, I could be ruthless, if
I let myself. Take what I want, and not think about the
consequences.''

"Haven't you already done that?" she asked. "Haven't we both?"

"But there aren't any consequences. Not yet." He touched her hand again. "I want things from you so profound there are no words for them—but I can't guarantee what I can give in return. And you'd let me, wouldn't you? I can feel it, Emma. You'd let me take and take."

"I want you to be happy," she conceded. "I understand your situation right now, but I still don't want to play it safe. Is that wrong?"

"It is if you get hurt," he said. "If I drain you, if I let you compromise your plans for me."

Emma smiled ruefully. "Thank you for protecting me against myself."

"Damn it, I don't *want* to be nice." He stared at her with an intensity that riveted Emma in her seat. "I want to take you somewhere alone, explore you, teach you, learn from you."

At that moment she wanted him almost painfully. It was physical but more than that, too. It was a yearning to melt into someone else, to please and excite him.

Emma folded her hands tightly in her lap, squeezing them until the pain brought her to her senses. Eric was right, of course. That nurturing instinct of hers would betray her own best interests, if she let it.

"So we get to gaze at each other from afar and pant?" She tried to make her tone light.

"I make no promises." Eric smiled. "Okay. I promise I won't attack you right here in the mall."

"But?"

"We don't have to act like nuns," he said. "Just like responsible adults."

"That sounds so damn sensible." Emma stood up. "Let's go look in windows. I'd better keep moving."

As they walked hand in hand, examining the displays, Emma forgot about yesterdays and tomorrows. Right now, there was only the pleasurable hum of the crowd, the bright good cheer of the mall lighting and the incredibly sensual pleasure of feeling Eric's breath move against her neck whenever she turned.

She wished this moment could last forever.

"SEVEN MONTHS. Can you believe it?" Josie held Greggie above her head, where he chuckled happily.

They'd chosen the beach for this Saturday outing. It was a splendid day, one of those occasions when she could hardly remember that it was March.

Despite the warm weather, the three women had a wide expanse of beach to themselves. They'd done a good job of filling it, too, with their assorted blankets, towels, diaper bags and picnic baskets.

Kiki, Otto and Roy dug intently in the wet sand, surrounded by an array of buckets and shovels. They were making a castle, which to adult eyes looked more like a series of lumps.

"He sure has grown," Betsy said. "Seven months old." Her dark, pretty face creased in a frown. "Oh, Josie, I'm so envious."

"Sam's coming home tomorrow," Josie said.

Her husband had been gone two months this time. "You must be excited." Emma applied more sunscreen to her nose.

"I'm dying to see him," Josie agreed. "But I wish I didn't resent having our schedules interrupted. The problem is that he walks in and wants to play instant father and tell me everything I'm doing wrong. I know he means well...."

"He *is* older than you," Betsy pointed out. "I guess he thinks that makes him wiser."

"Well, he doesn't know the kids like I do." Josie brushed some sand off her shorts. "I just want him to respect my judgment a little more."

"Uh-oh," Emma said. "Rebellion in the ranks."

"He still sees me as a young girl, someone he has to shape and advise," her friend continued. "But I've changed. Maybe the problem is that we're apart so much, we don't have time to really know each other. The kids are growing up—Kiki's going to be four soon—and he's almost a stranger."

"Are you sure you're not just feeling restless because of Emma's good news?" Betsy wasn't one to sidestep difficult issues. "I mean, both of us being homemakers, it's bound to stir up some dissatisfaction. Not that we aren't thrilled for you, Em, but—"

"I know," Emma said. "Remember, I was home with Otto for a while. I used to get those vague yearnings myself."

"I don't think that's it—" Josie broke off as Kiki darted over for something to drink. The boys followed, and after a few swallows of apple juice admitted they were hungry, as well.

The picnic baskets came open, and only when the last peanut butter-and-jelly sandwich had been consumed did the children return to their play.

Despite his sometimes contrary disposition, Otto meshed smoothly with his friends. Emma was pleased to see that he shared his toy shovel with Roy and Kiki and happily obeyed their command to fetch more water in his little pail.

"I don't want a career," Josie said when they could talk again. "I prefer being home. I just don't like this up-and-down life, with my husband popping in every few months like some traveling salesman."

The three women fell silent then, letting the sunshine wash across them. Emma reveled in her own rare relaxation.

Maybe it was the rhythmic murmur of the ocean or the playful tang of the breeze, but she felt far away from her usual concerns.

Down by the water's edge, a young couple walked hand in hand. Emma wished Eric could be here. She'd like to walk that way with him, smelling the fresh air from the sea, letting the breeze blow away the years and responsibilities for a little while.

It was only a fantasy, of course. Emma shaded her eyes and studied Otto, who was patting sand into place next to Roy.

"I'm a Gummi Bear and I'm going to make Gummi berry juice!" his throaty little voice said. "We'll stir it and then I'll drink it all up myself."

"I've got the Gummi medallion," Roy said. "And if you want to share it you'd better be nice to me."

"This is my pony." Kiki waved a knot of driftwood. "And he rode all the way across the ocean from Japan and now he's going to Disneyland."

"And he's going to ride in a teacup and hug Mickey Mouse," Otto added.

The three of them went right on chattering, absorbed in their play, three bundles of eagerness and energy.

Had she ever lived in a world without her son? It seemed as if Emma had always known him in some corner of her mind.

"I guess we'd better get going." Betsy rose reluctantly. "Two of the partners in Matt's law firm are coming for dinner tonight and I've got to get ready."

"He's going to be promoted, isn't he?" Emma knew Betsy's husband was determined to get to the top.

"He'd better." Betsy gathered her towels and shook them out. "That man would fall apart if he couldn't be the biggest success in the world."

"He reminds me of Eric." Emma, too, began packing up.

"Men," Josie pronounced. "That's the way they are."

The other two women hooted. "Now that sounds like something my mother would say," Betsy teased.

"Well, it's true." Josie shrugged, not embarrassed by the fact that, unlike the others, she'd always wanted a traditional woman's role. "Come on, admit it. Women aren't as ambitious. We have different values."

"What we are, is realistic." Betsy often engaged in friendly debates with their younger, more sheltered friend. "We—"

"I have to go potty," Roy announced, marching up.

Kiki and Otto decided they had to go, too, and the women finished picking up in a hurry and shepherded their brood to the restrooms. The conversation was suspended until next week.

It was nearly two o'clock by the time Emma had dusted most of the sand off Otto and strapped him into the car. The sun hadn't been terribly hot, but she felt drained, even a little sick to her stomach.

Boy, she thought with a twist of amusement, this is almost like being pregnant.

As she backed out of the parking space, a thought hit her. Hadn't her period been due three days ago?

Emma remembered seeing the notation on her calendar, but in all the excitement over her new job, she hadn't give it much thought.

Three days. That wasn't much. Except that Emma's periods always came like clockwork.

She counted back to the night she and Eric had made love. Two weeks ago. Right at the most dangerous time....

"Don't be silly," Emma said out loud.

"What?" asked Otto. "What do you say, Mama?"

"I have to stop at the drugstore."

IT COULDN'T BE. Emma held the blue stick up to the light, as if doing so might make it turn white again, but of course it didn't.

She reread the package instructions carefully. No, she hadn't followed them exactly. You were supposed to wait for your first morning's urine, and she'd been too impatient. The fact that the stick had still turned blue meant she must have a zillion hormones thrumming through her system.

Emma wrapped her arms around herself and stood silently in the bathroom, unable to absorb the news all at once.

From the bedroom, she could hear Otto's regular breathing. In the kitchen, the refrigerator grunted and plopped some ice cubes into a tray.

Pregnant. Oh, God.

How many times had she stood here, in this same bathroom, looking at a stick like this one? The first time, she'd been thrilled to death. Then, after the miscarriage, she'd approached the second pregnancy with cautious optimism.

The third time, the sight of the blue stick had filled her with dread. She'd almost wished, perversely, that she couldn't get pregnant at all so she wouldn't have to go through the agony of losing another child.

But she hadn't. There'd been some light spotting at eight weeks, enough to throw her into a panic, but then it stopped. Seven months later, Otto was born, a wonderful, miraculously perfect baby who cooed and waved his little arms and filled her with a tremendous surge of joy.

What would this pregnancy bring? Emma couldn't imagine that she was really going to have another child. What would she do with it? How would she balance her sitters, pay all those bills, find enough time for two kids?

And yet, a baby. She remembered the muffin-fresh smell of Otto when he awoke in his bassinet and the delight in her heart the first time he smiled at her.

A baby. A whole universe.

But what, dear Lord, was Eric going to say?

Briefly, crazily, Emma considered taking Otto and disappearing. Running off to Miami to stay with her stepmother.

But of course, she wouldn't. She couldn't do that to Alyssa, or to Otto—and especially not to Eric.

He was going to be a father, like it or not.

Chapter Seven

Peter spread his magazine across Eric's bed. "Don't you see? You're always designing those futuristic cities anyway!"

"It's to keep my brain from atrophying." Eric leaned back in his desk chair, his eyes sore from the blinking of the computer's cursor light. He was too tired to work tonight, after unstopping sinks and unclogging toilets for twelve hours.

"But this contest—it's perfect." Peter held up the magazine so Eric couldn't miss the two-page spread about the science-fiction convention, FutureCon, scheduled in September in nearby Anaheim.

For the past fifteen minutes, Peter had been trying to talk him into entering a competition to design the city of a hundred years from now. The winning design would be featured at the convention, and would bring a prize of a thousand dollars.

"What I've been doing—these cities—they aren't for a hundred years from now," Eric pointed out. "I look ahead ten, twenty years. I make projections based on technology that's already available."

"So? Guess a little." Peter grinned at him. "Come on, Ricky. You've got a few months before school starts. Take a chance. Besides, think how you'd impress your professors if you win."

"My professors won't give a darn about some science-fiction contest," Eric pointed out, but his mind, in defiance of every shred of common sense, was racing ahead.

A hundred years from now, how *would* people live? What kinds of materials would they build with, how would they organize their communities, what forms of transportation would dominate?

"Besides," he added more for his sake than for Peter's, "futurism isn't my field. There'll be lot of entries from people who specialize in it."

"Well, nobody guaranteed you'd win," Peter reminded him. "Eric, you've got your nose pressed so tightly to the grindstone, I'm surprised you can still breathe. Wouldn't it be fun?"

"And wouldn't you like to brag to your friends if I won?" Eric teased. "Oh, why not? If I have time, well, I'll think about it."

The phone rang in the adjacent den—not their business line but the private one. Peter took off at a lope, but returned a moment later. "It's Emma."

"Emma?" Why would she be calling at this hour? Eric wondered as he went to answer it. Nine-thirty. Otto would be in bed....

If she wanted company, he hoped he was up to it. Right now his back ached from bending over drains and his brain was fuzzy as a peach. But he wouldn't mind holding her in his arms and pressing his cheek against the softness of her skin. No, he wouldn't mind that at all.

"Hi," Eric said into the handset.

"Could—could you come over?" She sounded shaky.

"What's wrong?"

"I—I have to talk to you."

"You're not sick? Otto—?"

"Nothing like that." Her voice came across stronger now, but the tension gave him the impression she was straining to get the words out.

He'd talked to Emma earlier in the day, on a break between jobs, and they'd agreed they would both be too tired to get together tonight. She hadn't needed to discuss anything then. What could have happened this late on a Saturday night?

"Please, can you come?" she asked. "I mean—I guess we could wait till tomorrow, but I thought you might have some emergency calls."

What she meant, obviously, was that she didn't want to wait until morning. Whatever had occurred, it must be serious. "I'll see you in a few minutes," Eric said.

As he went out to his van, he found himself wanting to run. Whatever was wrong, he hoped he could help.

"I DON'T UNDERSTAND," Eric said, although Emma had explained the situation clearly. "How could this happen?"

"We didn't use contraception." Emma sat on the couch fiddling with the ridiculously elaborate silver tray she'd fixed with a pot of coffee, cups, sugar, cream, tea cookies, even frilly little napkins, as if she'd invited the queen of England to tea.

"Yes, but women don't get pregnant that easily." He knew he wasn't making sense, that you couldn't argue away the blue stick she'd shown him, but his mind kept grasping for a way to make it disappear. "The odds against it, from one time, must be astronomical."

"Right. And half the women I know are seeing infertility doctors," Emma added. "You don't have to tell me."

There was an air of fragility about her tonight that made Eric want to protect her. At the same time, she held herself erect, chin up. She looked so damn adorable and so damn scared.

How could he have done this? Why hadn't the possibility even occurred to him?

Something else nagged at him, a feeling he didn't like at all. The sense that fate had trapped him again.

It wasn't Emma's fault. It wasn't anybody's fault, just an accident. But he didn't intend to spend the rest of his life fixing toilets.

"What—what do you want to do?" he asked, and immediately despised himself for putting the burden on her. "I mean, of course we'll get married."

"No." Emma shook her head firmly. "This isn't a good enough reason."

"It's not as if we don't care about each other," he reminded her. He knew he ought to say he loved her, but his tongue felt thick and his thoughts wouldn't come into focus. Right now Eric wasn't certain how he felt about anything, except that he wasn't going to spend the rest of his life running J&J Plumbing.

"Look," Emma said, "I know I'll need help. Having a baby isn't easy, in spite of all those books that make it sound like the next best thing to a nature hike. I've had two miscarriages, so there's always the danger of that, and my emotions may give me a real roller coaster ride."

"I can help with expenses," Eric said, thinking out loud. "And take care of Otto sometimes, and provide moral support. Sure. I can do that." The truth was, he couldn't imagine what a pregnancy would be like, let alone having a child. "I guess I'm not being very romantic," he added. "Maybe I should go out and buy champagne."

"Thanks, but I can't drink while I'm pregnant." Emma smiled apologetically. "The hardest part is going to be giving up coffee."

"That's inhuman." Eric didn't see how a person could function without coffee. "Is that really necessary?"

"I don't even like to take an aspirin when I'm carrying a baby." He noticed that Emma's skin had taken on a translucent quality, like a madonna. Or was that his imagination? "I'm even concerned about the effects of hair spray, but I guess I'll have to chance it."

"Can you still work? Do you want to?" Eric was dismayed to realize he hadn't given any thought about how the pregnancy was going to affect Emma's life, only his own. "What about your big break? You can't give that up."

"I won't have to," she said. "Actually, working with one client will be a lot easier than being on my feet in the salon all day.... Eric, you look like a bomb went off in your underpants."

He couldn't help laughing. "It's not that bad."

"But almost?"

"I'm in shock," he admitted.

"So am I."

They sat together, holding hands. Eric tried to organize his responses into a logical sequence that he could deal with, but his thought processes refused to cooperate. Suddenly he began to chuckle.

"What?" Emma said. "I could use a laugh."

"I was thinking about Mom," Eric said. "She's dying for a grandchild."

"Does that mean you're going to tell her?"

"Not right away. Not until I've absorbed it myself."

The humor left her eyes. "Eric, I'm sorry. I never meant for this to happen."

"Oh, Emma." He drew her against his shoulder. "Never, never apologize. Do you think I blame you?"

"Some men would."

"Well, guys like that are—can I swear? Do you think the baby can hear us yet?"

She burrowed against him. "Not yet, I don't think."

"I suppose I'd better start developing good habits if I'm going to be a father...."

That was when it hit him, the gut-twisting mix of eagerness and anxiety. *A father. Me.*

He went home a while later, still trying to imagine a little boy or girl who resembled him and Emma. Instead, he kept picturing Otto, with his cute big eyes and his sometimes annoying, sometimes endearing way of thrusting himself into the middle of any situation.

During the next few days, Eric dropped in to see Emma a few times and was surprised to find her unchanged. She didn't look pregnant, and she seemed to be handling things matter-of-factly.

His life, on the other hand, shifted completely off center.

On house calls, he regarded children differently. That small girl hugging her teddy bear—would his baby act like that? Or would it be defiant like the boy who screamed and threw toys at his sister?

Whenever he walked past a baby carriage, Eric found himself peering inside and inquiring about the child's gender and age. Although he feared it might be rude, he couldn't help asking pregnant women when they were due and whether it was their first child.

Emma's due date was November 10.

Eric circled it on his calendar. He'd be back in school by then . . . if he was going back.

But he had to. Coming home late on Wednesday night, helping himself to a bagel and cream cheese from the refrigerator, he knew he would sacrifice anything but that for Emma and the baby.

Not his future. Not the thing he'd worked for all these years, the success that would have made his father proud.

Eric sat down in front of his computer and turned it on. As he waited for the program to come up, his heart started to pound the way it sometimes did in the middle of the night. He would wake from racing against a fierce opponent, right on the verge of winning....

When the computer was ready, Eric examined his city of twenty years in the future. The shapes of the buildings, the layout of the streets didn't show enough originality to satisfy him. Things probably wouldn't change dramatically in the next two decades, anyway.

But a hundred years from now...

His child would have died of old age by then. Good Lord, his great-grandchilden would be growing up as the twenty-second century approached.

What kind of world would they live in?

The project Peter had suggested no longer seemed far-fetched and frivolous. His offspring would be living in that era, and Eric wanted to be a part of it, at least in some small way.

Maybe if he were creative and insightful enough, some of his ideas would have real consequences. A scientist might take a new direction, an urban planner might be jolted out of his complacency...

Pushing the realities of the next nine months out of his thoughts, Eric bent over the computer and went to work.

IT TOOK A FEW WEEKS before Emma mentioned her pregnancy to Alyssa, and when she did, the singer hardly noticed.

"Oh? Well, congratulations," Alyssa said as Emma gave her hair a final spraying in the trailer. "Could you do something about that piece of hair behind my ear? It curls funny."

Corinne, informed of the news as soon as Alyssa had departed for the set, gave Emma a big hug. "I'm thrilled for you. At least, I presume you're happy about it. There's no husband right now, is there?"

"No," Emma admitted. "But my...friend is going to see me through it. He offered to marry me, but I couldn't accept."

Corinne wrinkled her nose. "How old-fashioned of him. I like that."

Old-fashioned. Emma supposed it was. Over the past few weeks, she couldn't help wondering if she should have been so quick to turn him down. More and more, she missed the solid comfort of a body sleeping next to hers, wished she could touch his rumpled hair at breakfast and kiss him goodbye when they both went off to work.

But she couldn't take advantage of Eric. Even now, he didn't really grasp what having a baby was going to mean. She could tell from the dazed look that crept into his eyes when he took her and Otto out for meals or joined them for an evening.

Heck, she wasn't sure *she* grasped what it meant this time around. But she did know that the last thing she needed, with her life in so much turmoil, was to take on a marriage that neither of them was ready for.

"Thirsty?" Corinne asked, and she nodded.

They left the trailer and took up their stations in the lunchroom, where Emma drank decaf and Corinne tackled her third cup of coffee for the day. It was only nine o'clock.

Working for Alyssa wasn't turning out to be nearly as exciting as Emma had expected, but right now she didn't mind. With Otto, she hadn't felt more than a few twinges of morning sickness, but this past week her stomach had taken to dancing the fandango at unpredictable intervals.

Like right now. "You're turning green," Corinne said. "Can I get you something?"

"Bread," Emma said. "A muffin. Something starchy."

The other woman returned a minute later with a sweet roll. "I'm afraid that's all they had."

Emma took a bite. "I'm going to look like a blimp."

"Just don't throw up on Alyssa."

They both laughed.

The morning went slowly, as usual. Lunch was a busy time, with Alyssa needing touch-ups. Also, today as for the past few days, her costar Ford Burgess visited the trailer, making himself at home on the couch.

Ford played the role of Jon, the fiancé of Alyssa's character, Janelle. Although thousands of women wrote him love letters every week, Emma wasn't impressed with his slick good looks or the way he ignored her, Corinne and the makeup artist as if they were part of the furniture.

Alyssa, however, grinned at his jokes and practically purred whenever he came close. Emma felt like an intruder, and was relieved when it was time for taping to resume.

Following Alyssa out of the trailer, she nearly collided with the two actors, who had stopped directly in front of her. They were staring at an enormous trailer being towed onto the lot.

"Who does that belong to?" Alyssa said.

"Nobody said anything to me about a new character," Ford grumbled.

"I'm going to find out." Alyssa stalked across the lot to where the producer, Barry Gray, stood talking with the director. Emma trailed behind, not wanting to eavesdrop but concerned about what changes in the program might mean to her employer.

Barry gave Alyssa a Hollywood peck on the cheek. "I know you'll be pleased," he announced too heartily. "We're so excited about your character that we want to give her a really socko story line."

"Oh?" Alyssa regarded him uncertainly. Her first episode wouldn't air for a few weeks, and Emma knew she lived in a state of anxiety about how critics and the public might respond.

"I had a meeting with the writers last week and we decided you need more conflict." Barry laid an arm lightly around Alyssa's shoulders. "We can't have your engagement going too smoothly, you know."

"Why didn't you tell me?" Alyssa asked.

"We had a particular actress in mind to play your rival, but we weren't sure she'd be available." Barry's words carried clearly to where Emma stood watching the new trailer being angled into place.

"So what's the story line exactly?" Alyssa asked.

"One of your father's discarded mistresses comes back to town." The producer gestured expansively. "She's considerably older than you but a real vamp. She decides to take her revenge on Hoover by cheating his daughter out of her marriage. So she seduces Jon."

"Oh." Alyssa nibbled at her lower lip. Emma caught sight of the makeup lady watching with professional concern. "Who's the actress?"

"That's the beauty of it." Barry pasted a big smile across his face. "Your mother!"

"My what?" Alyssa said. "Genevieve?"

"The public will love it." Barry pretended not to notice her flabbergasted expression. "Mother and daughter rivals for a man. We'll get tons of mileage out of it, publicity-wise."

"My mother's retired," Alyssa said.

"We talked her out of it. Oh, and by the way—" Barry waved to someone Emma couldn't see "—she asked to share your hairdresser. I assured her you wouldn't mind."

"Now look here—"

"Ratings, Alyssa," he said. "This is going to give the ratings a big boost. Trust me." Without waiting for an answer, the producer strode off. Coward, Emma thought.

Alyssa stood rooted to the ground, her fists clenched, until Ford ambled up. "I heard," he said. "Isn't it terrific?"

"Is it?" Alyssa snapped.

"Me, at the middle of a mother-daughter tug-of-war." Ford preened himself. "He's right, you know. It'll make terrific press."

"This is my big part." Alyssa pressed her lips together. "My break. I know Genevieve wanted to get back into acting. I'm glad she'll have the opportunity, but why does it have to be on *my*—"

"He probably had this in mind from the beginning," Ford told her. "I wouldn't put it past old Barry. Hey, I've got a scene. See you later."

Alyssa turned angrily toward her trailer, and it was then she spotted Emma.

"Well, congratulations." Alyssa's voice was as cold as her eyes. "I guess you're the hottest thing around. Looks like you're going to be styling my mother *and* me."

"They could have asked me first," Emma pointed out. "Alyssa, I promised to work for you. I consider your mother my friend, and I do owe her a certain loyalty, but I won't go against your wishes."

The singer's expression changed abruptly from resentment to astonishment. "Really? You'd turn her down?"

"If you want," Emma said. "You're the boss."

"Oh." Alyssa tapped her foot against the blacktop. "There's no point in getting on Barry's bad side. I suppose it's all right." She marched back into the trailer, followed by the makeup lady.

"Brilliant." Corinne appeared from around the corner of the trailer. "You handled that like a diplomat. Sorry, I couldn't help eavesdropping."

"Who can, with so much intrigue around here?" Emma shrugged.

"I'd better go see if I can pull the splinter out of the lion's paw." Corinne grimaced. "She'll be in a snit all afternoon. I'll have to make her see it's in her best interest."

"Is it?" Emma asked. It surprised her that Genevieve, despite her eagerness to make a comeback, would have accepted the role without consulting her daughter. Surely Genevieve didn't want a feud, but, on the other hand, she might figure their relationship went through ups and downs anyway.

"You can't add a big star like Alyssa to a show like *Hotel Marango* and not give her a shocker of a story line," Corinne said. "My personal opinion is that they made her character too bland, and she isn't experienced enough to add the kind of shading it needs. So they're bringing in the heavy artillery."

"Artillery is the right word," Emma said as her friend went into the trailer, and wondered when the first shots would be fired.

"DID YOU SEE *MARANGO* last night?" Josie demanded as they spread their blankets across the grass at Oeste Park. "Oh, of course you did, Emma. Betsy?"

"No," the other woman said shortly and busiest herself unpacking Roy's picnic lunch.

"Uh-oh." Josie lifted an eyebrow.

Emma, too, could see that something was troubling Betsy, but she didn't want to pry. Besides, last night had been the first episode to feature Alyssa and she was eager for audience reaction. "What did you think of it?"

"She's pretty good." Josie pushed a toy train in front of Greggie. "Kiki, eat your sandwich. No, you can't play until you finish."

"I'm done, Mommy." Otto tried vainly to wipe off his peanut butter-and-jelly mustache with a napkin. "Could you clean me up?"

"Sure." She mopped him down. "Why don't you wait for Kiki and Roy?"

"Uh-uh." He dashed off to the slide.

"But her character's a little too goody-goody, don't you think?" Josie went on as if they hadn't been interrupted. "I think she could get boring."

"Haven't you heard?" Emma said. "Genevieve's going to seduce her fiancé."

"Wow. Really?" Josie caught Greggie as he tried to stuff a leaf in his mouth. "No, no, baby. Here, have some bread."

Emma stretched her legs, wondering how much longer she'd feel comfortable sitting on the grass. As she recalled, it wouldn't take long before she'd have to confine herself to benches and straight chairs.

At least her stomach wasn't bothering her today. At ten weeks, the morning sickness was fading.

"That sounds great," Josie went on. "Alyssa didn't mind about her mother?"

"She minds," Emma said. "They've hardly spoken to each other since Genevieve came on the set."

As if her life wasn't complicated enough, now Emma had to deal with two clients who battled each other for every privilege and every advantage. They both insisted that Emma linger over their hair as long as possible; each wanted the producer to send fresh flowers every day, and then they complained about the size of the bouquets.

It amazed her that the usually gracious Genevieve could be so petty. The older woman had plunged full-force into a rivalry with her daughter that even extended to flirting off-camera with Ford, keeping him entertained with anecdotes about leading men of the past with the implication that he was the handsomest of the lot.

For all her fame and accomplishment, Alyssa was only twenty-three, and it showed. She might be younger and prettier, but she couldn't match her mother for sophistication. Whenever they sparred, Genevieve came off looking like a winner, and her daughter knew it.

The producer wore a Cheshire-cat grin, and Emma had to admit that the intramural resentment was not only attracting the attention of gossip columnists, it was also sparking up the show. But to her it seemed cruel.

"Roy!" Exasperated, Betsy snatched a bag of potato chips away. "Don't pig out on chips! Eat your sandwich."

"But, Mommy, I finished my bologna," the little boy pleaded.

Betsy glanced at his plate, embarrassed. "Oh. I guess you did. Well, why don't you go play?"

"Okay." Taking a last slurp of milk, Roy trotted away.

Emma and Josie gave Betsy meaningful looks until she stopped pretending nothing had happened.

"Okay, okay," she said. "So I'm cranky. Matt and I had a fight."

There was no need to ask what about. "Who won?" Josie said.

"Nobody wins in family fights," Emma sighed. "Either you both win or you both lose."

"We both lost," Betsy confirmed. "He's adamant about not wanting another child. And the more he refuses, the more I want one. Every time I see a baby, I nearly go crazy. It's even hard for me to look at Emma, I'm so envious."

"But I don't have a husband," Emma pointed out.

"Sometimes I think I'd rather have the baby than the man." Betsy waved her hand. "Don't misunderstand. I'm not thinking of leaving him. But he's not the one at home all day. He's got his job, but this is mine, and one kid doesn't feel like enough."

"Funny how life works out," Emma said, and then stopped with her mouth open.

Striding toward them across the grass was Eric, carrying a paper bag and wearing an uncertain expression.

Betsy let out a low whistle. "Who is that gorgeous thing?"

"He's mine, girls," Josie said. "I saw him first."

"Actually, I did." Emma got stiffly to her feet. "About ten years ago."

"Oh, *him,*" Betsy murmured.

Eric stopped a few feet away. "If I'm interrupting, just tell me. I had a job near here and I needed to eat lunch anyway, so I thought..."

"Join us," Emma said, and drew him down onto the blanket.

As she made introductions, she found herself touching Eric in little ways—picking a leaf off his shoulder, bumping against him as she shifted position. Even though she knew her friends must be noticing, she couldn't seem to help herself.

In the sunlight, his sandy hair took on red highlights, and his legs seemed longer than usual, stretched across the blanket she usually shared with Otto. She was glad he'd come, but now she didn't know what to say.

"Go on," Eric said. "Please, talk about whatever you usually talk about. Act like I'm not here."

The women exchanged glances.

"Well..." Josie took a deep breath. "Sam—my husband—he's home from Japan right now. We always go through this honeymoon period when he first gets back, and then—"

"Then you get real," Betsy finished.

"Which is probably the point you're at about now," Emma noted.

Josie nodded. "He thinks I'm too lax with the kids."

The other women smiled. "Of course," Betsy said.

"Why 'of course'?" Eric paused between bites of his hamburger.

"That's the way fathers are," Emma explained. "They're not with the kids all day. They don't understand how tough it is to play disciplinarian all the time."

"Besides," Betsy added, "sometimes you know the kid's worn-out, or coming down with a cold. You have to make allowances."

Eric gazed across the park at the play area, where the children had tired of the swings and retreated to a shady area under the slide. There they dug avidly in the sand with plastic shovels.

Suddenly Otto hopped up, grabbed a beach bucket and started off across the playground. The other children raced after him, and soon they were filling up their buckets from the water fountain.

"Isn't that too far for them to go by themselves?" Eric asked. "Shouldn't one of you go with them?"

"It's not that far," Betsy said.

"Yes, but it's right by the parking lot. Someone could snatch them."

"Sounds paranoid," Josie teased.

"Actually, that's how I used to feel," Emma said. "But they trek back and forth to that water fountain about twenty times an hour. We'd wear ourselves out."

As they watched, a motorcycle veered into the parking lot. Eric started to rise before he spotted a policeman dismounting and heading for the rest rooms.

"I guess it's pretty safe around here," he conceded, finishing up his French fries.

Josie couldn't contain herself any longer. "How do you feel?" she asked. "Do you really want this baby? Do you think you'll make a good father?"

"Whoa." Eric raised his hands playfully as if to defend himself. "What did I get myself into?"

"You'll find we're kind of protective," Betsy explained. "We've been through a lot with Emma."

"Eric," Emma said. "You don't have to discuss this." She shot Josie a warning glance.

"The answer," Eric mused, "is that I guess I want the baby but I'm not sure I want it right now. And I have no idea whether I'll make a good father, but I'll try."

"He's honest." Betsy nodded approvingly.

The fact that Eric would calmly submit to her friends' questioning moved Emma. That he cared about the opinions of those close to her meant he wanted to be included in all aspects of her life.

Yet there was a part of him she knew she hadn't reached, an inner zone where his driving need to prove himself lay semidormant. It would break out—perhaps soon. Only if he had to choose, and if he chose her and the baby, would she have the answer she wanted.

But in the meantime, she treasured this side of him, the Eric who worried about the children and wanted to please her friends.

A shrill beep-beep sounded from his pocket. "Rats." He checked the pager. "I've got to call my brother. Looks like he has another job for me."

"Just when things were getting interesting," Josie said.

"Do I sense a certain hostility?" Eric regarded her directly. "Is it me in particular or men in general?"

"It's..." Josie shrugged. "Men get off so lightly. They have their work, and we women end up carrying the burdens."

"You sure are in fine form today," Betsy said. "And I thought I was the cranky one."

"I don't like Sam telling me what to do." Josie caught Greggie as he tried to crawl off her blanket. "He's got all these great ideas about how to reorganize the household. Then he can fly off and leave me to carry them out."

"And you think I'm doing that to Emma?" Eric tossed his lunch bag into a trash can.

"Well, look at her," Josie said. "She's turning green around the gills, in case you hadn't noticed."

The last few minutes, Emma's stomach had reverted to roiling and churning. She didn't think she would throw up, but she couldn't imagine how she was going to collect Otto, fold up her gear and pack everything into the car.

"Would it help to lie down?" Eric said. "Can I drive you home?"

Emma lowered herself gratefully into a reclining position. "If you could get Otto..."

"Sure." Eric and her friends sprang into action. Within minutes, everything was stowed in place and Otto had been strapped into his seat.

Emma sat up slowly. "I feel okay now." Still, she didn't object to leaning against Eric while Betsy folded her blanket.

As he helped her to the car, Josie walked alongside. "I'm sorry," she said. "I was kind of tough on you."

"I can take it." Eric smiled. "As for your husband, if you're as straight with him as you were with me..."

"I'm not," Josie said. "He's a lot older than me and sometimes I feel more like his daughter than his wife."

"Whose fault is that?" Eric challenged.

"Okay, okay." Josie held the door for Emma. "Are you sure you can drive?"

"That's my line," Eric said.

"Yes to you both." Emma slid into her seat, feeling tired but in control. "Thanks."

On the way home, she pulled into a drive-through dairy and bought milk and ice cream. Otto insisted on holding the bag and she didn't argue, even though his body heat wasn't going to do the contents any good.

At the house, Emma unloaded the car and put Otto in bed. She was getting ready to take a nap of her own when she made the discovery.

Several small spots of blood flecked her underclothes. Emma stared at them numbly for a minute before the import sank in.

No, she couldn't lose this baby. It might be unplanned, it might complicate her life, it might even drive Eric away forever, but she realized with a start that she'd already fallen in love with it.

Chapter Eight

Eric arrived within minutes. "Why are you answering the door?" he demanded. "You should be in bed. Did you call the doctor? What did he say?"

Emma allowed herself to be escorted. As Eric pulled back the covers for her, she realized it was the first time he'd been in the bedroom with her. That seemed strange, considering how intimate they'd become.

Sliding under the covers, Emma said, "He told me at this early stage, there's not much they can do. I'm supposed to stay in bed for a day or two. Really, I shouldn't have called you."

"Peter can take over." Eric tucked her in. "Where's Otto?"

"Watching cartoons." Tension stiffened Emma's body. "Eric, I don't want to lose this baby."

"Maybe you should call another doctor," he said. "Couldn't they run some tests? One of those ultrasounds?"

"It wouldn't do any good." Emma closed her eyes for a moment. "Either I'm going to miscarry or I'm not."

To her embarrassment, tears streamed down her cheeks. Eric gathered her into his arms.

"You won't lose it," he said.

Old feelings rushed back, nearly overwhelming Emma. That first miscarriage—her disbelief—and then the second, bringing the stark terror that she'd never be able to have a child. "I'm sorry," she said.

"Mommy?" Otto peered over the edge of the bed. "Why are you crying?"

"Your mommy doesn't feel good," Eric said.

"Does she have a cold?"

"Something like that," Emma said.

Otto nodded sagely. "You should take some medicine. Can I hug you, Mommy?" When she agreed, he climbed onto the bed and lay down beside her, wrapping his arms around her neck. He felt small and warm and wonderful.

When he finally climbed down, Otto announced that he was hungry.

Eric stood up. "I'll fix it. What would you like, sport?"

"Shell noodles," Otto said.

"That's all?" Eric followed him out of the room.

"Eric!" Emma called. "Open a can of minestrone soup and add a handful of shell noodles. They soak up all the liquid, and that way he gets his vegetables, too."

"Okay."

From the kitchen came the click of the pantry door, the whirr of the electric can opener and the bang of pots. Otto's high-pitched voice rose and fell with one question after another. Emma could hear Eric's deep rumbling responses, but couldn't make out the words.

Sunlight fell across her face and outside, birds were celebrating the arrival of April, but the thought of spring left a cold taste in her mouth. Spring was the time for new life, for babies, and she was losing hers—

No. She had to think positively. Besides, she was so tired.

Imagining a cooing baby in bed beside her, Emma fell asleep.

When she awoke, evening shadows lengthened across the room. She felt disoriented, lying there in the dark bedroom. Where was Otto? Dinner needed to be fixed and there were other chores.

Eric peeked in. "You awake? You slept for hours."

As soon as he said it, panic spread across Emma's chest. "I'd better go check if I'm bleeding."

"It doesn't hurt?" Eric came to help her.

"No. But it never did." Her arm around his shoulders, Emma slid out of bed and stood up. She felt heavy with tension. Leaning against Eric, smelling his fresh after-shave, she experienced a wave of regret.

They should have had months to get to know each other and to explore their friendship and their passions. Instead, they'd been thrust into a situation that would strain even a well-established relationship. And yet he'd been so loving and supportive, she felt as if in some way they *had* been building a friendship all these years.

As they shuffled by Otto's room, Emma saw him adding Lego pieces to a huge castle. "You two have been busy."

"I love those things," Eric said. "Blocks, erector sets, you name it."

In the bathroom, Emma found no more blood. "Looks okay," she said, not quite daring to believe her good luck. Was she really, truly going to have another sweet, bright-eyed baby to hold in her arms?

"You'd better stay in bed tomorrow." Eric waited until she came out. "Now, what would you like for dinner?"

"You mean you cook?" she said.

"I know how to make shell noodles."

They both chuckled. "Maybe you could whip up a pizza," she said. "There's a coupon in the silverware drawer. They deliver."

"My best dish." Eric returned her to the bedroom and went to place the order.

When the pizza came, they ate it sitting around the bed. Eric had spread out a towel to absorb Otto's mess.

"It's just like a picnic!" Otto said. "Mommy, will you still be sick tomorrow?"

"Looks like it." Eric adjusted the boy's bib.

"Oh, good." Otto attacked his second slice. "Can we have doughnuts for breakfast, Eric?"

After a quick glance at Emma, Eric said, "Just might."

Under Emma's supervision, he got Otto ready for bed. Listening to him read *The Little Engine That Could,* Emma felt a wave of warmth.

He was so patient with Otto tonight, so clearly enjoying the role of substitute parent. Eric had a gift for spontaneity that Bill had lacked. He would be a wonderful father, she thought.

On the other hand, today was a kind of holiday for Eric, a break from his routine. Would he have the same kind of patience when parenting tasks lost their novelty?

After Otto fell asleep, Eric came into the bedroom and began taking off his clothes.

"Whoa." Emma quirked an eyebrow. "Not that I mind, but you really can go home now."

"You're kidding." Eric paused with one sock off and one foot in the air.

"I won't bleed to death," she told him. "Whatever's going to happen is going to happen."

"You think I'd just leave you here? You and Otto?" He wasn't kidding, she realized. "Emma, you know, it's all right to depend on someone else once in a while."

"But you don't have your things with you."

"I'll survive." He removed the other sock and prowled through her closet, where he discovered an old bathrobe of Bill's. "Is this sentimental? Would it bother you if I wore it?"

"Please do," she said. "I like to snuggle up in it some-times when I'm cold. That's the only reason I keep it."

He slid into bed beside her, carrying a science-fiction magazine. "I want to show you something."

He opened it to a center spread and told her about a pro-ject he'd taken on, designing a city of the future. As he talked, Eric's eyes glowed with a radiance she'd only seen there when he discussed his dreams.

"It's the essence of architecture," he said. "It's how people relate to each other, how they move around, their behavior patterns. I mean, think back to a hundred years ago when people depended on horses. They often lived where they worked—on farms, over stores. People had ser-vants, so the kitchens were in remote parts of the house or even in a separate building. Now, think how different things will be a hundred years from now...."

Fascinated, Emma listened until she felt sleepy again. Fi-nally, reluctantly, she said good-night.

She loved the fact that Eric shared his visions with her. But it troubled her that he was taking on this major pro-ject. Where would he find the time, with his long hours and her need for help?

Burrowing under the covers, Emma let her foot rest against Eric's leg. Maybe she was getting greedy, wanting more and more of him. Just having him here tonight gave her a sense of security she hadn't felt in years.

She had no right to try to tie him down. Eric was keeping his word, standing by her. But his spare time and his dreams were his own, as hers belonged to her. That was the way she wanted it.

BY SUNDAY NIGHT, there had been no more bleeding. Eric spent the day catering to Emma and keeping Otto enter-tained, but by evening he was pacing restlessly.

"I think we're all right." Emma couldn't quite grasp the sense of relief that the baby was safe.

"Are you sure it's okay to stay up?" But Eric didn't press the point as she sat in a kitchen chair instead of returning to her room.

"This happened with Otto." She eyed the refrigerator wistfully, wondering if she had any orange juice left. "It's called spotting."

"And you never had trouble after that?" For the first time that weekend, he didn't notice that she wanted something, and Emma realized how worn out he must be. Taking care of other people could wear you down in a hurry, as she well knew.

"No." She laid her hand over his on the table. "Eric, thank you. I needed your help, and I appreciate it. But I'm sure you want to get back to your project."

"Well, I *have* come up with a few ideas I'd like to program in." He stretched lazily. "Emma, are you sure you shouldn't call that doctor again?"

"On Sunday night? Besides, I'm not bleeding."

"Well, I don't think they're taking very good care of you," Eric said. "They ought to do more."

"I'm fine." She touched his cheek. "It's all right for you to go. Eric, I'm a grown woman. I've been through this before."

Unexpectedly, he kissed the palm of her hand. Emma felt herself grow soft inside. Impossible as it seemed, she wanted him. And darn it, she wasn't going to be able to do anything about it, not until all danger had passed.

"This could get frustrating," Eric said.

"Go home. Charm your computer."

"It's almost Otto's bedtime. He might get upset." As he spoke, Eric shifted in his chair. Clearly, he wanted to leave but felt uncomfortable about it.

"Do I have to come after you with a broom? Beat it, buster!"

He leaned forward and kissed her. "You have my pager number?"

"Eric!"

"All right, all right."

After he was gone, Emma stood up slowly. The house seemed empty without him.

After drinking the orange juice, she checked one more time and was grateful not to find any blood. Positive thinking—that had helped, she felt. She believed in this baby.

Standing outside Otto's room, listening to him chatter aloud as he played with his toy space station, she tried to imagine a baby in the spare room across the hall, the room that had been Bill's office. A little brother, chunky and stubborn, or a girl, sweet-natured and elfin. A wiggly body to fit into the terry sleepers and tiny T-shirts she'd saved from Otto's infancy.

Impulsively, at bedtime, she told Otto that she was carrying a baby inside her.

"Where?" he asked.

"It's called the womb." She held him on her lap, determined to cuddle him as much as possible while she still had one.

"Someday I will be a mommy and I will have a baby in my womb," Otto announced.

Emma shook her head, smiling. "You'll be a daddy."

"I don't want to be a daddy," he said. "I want to be like you."

She rocked him for a while, but Otto was too independent to be held for long. Soon he found his way into bed.

"Where's Eric?" he said. "I want a good-night kiss."

"Eric went home." She waited for his reaction.

"Well, he can come back sometime," Otto answered.

Yes, Emma thought as she turned out the lights, he can come back sometime.

THE RATINGS ROSE with Alyssa's debut, dipped the following week and then shot sky-high with Genevieve's first appearance on the show. And there they stayed through May.

Suddenly the mother and daughter had become the hottest thing in television. Gossip columnists hounded them; their mailboxes bulged with fan letters; requests for interviews poured in.

Nothing soothed Alyssa's ruffled feathers at having to share the spotlight with Genevieve. And in all honesty, Emma suspected the producer was egging the two of them on, relishing the publicity that came from their sometimes public quarreling.

She sighed, thinking about it while on her way to style the two of them for a photo session one Saturday. A reporter and photographer from *Weekend Magazine* were coming to prepare the cover article for an upcoming issue.

Weekend Magazine, the latest entry in the crowded entertainment market, had been launched a year before with a publicity splash. Since then, it had soared to a huge circulation with its unexpected angles on popular stories—a prospect that filled Emma with uneasiness.

Alyssa lived in a rambling, ultramodern wood-and-glass structure on a hill overlooking Hollywood. To get there, Emma navigated a narrow, winding road between thick hedges, praying all the while that she wouldn't suffer a head-on collision with one of the sport cars that roared by.

In some ways, the semirural neighborhood reminded her of the area around Genevieve's home, but she knew better than to say so to Alyssa.

As Emma rang the doorbell, she could hear voices from inside the house.

"There's nothing wrong with the light in my guest bedroom!" Alyssa was saying. "I use it sometimes myself!"

"The least you could do is provide a makeup mirror!" came Genevieve's commanding voice. "Honestly, Alyssa, you just don't think sometimes."

"Why didn't you bring your own makeup mirror? You're supposed to be the old pro around here. With emphasis on 'old'!"

Corinne opened the door. "Thank goodness," she said. "I'm afraid they're going to snarl each other to death."

They hurried through oversize rooms arrayed with wicker furniture and exotic plants. The effect was tropical and unmistakably expensive.

Emma found Amalie trying to improvise a makeup mirror for Genevieve with lamps. "You'd better style my daughter first," said the actress. "She has a bad case of starlet-itis, as we all know."

Resisting the impulse to click her tongue, Emma left the room wondering why the two of them always managed to bring out the worst in each other.

Alyssa's vast bedroom, on the opposite side of the house, featured a round, velvet-covered bed with a mirrored canopy, which Emma found in rather bad taste. The adjacent dressing room sported another huge mirror blazing with light. Visible through a door into the bathroom was a whirlpool tub set with black and white tile.

"Well!" Alyssa waved her in. "I was afraid my mother would haul you off first. I mean, she always looks great, doesn't she? For her age. So why is she making such a fuss about it?"

Emma ducked her head and went to work. Alyssa had already washed her hair and let it air dry. Styling it required gel, judicious use of a curling iron, a bit of dampening and blow drying, and lots of spray.

With no one else around, Alyssa sat quietly for a while watching her image in the glass and then said, "I suppose you and your mother get along beautifully."

"Actually, my mother died when I was thirteen." Emma didn't want the response to sound like a rebuke, so she added, "We did use to quarrel. I felt guilty about it later."

"What did she die of?" For once, Alyssa focused on her hairdresser's words.

"Cancer. It was very quick," Emma said. "I always thought it took years."

"You were only thirteen," Alyssa said. "Was your father strict, or did you get to enjoy yourself? My mother practically roped and tied me when I was a teenager."

Emma doubted that very much, but she knew better than to say so. "It wasn't so much that he was strict, but I felt responsible for him. I used to go home after school and do laundry, clean and fix dinner. I guess I like taking care of people."

"Lucky for me," Alyssa said. "I'm not very good at complimenting people but—you're the best hairdresser I've had."

"Thanks. That means a lot."

When Emma had finished, the singer regarded herself for a moment. "I don't know how you do it. When I try, it ends up looking like hay."

"You could learn, but you don't need to," Emma said.

Corinne peeked in. "I'm sorry, Alyssa, but your mother's asking to have her hair done."

"We're not quite finished," Alyssa said, and her assistant retreated.

Emma refrained from commenting as she packed up her gear.

"Did you always want to be a hairdresser?" Alyssa asked "How did you know you'd be good at it?"

"I used to fix my dolls' hair." Emma smiled at the memory. "And my girlfriends'. I was popular at slumber parties because I could do French braids."

She didn't feel like telling Alyssa about her dream of working with performers, or how she got sidetracked for so long. Some instinct warned to keep a subtle but definite distance from her employer.

Amalie appeared a moment later. Instead of asking, she said, "Oh, good, you're done. Emma, Genevieve's getting anxious."

The doorbell rang, and Alyssa beamed. Obviously the reporter and photographer had arrived, and she would have the spotlight to herself for a while.

Genevieve sat fuming in front of her dressing table mirror when Emma entered the room.

"Look at this!" she snorted, gesturing at all the lamps. "I feel like some weird old lady with a fetish for light. Wouldn't you think my own daughter would invite me to share her dressing room?"

"There'd be blood on the floor." Emma set up her equipment.

Genevieve chuckled. "Well, I suppose. Do you believe that little fool? She's preening herself on being first to talk to the reporter. Doesn't she realize that allows me to make an entrance?"

Although Emma refrained from saying anything, she observed silently that one could easily see where Alyssa got her competitiveness.

After Genevieve's hair had been curled and styled to perfection, Emma prepared to leave. "Oh, no!" the actress said. "Don't forget we're taking a cover photo. We'll need touch-ups."

"Oh, of course." Emma tried not to think about Otto, who was playing at Josie's house. He wouldn't mind staying longer, and Josie had told her not to rush back.

Emma joined Corinne and Amalie in the kitchen, where the housekeeper served coffee. From where they sat, they could hear the interview and catch glimpses of the reporter—a gaunt woman in her late thirties with dyed blond hair.

The initial questions were matter-of-fact, and Emma had begun to relax when she heard the reporter say, "I hear your musical special was postponed. Industry gossip says there may be problems with it. Any comment?"

"There aren't any problems," Alyssa snapped. "I don't know who's saying that. People just love to dish the dirt at whoever's on top, don't they?"

"What my daughter means," Genevieve said, "is that we've been assured that the network loves the show. They ran into some scheduling problems and decided to hold it for the fall ratings' sweeps."

The reporter waited a moment and then, when no further response was forthcoming, she said, "We understand the two of you fight over almost everything, even who gets her hair styled first."

"Nonsense," Genevieve said. "We have the usual disagreements you'd expect, with all the pressure of performing in a hit show, but we'd never quarrel over anything so petty."

"We could certainly each have our own hairdresser," Alyssa added. "We just happen to like the same one. She works for me, actually."

"But I discovered her," Genevieve said.

"Could I meet her?" the reporter asked.

Emma shot an alarmed look at Corinne and Amalie, but there was nothing they could do when Alyssa came to fetch her.

Stepping into the living room, Emma could feel the tension in the air. The reporter studied her piercingly as if seeking some new and shocking angle for her readers. Genevieve sat smoothing her skirt, wearing her patented gracious expression, while Alyssa propelled Emma forward possessively.

"Here she is," the singer said.

"Emma Lindt?" The reporter double-checked the spelling and asked a few questions about Emma's training and experience before saying, "So you're new to Hollywood? You've certainly landed in the big time!"

"I've been lucky." Clearly, the reporter expected to hear more, so Emma added, "Alyssa and Genevieve have both been very kind."

"Do they have the same kind of hair?" The reporter checked her tape recorder and then resumed questioning. "Who's the easiest to style? Are you the one responsible for Alyssa's softer look?"

Emma answered as diplomatically as she could, all the time wishing she could fade into the background. The worst moment came when the reporter said, "I'd like to have you in the picture. The Loos women and their shared hairstylist."

"The article isn't about me," Emma pointed out quickly. "And I'm not dressed for a picture." Mentally, she cataloged her apparel: jogging shoes, blue jeans, a rather flattering green blouse with matching earrings. At least she'd done her makeup and hair this morning.

"You look fine," the reporter said. "Doesn't she?"

Reluctantly, the two stars nodded. They weren't any more thrilled about this than Emma was.

The magazine's photographer directed them all out to the pool area. Set into the side of a slope, the backyard had been designed with a series of hidden glades, featuring pools linked by small waterfalls. Lush greenery shaded the mild May sunshine.

They must have spent an hour posing and smiling, until Emma's jaw ached and her neck felt stiff. She tried to blend as much into the background as possible, and slipped away with relief when the photographer finally decided to take some pictures without her.

"Do you think Alyssa was offended?" she asked Corinne before leaving.

"Oh, she's not too thrilled, but she'll survive." The other woman walked Emma to her car. "She can hardly blame you."

"I felt like an interloper," Emma said.

Corinne shook her head. "You told me you've always wanted to style celebrities. Well, that means you've got to become something of a celebrity yourself. Stars like to surround themselves with glitter."

"You mean I should promote myself more?" Emma asked in dismay.

"Well..." Her friend smiled. "I wouldn't want you to do things that make you uncomfortable, but a little publicity wouldn't hurt. Let people know how talented you are. Otherwise they won't value you."

Driving home, Emma realized her instincts were telling her the same thing. Alyssa might prefer the way Emma did her hair, but there was always the danger she might defect to someone more prestigious, unless Emma herself developed a certain *cachet*.

Still, she couldn't help wondering how the article would portray her, and how she could balance her natural tendency toward modesty against her professional need for recognition.

The irony amused her. A few months ago, there would have been no question. She'd been determined to make up for lost time, even if it involved some sacrifice in her personal life.

But now, well, life had a way of changing one's perspective.

Emma touched her abdomen. She knew it was early, but sometimes she thought she felt little wisps of movement, the first tentative stirrings of the baby.

Part of her still wanted the glory, even at the cost of public exposure, longer hours and greater stress. And part of her wanted to nestle down in her cozy home and treasure every moment of her babies' childhoods before they fled forever.

She gritted her teeth as a car merged in front of her, going five miles under the speed limit. Instinct urged her to veer around it, to get on her way in a hurry.

Instead, Emma paused to check her mirrors and look behind her carefully. She couldn't afford to take risks now. She was carrying too precious a cargo.

Chapter Nine

"Mommy," Otto said. "There's somebody on the phone."

Emma poked her head out of the shower. "Did they say who it was?"

"She said to tell you...um...somebody's calling." Otto bounced up and down.

"All right." Emma wrapped a towel sarong-style around her swelling body and hurried out. She wondered why anyone would be calling so early on a Sunday morning.

The last month hadn't been easy. With taping of *Hotel Marango* on hiatus, Alyssa had taken over hostess duties on a late-night rock video show as well as making guest appearances on variety shows. Genevieve, meanwhile, was starring in a revival of *South Pacific* in Long Beach; and both of them insisted they couldn't go on without Emma's services.

Emma picked up the phone. "Hello?"

"Hold for Susan Salonica," said a female voice on the other end.

Emma nearly dropped the phone. Susan Salonica, the vamp star of a daytime soap opera, was currently shooting her first feature film amid lots of publicity about her quarrels with the director.

A sultry voice came on the phone. "Miss Lindt? This is Susan Salonica."

She could hardly speak. Big stars like Susan Salonica didn't usually go around calling hairdressers, on Sunday or any other day. "Yes. I mean, good morning. What can I do for you?"

"I saw the article in *Weekend*," purred the voice. "I'm having some problems with my stylist. Frankly, I need someone a bit more flexible. Would you be interested?"

Mentally, Emma ran through her schedule. If she tried to fit anyone else in, it would mean working a twenty-hour day, and not being available whenever Alyssa needed her.

"I'd love to, but unfortunately I'm on salary with Miss Loos," she said. "She has a hectic schedule right now and I'd be doing you both a disservice if I took on any more work. But if you have any special occasions, one-time events, perhaps I could work you in."

She expected the actress to react with a curt dismissal. The response, instead, was, "Oh, I will. Really, I'm dying to try you out. You will promise to let me know if you get free? Here, I'll have my secretary give you my phone numbers."

The numbers included not only her studio but also her home and car phones.

Emma hung up, amazed. Being turned down had only made the actress more eager.

Then it struck her. The article had come out! A pang of anxiety warned that if it focused too much on her, Alyssa wouldn't be pleased. In fact, Emma might soon find herself with lots of spare time for Susan Salonica.

About to return to the bathroom, she stopped as the doorbell rang. The thought crossed her mind that someone else might have come as a result of the article, but she dismissed it as unlikely.

Emma padded through the house and peered through the viewhole, relieved to see Eric. She slipped open the door and let him in.

They'd met for dinner twice over the past few weeks, with Otto on hand, but otherwise their schedules hadn't meshed. Complicating matters was Eric's increasing fixation with the futuristic city in his computer.

While Emma relished his enthusiasm, she hadn't appreciated spending a rare free evening alone the previous week because he had to input some startling insights. Seeing him now, his hair newly washed and his eyes bluer than usual in the bright morning light, she realized how much she'd missed him.

"Have you seen this?" He offered a stack of magazines. "I bought you some extras, just in case."

Clamping her towel in place with one hand, Emma picked one up. Staring out from the cover were the familiar countenances of her two clients and, above and behind them, her own softer face.

In bold type was printed, "Alyssa And Genevieve: Sharing A Stylist And A Man."

"A man?" Emma flipped to the article.

Eric leaned over, his breath tickling her ear. "It's a real come-on. They're talking about the character of Jon on the show."

Skimming the article, Emma found several flattering references to her, along with the strong implications that the two women were more enamored of her hair styling than of any member of the male sex.

"It makes them sound so egotistical," she said.

"It makes you sound brilliant." Eric bent down and nuzzled her neck. "Mmm. I like that perfume."

"It's my soap." She laughed as his nibbling tickled her throat. "Eric!"

Dropping the magazines on an end table, he wrapped his arms around Emma. Inhaling his masculine scent, she felt all the tension seep out of her body, replaced by a languid, slowly intensifying desire.

Her lips met his in a hungry kiss. Pressed against him, she could feel his eagerness matching her own.

Eric lifted his head, his breathing ragged. "Damn," he muttered. Then she heard it, the thump-thump of Otto bounding down the hall. Reluctantly, she stepped away.

Otto halted inches short of a collision. "Can I have some crackers?"

"Sure." As she tucked her towel tighter, Emma wondered how much he'd seen and what he thought, but her son trailed quietly behind her into the kitchen.

"Can I watch cartoons?" he asked after she handed him the crackers in a plastic bag.

"Okay." Emma didn't like him to watch too much television, but she needed some time with Eric. "How about Winnie the Pooh?"

"Chip and Dale," he corrected. "And the Rescue Rangers. Okay, Mommy?"

When he was settled, Emma retreated to her bedroom to change. Eric came inside with her and closed the door.

"I was going to dress," she said.

"I've seen you nude before." He tilted his head. "Are you being shy?"

"You—you haven't seen me pregnant."

He moved toward Emma. "That's right, I haven't."

Without thinking, she backed away, and he halted. "I'm sorry," she said. "I don't know why I did that."

Eric reached out and removed the corner of the towel from her hand, letting it fall to the floor. Irrationally, Emma wanted to retreat.

She could feel Eric's gaze on her body as if he were touching her, trailing down her enlarged breasts and rounded abdomen. Her skin tingled and she knew her nipples were hardening.

"You look like a fertility goddess." He spoke almost reverently. "Your skin is velvet."

"Eric—"

He drew her toward him. "Can we?"

"Make love?" The words sounded hoarse in her own ears. "I—I haven't had any more bleeding but—" The sense of lumpishness had vanished; in Eric's arms, Emma felt voluptuously earthy, in need of fulfillment. "And then there's Otto. I can't—"

"I know." He uttered something between a sigh and a groan. "He's a great kid, but we need time alone. Can't we send him somewhere?"

Emma's sense of languor vanished. "You don't just send a kid out like laundry."

"I suppose not." Eric ruffled his fingers through her hair. "Doesn't he need a nap or something?"

"At nine o'clock in the morning?" Turning away, Emma dressed quickly. "I know kids can be inconvenient sometimes."

"That's putting it mildly." Eric gave her a rueful grin. "I suppose babies are even worse."

"You suppose right." Emma tried to ignore the need that still pulsed through her body.

The phone rang.

"Now who—?" Emma picked it up. "Hello?"

"Emma Lindt?" The woman's tone was strident and commanding. "This is Barbara Lisle. I write the Town Crier column for *Hollywood After Sunset*."

"Yes?" She made a face at Eric.

"Tell us the story behind Alyssa's new hairstyle. We hear that her hair was falling out—that she was on the verge of going bald."

"Nonsense." Emma shivered inwardly, concerned that anything she said might be twisted. "Alyssa has beautiful hair. She simply wanted a different look."

"Whose idea was it? Was it Genevieve's?"

"I'm sorry," Emma said. "I can't discuss my clients this way. It isn't fair to them."

"Now look here," the woman snapped. "It's in your own best interest to be mentioned in my column, young lady. If you want any press from me, you're going to have to co-operate."

On the verge of replying sharply, Emma stopped herself. It would be foolish to antagonize such a powerful woman. "I'll tell you what," she said. "Anytime you want me to confirm or deny a rumor—if I can—I'll help you out. But I can't betray my clients' trust by telling stories out of school. I'm sure you understand."

"Well..." A tongue clicked in frustration. "Yes, I suppose I have to admire your integrity. I don't run into that very often. But really, if you want to make a name for yourself, you may have to step off your high horse one of these days."

Before Emma could reply, she heard a click at the other end.

"High pressure?" Eric asked and she nodded.

When she'd finished dressing, they pried Otto away from the TV and took him on a forty-five-minute drive to the beach. A sharp ocean breeze made the air too cold for swimming, but he played happily in the sand for an hour and then they ate fried clams and potatoes from a restaurant at the Newport Pier.

By the time they got home, Otto was nodding off, and Emma tucked him into bed with relief. "He's a deep sleeper," she told Eric. "He'll be out for a couple of hours at least."

They walked down the hall to the bedroom together. Emma could feel Eric's yearning, as well as her own. She wanted to please him and satisfy him, to draw away all his frustrations until his body echoed with happiness.

She felt a little awkward at first as he undressed her, stiffly aware of her bulky body and of the few light butterfly movements inside that signaled the baby's wakefulness.

Sensing her discomfort, Eric massaged Emma's shoulders and back until her muscles loosened. Then his hands cupped her breasts, circling gently, and his mouth teased kisses along her stomach.

With a great sense of release, Emma fell back on the bed, giving herself over to the sensations rioting through her nervous system. By the time Eric joined their bodies, she had forgotten all about caution. They merged like a great force of the earth, the sea pouring into a bay, unstoppable and wild.

Emma wanted more and more, surprising herself with the demands she made, until neither could hold back any longer and they flashed into ecstasy together.

"Oh, God," Eric murmured. "Did we have an earthquake or what?"

She smiled. "At least we don't have to worry about me getting pregnant."

He shot her a baleful look, then chuckled. "I never thought about it that way."

They tiptoed down the hall, past the room where Otto lay snoring lightly, and showered together. As they soaped each other, Eric said, "This tub drains great."

"I know a good plumber." They both laughed.

By five, he was back on duty, handling an emergency call from an elderly lady whose toilet had overflowed. "Such a romantic way to cap the day," Eric grumbled playfully as he kissed Emma at the door. "Give Otto my regrets."

"I will. He'll miss you at bedtime."

Emma stood by the window, staring out at the street as his van pulled away, trying to sort out her emotions.

The problem was that she wanted things tied up neatly, and her life wasn't working out that way. Did she love Eric?

Of course, in a way, but not enough to commit herself to him. Not enough to build her life around him.

The fact that she'd made love this afternoon, pleasurable as it had been, scared her. *Had* it been safe? Why had she overridden her own common sense?

Passion was part of it, but not the whole story. Instinctively, Emma had sensed Eric's needs and made them her responsibility. It wasn't her job to take care of everybody. Why couldn't she say no sometimes?

Well, she'd said no to Susan Salonica, Emma told herself as she reopened the magazine Eric had left on the coffee table. Then she read the article again—every single word.

DURING THE NEXT MONTH, Emma found herself saying no a lot. She said no to an aging rock star who wanted her to accompany him on tour; she turned down a sitcom starlet known for her bad temper; she refused a full-time position at a top Hollywood salon.

The only exception Emma made had come two weeks ago, when she'd spent a free night styling Susan Salonica's hair for an awards banquet. The actress had crowed about snaring the hottest stylist in Hollywood, and heaped praise on the subtle but very flattering improvement in her coiffure.

Being welcomed with open arms had given Emma a taste of the benefits of fame. More and more, she was finding it hard to reject the tempting offers that came her way.

"Maybe I'm being foolish," she told Corinne one day in June as they waited backstage for Alyssa, who was participating in a charity concert at the Universal Amphitheatre.

With only a minimum of grumbling, Alyssa had agreed to share a dressing room with two other rock stars, and the place was a mess. One singer's assistant had shown up half-loaded and the other assistant had marched herself away with her nose in the air, too proud to hobnob with a mere hairdresser.

Fortunately, Alyssa and her friends scorned drugs, a matter that had concerned Emma when she first went to work for the singer. She was pleased to find that more and more performers understood not only the dangers of drugs but also their responsibility to their young audiences.

Swallowing a long draft of diet soda, Corinne took a seat beside Emma on the dressing-room couch. "It's a tough thing in Hollywood. Loyalty is great, but too much of it can work against you."

"You think I'm making a mistake?"

The blond woman answered with a shrug. "Who knows? Right now, Alyssa and Genevieve are hot, and they're carrying you with them. You're wise not to alienate them."

Emma glanced at the dressing counter, with its jumble of creams and lipsticks, powders and glitter. It looked so exotic, even a little decadent. What was Emma Conrad Lindt doing here?

She felt as if she were standing on a ledge in a high wind, struggling to maintain a precarious balance. Not just in her career, but in her life. The baby spent most of its nights tumbling around, leaving her grateful for its obvious health but dismayed at her sleeplessness. Otto resolutely refused to discuss either the baby or Eric, choosing to spend as much time as she allowed in front of the TV. And Eric himself, since their passionate encounter in June, had developed a lusty appetite that Emma could never refuse.

Darn it, she didn't *want* to refuse. But a nagging voice inside lectured on her cowardice. So far, she hadn't worked up the nerve to ask the doctor if it was safe.

Corinne sprang up as Alyssa stormed in. "Did you see that?" the singer demanded. "That idiot running the spotlight kept missing me. Can you believe it? I felt like the original amateur night, running around the stage, trying to stay in the spotlight!"

"It's for a good cause," Emma ventured, since the concert was to raise money for the homeless.

"Why do I do these things?" Alyssa dropped into her chair with a thump. "I could just make a donation."

Her delicate face wore a strained expression. For the first time, Emma noticed a hint of fine lines around her eyes. Since scoring a hit on *Hotel Marango*, Alyssa had been driving herself at a furious pace, as if trying to prove she didn't have to sacrifice her music for her acting.

Like the first time they'd met, it struck Emma that Alyssa was running scared. Insecurity was a funny thing; it made no allowances for talent or success.

Besides, she supposed that when you reached the top, the way down looked awfully steep.

"Your name means a lot," Emma ventured. "Hearing that you're participating will make people think more about the homeless. You can do a lot of good, Alyssa."

The singer dropped her chin into her hand, leaning forward and making a face at herself in the mirror. "Do I look like Mother Theresa to you?"

"Not hardly." Emma smiled, and to her relief, Alyssa smiled back.

"How's the kid?" Alyssa straightened as Emma began recurling her hair for the grand finale at the end of the show.

It was safe to assume her employer meant the baby, since she'd never shown much curiosity about Otto. "Pretty lively."

"You must be—how far along?"

"Twenty weeks. Halfway." Emma shook her head. "On the one hand, that doesn't seem possible. On the other hand, it feels like I've been pregnant forever."

She caught Alyssa's wistful gaze in the mirror. "I guess— I mean, someday—well, I suppose I need to meet the right guy first."

Corinne, watching from the next chair over, made a clucking noise. "You should see the proposals she gets in the mail, Emma."

Alyssa waved her hand. "Nerds and love-struck fourteen-year-olds."

"It'll happen," Emma said.

The singer bit her lip, and Emma thought of Ford Burgess. Had Genevieve's on-screen seduction of him and her off-screen flirting spoiled a potential romance? No, not likely; the only one he would ever fall in love with was himself.

"I dream sometimes about finding the right man. But will I know him when I do? And why is it taking so long?" Alyssa mused.

"They say you have to kiss a lot of frogs before you find a prince," Emma said.

The other two women giggled. "A frog," Alyssa said. "Yep. That fits a certain I know."

"Close call," was Corinne's judgment after their employer headed back to the wings.

"Does she always have these mood swings?" Emma tucked her equipment into its case.

"Show business is hard on the emotions." Corinne wrapped the cord around the curling iron and handed it to her. "You're always on trial, always on show. And you have to keep your emotions close to the surface because they're the tools of your trade."

"Why do you suppose—" Emma searched around the counter, finally finding the cap to the hairspray. "Why would Genevieve make things so hard on her? She must understand the tightrope her daughter's walking."

Corinne grimaced. "Alyssa's poaching on her territory. Frankly, I think it's jealousy."

"Of her own daughter?"

"It's not unknown," Corinne said. "No one can drive you crazy like your nearest and dearest. They know all the buttons to push."

Emma reflected on her employer's emotional fragility all the way home. Then, walking into the house, she felt a slight but distinct cramp that drove all thought of work from her mind.

A check revealed that she was spotting again. Only a little bit, but she knew any bleeding could be a danger sign.

ON THE WAY to the hospital, Eric gripped the steering wheel so hard it cut creases into his hands. Why had Emma waited until morning to tell him? At least she could have let him drive her, but she'd insisted her friend Betsy would drop her off.

Darn it, he shouldn't have been dragging her into the bedroom all month. He had to learn to put her needs first.

Eric didn't like the feeling that came to him, that despite his occasional helpfulness he'd left most of the burden of the pregnancy to Emma. Sure, he picked up a fast-food dinner for her sometimes, and he'd helped out during the threatened miscarriage. But mostly he'd gone about his business as always, spending endless hours building the model for his futuristic city before finally shipping it off right before the deadline.

Emma didn't have the luxury of that kind of time. When she worked long hours, he knew, it was only by juggling preschool and babysitters. When she did have a day off, she devoted it to Otto.

What *was* it like, being a woman? Did she resent the demands of family, as he suspected he might in her situation? And how did it feel to carry new life inside you? Although Eric had never considered himself a traditionalist, he'd read that there were emotional and psychological differences between the sexes, and he supposed pregnancy must intensify those. If only he could see through Emma's eyes for just one day, maybe he'd understand better.

An unfamiliar wistfulness touched him. He'd never considered it before, but it didn't seem quite fair that a man could never know the miracle of feeling life grow within. He supposed women would hoot at him and remind him of all the aches and inconveniences that came with pregnancy, but at the same time it must feel—transcendent.

At the hospital, a receptionist directed him down the elevator to the radiology lab in the basement. Eric felt the muscles tighten in his jaw as he entered the waiting room.

It was full of people, most reading magazines, some conversing quietly or watching TV. He caught expressions of fear, of impatience, of passivity.

Then he spotted Emma, tucked into a corner seat flipping through a glossy hairstyling magazine.

She'd dressed meticulously in a crisp pink maternity suit. Actually, he thought, she looked robustly healthy compared to everyone else in the room.

Then she peered up and he saw the tension around her mouth. "Hi." Eric strode over and sat down, taking her hand. "How are you holding up?"

"Going through the motions," Emma said, her delicate face pinched with worry. "I didn't tell Otto anything but I think he suspected. I wish he'd talk to me more. He won't discuss the pregnancy at all."

"It must be hard for him." Eric tried to imagine himself in Otto's place, but it wasn't easy. "In the last few years he's lost his father—"

"He doesn't remember it," Emma said.

"Still, there's a gap in his life," Eric pointed out. "And then I've barged in, and I'm sure he doesn't know what to make of me yet. And now this baby."

Emma ducked her head. Was that a tear glittering in her eye?

"You're not going to lose it," Eric said. It was only a guess about what she might be thinking, but her panicked expression confirmed his suspicion.

"It's too early for the baby to survive outside me," she choked out.

"Don't talk that way!"

"But why am I bleeding again?" she asked. "That didn't happen with Otto. Once I was past the first trimester—"

"Emma Lindt?" called a female technician from the front of the room. "This way, please."

Eric helped Emma to her feet and they walked through the door, along a short hall and into a room filled with sonogram equipment. It looked rather like his computer, with a viewing screen and a control panel, and he felt a little more at ease.

The technician plied Emma with questions—the date of her last period, whether she felt movement, why she'd come for the ultrasound.

"Will we get the results right away?" Eric asked, and then felt foolish. "I guess we can see on the screen."

"I haven't felt any movement this morning." The words came out shaky. "You don't think—?"

"Just climb up here on the table," the technician said, directing Emma to a footstool.

A minute later, she lay on her back with her blouse pulled up, her skirt pulled down and some kind of clear goo spread on her bulging midsection.

"I feel like a beached whale," Emma said. Eric squeezed her hand. He didn't seem able to speak right now. He couldn't recall ever feeling this tense before, except driving to the hospital the day his father was stricken.

Couldn't that technician work faster? Why was she fooling with her equipment for so long?

Finally she pressed a small scanner over Emma's stomach, moving slowly up and back. All Eric could see on the screen was a nebulous gray cloud, like muddy water rippling faintly.

And then, suddenly, there it was: a tiny but unmistakable hand waving, and then an arm and—the whole picture surged and roiled.

"Talk about active," said the technician. "This guy's a real go-getter."

Eric heard a funny sound in the room, kind of a rumble rising into an unmistakable laugh, and then he realized it was him.

"Wow," he said. "Guess the little guy's safe, huh, Emma?"

Her eyes glistened. "Guess so."

"Is it a boy?" Eric asked. "Can you tell?"

"Not this early." The technician pressed a button, and the picture on-screen froze. A moment later, the motion resumed. "I'm going to take some photos here for the doctor."

For the next few minutes, as the technician completed her work, Eric stared in fascination at the screen. Until now, he'd known intellectually that Emma was carrying a baby, but it hadn't seemed real.

Now he could make out wonderful details—tiny legs kicking, the round shape of the head, even the miniature thumb being inserted into the mouth. It amazed him that all those parts functioned so well.

His child. His very own little person.

"I think I see your problem." The statement broke his concentration, and Eric remembered why they were here. "Do you see this?" The technician pointed to a shadow. "That's the placenta. It's very low-lying, what they call a placenta previa."

"What does that mean?" Emma asked.

"The doctor will explain it," the technician said, and impatient as they were, they had to wait.

The appointment with the doctor was later that morning, in an adjacent building on the hospital grounds. Eric, glad he'd planned to take the morning off, noticed he wasn't the only man accompanying his wife.

Except that Emma wasn't his wife.

As they followed a nurse into the examining room, he tried to sort out the emotions doing battle in his mind. He loved Emma, and he certainly wanted to take care of her. But first he had to achieve things he could be proud of, to prove to himself and to the memory of his father that Eric Jameson wasn't a quitter. Otherwise he'd be offering Emma less than she deserved.

And yet, if he were really gifted, shouldn't he have found a way to succeed before now? Had he been held back by economics all these years, or had it been fear? He knew what his father would have said.

Eric frowned, clearing away the self-destructive thoughts, as the doctor came into the room. After introducing himself, Dr. Meyers held up what looked like a sheet of X rays.

"A placenta previa means the placenta, which provides the baby with food and oxygen, is covering part or all of the birth canal," he explained.

"Does—is that dangerous for the baby?" Emma ventured from where she sat on the paper-covered table.

"It can be," the doctor said. "But most of the time, during the course of the pregnancy, the placenta migrates upward and by the time you're ready to deliver, there's no problem."

"And if it doesn't?" Eric asked.

"Let's not worry about that now." The doctor put the diagram away. "We'll do another sonogram before delivery, just to make sure. In the meantime, no strenuous exercise and no intercourse."

"Oh." Emma glanced timidly at Eric.

Did she think he was selfish enough to resent being deprived? Eric barely restrained himself from glaring, afraid she might misunderstand. "Of course, Doctor," he said.

Afterward, walking out into the sunshine, he wrapped his arms around Emma.

"Are you happy?" he murmured. "Relieved?"

"Yes." She sounded hesitant. "I mean—I can't help being a little apprehensive. And—you don't mind—"

"Emma!" He caught her shoulders and looked her square in the eye. "It's my baby, too."

"Well, sure."

Words jumbled together in Eric's throat as he hugged her again. There were so many things he wanted to say—that he'd never imagined the sheer joy of seeing his child wiggle around a computer screen, that her big round body looked more beautiful to him than any swimsuit model on TV, that he half wished a dragon would come along right now so he could slay it.

The irony was that, easily as he could talk to Emma about dreams and plans, Eric found himself tongue-tied now. He had to content himself with tucking her into his car and driving her home, slowing down more than usual for the railroad tracks and a bump in the pavement.

Half a block from her house, they passed a man strolling along the sidewalk with a little girl riding piggyback on his shoulders, laughing and bouncing. In the soft June breeze, her blond hair fluttered around her head like a halo.

A wave of happiness so pure it was almost pain swept through Eric's heart, and he couldn't seem to stop chuckling for the rest of the day.

Chapter Ten

In typical Southern California fashion, the July morning began with a cool overcast, but by the time Emma and her friends met at the McDonald's in Anaheim, the sun baked the hamburger play tower, the slide and the merry-go-round.

"I love this place but I wish they'd put in umbrellas," muttered Josie as she smeared sunscreen on Kiki and Greggie.

"Feels nice to me." Betsy stretched her legs, keeping an eye on Roy as he munched his McNuggets.

"If you guys want dessert, let me know." Josie was treating today in celebration of Greggie's first birthday. Her husband was, as usual, out of town.

"Are you kidding?" Emma folded her hands over her belly. As with Otto, she looked bigger than her five months, probably because she was short and didn't have a lot of space in which to carry the baby. "Besides, Otto's birthday is next month, and I can't bake cupcakes without pigging out."

"I'll have some of those chocolate-chip cookies." Betsy waved her hand. "You don't have to come, Josie. You take care of the kids."

"Well, here." Josie handed her a dollar.

Letting out a low whistle, Betsy said, "See you guys in Las Vegas," and disappeared into the restaurant.

Otto dropped his empty hamburger carton onto the tray. "Can I go play, Mommy?" Without waiting for an answer, he dashed away, with Kiki in pursuit.

Emma sipped her milk and pondered what to do about Otto. Last night she'd read him a book about having a new baby in the family, hoping it would bring out whatever was on his mind. But Otto had merely listened and then promptly changed the subject.

She knew he must be concerned. Kids reacted to any change, and especially something so major. But he would simply have to talk about it in his own time.

She'd tried to keep things as normal as possible, and fortunately there'd been no further bleeding this month. She'd even managed to cut back on her work, since Genevieve was on vacation and, without her mother around to goad her, Alyssa wasn't pushing herself so frantically.

Eric visited more often, making a point of helping with the housework, with mixed results. At first, he'd managed to bake the dirt on the dishes by sticking them in the dishwasher unrinsed, and he'd turned a load of Emma's underwear pink when he washed it with Otto's new red shirt.

However, with his computer project behind him, Eric had devoted himself to learning the domestic skills, even to the point of whipping up an omelet and fried potatoes one night. Emma had tactfully excused the fact that the omelet was ready fifteen minutes before the potatoes by proclaiming that she loved to eat in courses.

Otto wavered between following Eric around like a puppy and hanging all over his mother possessively. She supposed that was normal, but she wished she could see inside the boy's stubborn little head.

Now she watched him whisk down the slide, whooping. Who would ever guess what a difficult life he'd led in his few short years?

"I don't know why I'm such a wimp," Josie said.

Turning toward her, Emma caught Greggie's hand before he could knock Betsy's drink off the table. "You still haven't confronted Sam, have you?"

"How can I?" Josie produced a toy for Greggie from the diaper bag. "I mean, we had this agreement when we got married. He hates it when people go back on their word. Besides, I'm not even sure what I want him to do. He'd never be able to find another job that pays this well. And I love him so much—I just want us both to be happy."

"Marriage isn't a business contract." Emma watched Roy, Otto and Kiki race noisily to the merry-go-round. "It's not a question of going back on your word. And what good is the money if he misses watching his kids grow up?"

Betsy slipped back into her seat, nibbling on a cookie. "What did I miss?"

"Josie's still waffling," Emma said.

"I had an interesting discussion with Matt." Betsy frowned at a ding in her nail polish. "Isn't this stuff awful? The brand always says they're extrastrong. I can't go two days without touch-ups."

"Matt," Emma prodded.

"I need to hear this," Josie added. "You don't seem to have any hesitation about confronting *your* husband."

"Maybe that's part of my problem." Betsy waved a cookie at Roy, but he was too absorbed in his play even for such a temptation. "Sometimes I come on a little too strong. So last night, after Roy was in bed, I poured some wine, lit the candles and dragged my husband into bed."

"You didn't!" Josie said.

Betsy regarded her, in confusion until understanding dawned. "No, no. I used the diaphragm. Honestly, Jos, I'm not that underhanded!"

"And?" Emma said.

"When it came time for pillow talk, well, I tactfully brought the subject up." Betsy tilted her face to the sun. "For once, he didn't get angry and dig in his heels."

"He's willing to consider another child?" Josie snatched Greggie back as he nearly tripped a woman carrying a tray. "Look at this kid! Are you sure you want another one?"

"They drive you crazy but they're wonderful." Betsy sighed. "Anyway, then it all came out."

She stopped as the children ran up, demanding their drinks.

"Excuse me a minute." Josie reached into her huge diaper bag. "I have a little gift for everyone."

"But you told us not to bring presents!" said Emma, who had in fact stashed a small package in her car to give Greggie on the way out.

"You can't have a birthday party without favors." Josie pulled out three Magic Bee masks. Magic Bee was the latest cartoon character to follow the Ninja Turtles and Tailspin in the hearts of the preschool set.

"Wow!" Otto grabbed one. "Mommy, can you help me?"

When all three kids had their masks in place, they bolted back into the fray, winning envious stares from the other children on the playground.

"Okay," Emma said. "What all came out?"

"You know Matt and I hail from different backgrounds," Betsy began. She'd described before how her parents, both professionals from the well-educated African-American middle class, had disapproved when she and Matt first began dating.

Unlike her, he came from a poor family and had to put himself through law school by working nights as a cab driver. Only when he finally passed the bar exam did her parents relent and accept him.

"Well, you know how hard it can be for black people—I don't mean that it isn't hard for lots of people, but unfortunately we have to overcome the same obstacles as everyone else and prejudice, too," Betsy said. "Matt's got it into his head that he has to work twice as hard as the other lawyers if he's ever going to make partner."

"He's afraid if you have another child he won't be able to spend enough time with the baby?" Emma asked.

"You know how lawyers are." Betsy sighed. "They consider an eighty-hour week to be routine. And it would just kill Matt if he got to the top and someone suggested he didn't really deserve it, that he'd been given special privileges because of affirmative action."

"I don't see how anyone could say that," Josie pointed out. "Matt's won some brilliant cases. Sam even read about him in a magazine."

"He can't adjust to the fact that he isn't poor and struggling anymore." Betsy shaded her eyes and checked on Roy as she spoke. "At least now I know what I'm up against."

"And you know it isn't because he doesn't like the idea of another child," Emma added.

"Sometimes I think..." Betsy shook her head. "No, I wouldn't trick him into it. I value my marriage too much. And then he might resent the child."

They mulled this over, absorbing the sunshine and watching their children chase each other through pretend castles. In a way, Emma reflected, Eric was like Matt. Eric hadn't come from a poor background, but he needed to prove something to himself, too.

She, on the other hand, loved her career for its own sake. She didn't want to give it up because she would miss the excitement backstage and the challenge of styling her clients for the camera, but her inner sense of worth wasn't tied up in her job.

She supposed that in some ways this pregnancy was easier on her than on him. Not physically, of course, but emotionally. She had no doubts about wanting the baby, but she could see the conflict in his face sometimes when he looked at her. Still, his eyes brimmed with pure delight when he pressed his hand against her abdomen and felt the baby kick.

Unexpectedly, tears came to her eyes.

"What?" Betsy demanded.

"I love this baby so much," Emma said. "I just—sometimes I get really emotional. And kind of irrational."

"Who ever said pregnancy was rational?" Betsy replied.

"IT'S JUST A BIRTHDAY party, Mom." Eric smiled indulgently as Stella Jameson, riding on the van seat beside him, patted her hair for the dozenth time.

He knew she'd spent all Saturday morning debating over which dress to wear, and she'd put on eyeshadow, which she almost never wore.

Actually, his mother looked terrific for fifty-one. Gray added distinction to her dark hair, and she kept in shape with visits to the health club. To Eric, she didn't look at all like someone about to become a grandmother.

Except for that one lunch at the mall, Stella hadn't had a chance to get to know Emma. His mother had hinted several times that he should extend a dinner invitation, but for some reason he'd wanted to keep Emma to himself.

He couldn't see why everybody in the world, from his second cousin Ellen to his Great-Aunt Melinda, considered it their business to nose into his private life. This miracle was happening to Emma and him; when they shared it with other people, Eric felt matters slipping out of his control.

Questions bombarded him: When were they getting married? Did they know if it was a boy or a girl? Had they picked out a name?

Even some of the plumbing service's regular clients had gotten wind of the forthcoming birth from Peter and offered congratulations. Not that Eric minded, and yet... Maybe if he were more sure where all this was going to lead and how he would deal with it, he wouldn't mind.

"You're awfully quiet," Stella said.

"I don't know what I'm going to do at a kid's birthday party," he said to avoid having to confess his thoughts.

"It's not a kid. It's Otto." She'd never said so, but he could tell his mother wouldn't object one bit to adding Otto to her soon-to-be-established list of grandchildren.

"Yes, but there'll be other four-year-olds." Eric hadn't thought to inquire how many, or what sort of activities Emma had planned. He found the whole prospect intimidating.

"I'm glad she asked us to come early," Stella said. "In her condition, she shouldn't be doing so much work."

"Mom." As they stopped at a red light, Eric turned toward her. "You've never said so, but you think we should get married, don't you?"

She considered briefly. "You did say it was Emma's choice not to."

"But?" He knew her too well to take her words as a conclusive answer.

"I don't suppose you pressed her very strongly." Stella twisted her purse strap in her hands. "Your father was always so hard on you. Much more than with Peter. I should have made an issue of it, but at the time—well, I didn't think it would hurt. So I know you feel you have to prove yourself."

"You think I'm wrong?" He pulled away from the light slowly. "Maybe I should postpone going back to school. Or give it up."

He didn't mean it, and his mother shot him a knowing look. "Right."

"Come on, Mom." They were almost to Emma's house, and Eric was losing patience. "I want to know what you *think.*"

"I think my opinions are all colored by the fact that I want my grandchild to be legitimate," Stella said, "even though I know nobody worries about such things anymore."

"And you want to mother Emma and Otto, which would be a lot easier if they were related to you," Eric added.

"Something like that."

He stopped in front of Emma's house and touched his mother's hand. "Mom, I know things have been hard for you. I want you to have all the joy in the world. But I have to come to Emma as a whole person, and right now I'm not."

"I keep wondering if I could have changed that." Stella opened the door. "But I suppose not. People have to find their own path."

As he and his mother carried their gifts to the house, Eric reflected that someday he, too, would be the parent of a grown child. He hoped he would have made the right choices to give that child a wonderful start in life.

As soon as Emma opened the door, he knew something was troubling her.

Tears darkened her eyes, and from behind came the angry squall of a childish temper tantrum.

"I don't want a party!" Otto was screaming from the middle of the living room. "I want to go to Disneyland!"

Emma greeted Stella briefly, then explained, "He's been awful all day. I don't know what's got into him. He's been looking forward to this party all week."

"I could take him to Disneyland next weekend," Stella offered.

"I don't want to go next weekend!" Otto howled. "I want to go now!"

"Well, maybe tonight—"

"No! It's my birthday. Don't I get to do what I want?" Tears glimmered in Otto's eyes.

Normally, Emma would probably have coped with him steadily enough, but she was pressing her hands against her temples as if she had a headache. Also, at six months, she looked to Eric uncomfortably large. A woman under that much physical pressure shouldn't have to cope with a head-strong child, too.

"Now look here." He knelt in front of Otto. "We're not going to bribe you. If my mother wants to take you to Dis-neyland next weekend, fine, but right now you've got guests coming and your mother's done a lot of work to make you happy."

"I don't want to be happy!" Otto said. "I want—I want—" He stopped in midsentence and clamped his lips together.

Until he'd come to know Emma, Eric hadn't spent much time with kids. The few times he'd seen one throw a temper tantrum, he'd figured the child was a brat and needed to be taught a lesson.

But this was Otto, not some generic child. Behind the outburst, he could see real misery in the child's eyes.

The pressure's getting to him.

"You want us all to go away, don't you?" he said. "Me, and the baby, and anybody else who takes your mother's attention. Right?"

"So, who cares?" Otto stared rebelliously toward the dining room, but his lower lip trembled.

"How would you like to beat me up?" Eric said.

The little boy's eyes flickered with interest. "Yeah?"

"In the backyard."

"Well, okay. I mean, not really beat you up, right? But like we're pirates or something." Otto dashed through the kitchen. "Come on out. My mom's got the balloons up, and the pitata."

"Piñata," Emma corrected with a smile.

The grassy yard had been transformed with black-and-yellow Magic Bee decorations, including a giant paper bee covered with ruffles. Card tables and chairs dotted the lawn, and chips and dip had been set out beneath a mesh umbrella.

Emma had even managed to find a piñata shaped like a bee. The paper-covered container, a popular item among Mexican families and others in Southern California, hung temptingly from a corner of the garage. A baseball bat rested against the wall, ready for a line of blindfolded children to use it to knock a hole in the piñata and spill out the candies.

Eric barely had time to brace himself before Otto attacked. The little boy squealed with delight as he pounded at the shoulder and arm with which Eric protected himself. Beneath the childish blows lay the pent-up frustration and resentment Otto couldn't express any other way.

When the blows began to weaken, Eric snaked his arm out and tickled Otto. The response was defiant laughter.

"You can't catch me!" Otto pelted away across the yard, and Eric gave chase, dodging around tables and chairs. He caught the boy next to the shade tree and they tussled and rolled on the grass, tickling and poking until they both ran out of breath.

"Well?" Eric demanded as they lay there, panting. "You still want to go to Disneyland instead?"

"Oh—I'll stay." Otto got to his feet. "Can I open my presents now?" He bounded away to pester Emma about the gaily wrapped packages that marked the gift table.

As he brushed himself off, Eric wondered what had happened between him and Otto. Perhaps because of the physical contact, he felt closer to the boy. It had been the preschool equivalent of an adult heart-to-heart.

Stella shanghaied Otto into helping her fill paper cups with M & M's. Emma finished giving the yard a final examination and turned to Eric.

"Thank you," she said. "I didn't know what to do with Otto. I guess he needed to slug it out of his system."

"It seemed to help, but I'm not sure why." He resisted the impulse to stroke her hair, knowing she'd probably spent half an hour fixing it. It looked even thicker and glossier than usual, and the sunlight brought out golden highlights.

"Otto's verbal in many ways, but not when it comes to his emotions." Emma's gaze followed her son as he paraded around the yard, setting the candy cups in place. "He needs to act it out, and you helped him."

"He's a real scrapper." Eric rubbed his shoulders, only half joking. "I may have scars."

"I'll give you a massage later, and maybe a little more," Emma teased, and then shook her head. "I keep forgetting."

Since the last episode of bleeding, they'd confined themselves to cuddling. "I keep forgetting, too." Eric angled an arm around her waist, and started as he felt a distinct thud. "The squirt kicked me."

"Don't tell me he—or she—is going to be as feisty as Otto." She laid her cheek against his chest. "Let's turn out all the lights and hide, okay? I don't want any guests today, after all."

"Neither does my mother." They both watched as Stella wiped a spot of chocolate off Otto's cheek, and replaced it with a kiss. "She wants to adopt you both."

"I'm glad I like my un-mother-in-law." Emma moved away as footsteps approached along the side walkway. "Oh, good. That must be Josie or Betsy. I forgot to put up the sign so people wouldn't trek through the house. Excuse me."

Before Eric could grasp that a full-scale invasion was under way, the yard quickly filled with what seemed like zillions of whooping, running children. By actual count half an hour later, there were five children Otto's size plus a sprinkling of babies, toddlers and older siblings, attended by appropriate numbers of grownups.

The children chased each other under tables, pedaled tricycles madly and made "bang-bang" noises as they played shoot-em-up with toy broomsticks and rakes. Eric, running interference whenever he saw a trouble spot, wondered how parents kept their sanity.

But of course he'd be patient and understanding with his own children, he told himself.

He caught sight of a two-year-old thwacking Otto on the arm, screaming, "You let go! It's mine!" The object of contention appeared to be a broken-off tree branch.

"Hey." Eric waded into the fracas. "Don't kill each other. It's just a stick."

"It is not!" Otto glared at him. "It's a Magic Bee stinger!"

"Mine!" said the toddler.

"No it isn't!" Otto pulled on the stick. "You can play with my toy rake, okay? Or my helmet. It's over there. Now let go!"

The funny thing was that Eric found himself entirely sympathetic to the children's points of view. After all, there was no better toy than a stick, something you could make into whatever your heart desired.

"Let's see if we can't find another stick," he told the toddler, who yielded the object of contention and waddled readily alongside him as they probed the ground, eventually finding a suitable twig. By then, Otto was chasing his

friend Kiki around the yard, making her shriek with terri-
fied glee at the prospect of being stung.

"Which one's yours?" asked a bearded man who wore a
broad smile and balanced a clear plastic cup in one hand.

Eric pointed to Emma. "That one."

"The baby? Congratulations." The man indicated a
blond boy with chocolate smeared across his face. "That's
Myford."

"Myford?"

"Kind of has an English ring to it, don't you think? What
kind of names have you picked out?" The man took a sip
of punch.

"I—I hadn't thought about it," Eric said.

"Better get started. Myford came a month early, so you
never know." The child in question was trying to dump potato chips into the punch bowl, and his father departed
hurriedly.

Names? Eric knew that parents usually tapped into family history or ethnic background, but just now the prospect
of saddling another human being with one particular name
for life struck him as an enormous responsibility.

What if the kid hated the name? Or suppose it became so
popular there were five children called Chuck or Sally in the
same kindergarten class?

Chuck or Sally. No, those were nicknames. His child was
going to need a distinguished name, but not something os-
tentatious like Myford. Wesley, perhaps. Samantha. Andrew or Diana, like British royalty, or...

Silence rippled across the yard and Eric looked up. Entering through the gate was a face so familiar he had to blink
twice before he realized he didn't actually know her. Alyssa
Loos.

And trailing behind came two men with cameras, a
woman with a notebook, and three men toting a Minicam
and sound equipment.

He glanced questioningly at Emma and saw her fleeting expression of shock before she started across the yard to greet her client.

Amid her entourage, Alyssa looked smaller than he would have expected. On TV, her eyes appeared huge and her figure a knockout. In person, she was certainly attractive, but he wouldn't have picked her out in a crowd.

She really wasn't any prettier than Emma. Probably more photogenic with her pronounced cheekbones, and her features had a faintly exotic cast, but he wasn't sure he'd want to look at her every morning over the breakfast table.

No, he'd take Emma over America's top female rock star any day.

EVEN AS SHE GREETED Alyssa, Emma ventured a peek at Corinne. The assistant shrugged helplessly.

When she'd sent invitations to Alyssa and Genevieve, Emma had never expected them to accept. She'd debated whether to include them or not, and then decided they might appreciate the gesture.

Alyssa handed her a beautifully decorated package. "I just couldn't miss this. I love birthday parties!"

"It's not particularly fancy." Emma blinked as a flash-bulb went off in her face.

"I hope you don't mind." The singer gestured at her entourage. "They're featuring me on *L.A. Today,* and my agent suggested I let a couple of photographers tag along as well. They're from *Show Biz Magazine* and *TV Tonight.*"

Emma didn't particularly like having her party turned into a media circus—at least, not unless some clowns and acrobats came with it—but there wasn't much she could do except smile graciously and offer Alyssa a glass of punch. Besides, she was touched that her employer would drive all the way to La Habra for Otto's birthday.

The other parents did their best to be friendly, but the photographers kept pulling Alyssa aside and trying to pose her. They induced some reluctant children into a game of kick-the-ball, which probably looked good on tape, and insisted on her sharing a cupcake with a squirming Otto, who risked getting a sunburn from all the flashbulbs.

As the guests were finishing up their hot dogs and guiding their children into line for the piñata, Genevieve arrived.

To her credit, she brought only Amalie, but the way she scanned the yard for the cameras told Emma the real reason for the visit.

"I hope you don't mind," she murmured to Emma as they kissed each other on the cheek, Hollywood-style. "Barry Gray suggested I drop by."

So the producer of *Hotel Marango* was behind this, fanning the flames to benefit the show's season premiere next month. Emma was surprised Genevieve had fallen for it.

"Would you like a hot dog?" she asked, but the actress declined. Genevieve lived on salads.

The rest of the guests, Emma noted, were watching with open curiosity as Genevieve crossed to her daughter and turned at the perfect angle to have her picture taken.

"I remember your fourth birthday," Genevieve proclaimed loudly. "You beat up all the boys and got sick on ice cream."

"I remember your fiftieth birthday," countered her daughter. "Oops. I'd better not say how long ago that was." In the background, Eric made a throat-slitting motion.

Emma searched her brain for a way to divert their attention. "Alyssa, maybe you could help Otto open the gifts."

"What fun!" Alyssa said. "I'd love to."

Soon the singer had folded herself onto a chair—she could hardly sit on the grass in her white silk slacks—at Otto's side.

Emma had to admit that Alyssa seemed to enjoy helping him rip open the brightly colored paper, quickly losing awareness of the photographers amid the children's excitement as each new toy emerged.

"She's so childish," Genevieve commented, close to the Minicam. "Or do I mean childlike?"

Alyssa's face tilted up, fury radiating out. Before she could reply, however, Stella moved to Genevieve's side. "It's hard watching one's children grow up, isn't it?" she said. "They ought to stay little much longer."

"They have no gratitude." Genevieve heaved a dramatic sigh. "You spend your best years raising them, and then they mock you for not being young anymore."

"I hear daughters can be difficult." Stella pretended not to notice the slurs against Alyssa. "I have two sons, myself. That's Eric over there. He's Emma's—friend."

"Ah." This time she'd succeeded in engaging Genevieve's full attention. "Are they getting married?" The actress didn't seem to care that Emma was standing within easy earshot.

"Perhaps someday," Stella said. "I'm just grateful I'm going to be a grandmother."

"I'd love to have a grandchild." There was no pretense in that wistful note.

It occurred to Emma that the mother and daughter might finally be reconciled when they had a third generation to cherish. She supposed they'd probably fight about how to bring up the children, but Genevieve might begin to see Alyssa as an adult, and the singer might gain some sympathy for the sacrifices her mother had made.

But that day, unfortunately, was a long time off.

Amalie summoned Genevieve away to be photographed among the children, and the parents kept both women busy signing autographs after that. Before Emma knew it, children were yawning and waving goodbye, except for Roy, who ran about the yard with Otto playing with the new toys.

Alyssa and Genevieve made a low-key departure, both rather strained by the commotion. After they were gone, Emma heaved a sigh of relief.

She noticed with only slight dismay that the yard resembled a park the day after a rock concert—blotched with brightly colored litter, tumbling balloons and plates full of half-eaten food.

"That was a surprise," Betsy commented as she shooed Roy toward the gate.

"The understatement of the century." Emma grimaced. "But Otto should be grateful. Alyssa gave him that amazing marble run, and Genevieve must have spent a fortune on that miniature tuxedo. She even got the size right."

"I'm glad I got to see them." Betsy snatched up a guilty handful of leftover candies and nibbled at them. "They aren't very happy, are they?"

"It's sad when a mother resents her daughter." Stella tossed another paper plate into the garbage bag she was hauling around the yard. "I suppose it's hard to see someone else take your place in the sun, but that's life."

"You think Genevieve's at fault?" Emma asked.

"Absolutely. Although I'm a big fan of hers." Stella poured some lemonade onto the grass before disposing of the cup. "She doesn't view Alyssa as a separate person, but as a reflection of herself. So she thinks she should get all the glory."

"And Alyssa's just defending herself?" Betsy asked.

"She acts more like a teenager than a grown woman, but she is rather young," Stella said.

"Twenty-three." Emma stacked Otto's presents into a box.

"No, no." Stella reached out to stop her. "You need to sit down. Go on. Get in the house and put your feet up. Not another word!"

Gratefully, Emma waved goodbye to Betsy and obeyed. Her ankles had swollen and her abdominal muscles ached. Propping her feet on the coffee table, she leaned back on the couch and promptly fell asleep.

When she awoke, the tantalizing aroma of bacon wafted through the air. Muddled, and beginning to realize she must have slept for several hours, Emma rose stiffly and went into the kitchen.

Stella, Eric and Otto sat around the table, consuming piles of pancakes with bacon. They looked up when she walked in.

"Eric helped me put my space station together," Otto said. "And my marble run, too. It's really fun. I think Alyssa's pretty and she smells nice."

"I'll tell her." Still sleep-dazed, Emma took a seat, not even protesting when Stella got up to pour her a cup of decaf.

"I enjoyed today," Eric said.

His face had taken on a relaxed warmth. He'd spent all afternoon with her son, and Emma could tell he'd actually had a good time.

"I wish—" she began and stopped, because she wasn't quite sure what it was she wished at the moment.

"I wish this day could last forever," Stella finished for her, sitting down again. "It's been so long since I've spent much time around children."

"Sounds like a volunteer baby-sitter to me." Eric smiled.

"Any time." The intensity in his mother's voice touched Emma.

Having a child affected so many people, made you part of the web of their lives and dreams. She felt close to Stella, and hoped someday they'd become even closer.

Otto yawned, and Emma saw that it was nearly eight. "Time for bed, buddy," she said.

"I'll clean up." Stella shooed the three of them out of the kitchen.

This time, Eric knew the ritual almost as well as Emma. He stretched it out, reading Otto two books, until the little boy finally insisted that they put out the lights.

"He's exhausted," Emma said.

"He ought to be." Eric turned in the hall and touched her cheek.

His mouth came down and brushed hers. Emma wished the baby weren't filling up the space between them. Right now she wanted to feel the hardness of his body, to stir up the masculine interest she felt quickening in his lips.

She had to turn sideways to embrace him, but it didn't matter. Lightly, his hands brushed the edges of her enlarged breasts, and a hot wave of desire consumed her.

A pan clattered in the kitchen, and they drew apart reluctantly. "You know," Eric mused, "I think I could get to like kids' birthday parties. But only if I can stay with the lady of the house afterward."

He and Stella left a few minutes later. Emma watched until their van disappeared from view, then switched off the porch light. She stood in the doorway, gazing out into the night. The August stars hung brightly over the neighbors' houses, and the moon verged on fullness.

How much would change next month when Eric went back to school? For a moment, selfishly, she wished he didn't have such demanding dreams. But then, he wouldn't be Eric if he didn't.

Chapter Eleven

Looking out through the tall windows, Eric's gaze raked over the sunny courtyard and the handful of students reading or talking in the small outdoor amphitheater. Ironically, after yearning to be back in the classroom, he found himself wishing right now that he were out lounging beneath the jacaranda trees.

He knew he ought to pay more attention to the instructor giving them an overview of second-year architectural design, but conflicting emotions and memories kept fogging his mind.

Eric hadn't expected to be slammed by chaotic feelings this morning when he walked onto the campus. After all, he'd visited several times before to register and get his books.

Today he could see that, on those visits, he'd felt like an adult dropping by. Now, suddenly, he was one of the students. Except that you couldn't just erase the eight years and all the changes in his life since he'd last sat in a classroom.

In a way, he felt that it gave him an advantage. But he'd have to get used to sitting still and paying attention at lectures, and right now that wasn't easy.

"At this point in your studies, we of the faculty believe you need to liberate your creative spirit, not to limit yourselves to problem solving based on conventional functions...."

Why did he keep tuning out that voice? He kept wanting to get down to work, to draw something or tackle a problem. It felt odd to sit here so formally in a classroom that looked more like an art studio, with stools instead of chairs, broad-surfaced tables for hands-on work, and telltale stained concrete floors.

Trying not to attract notice, he took an assessing look around the studio. There were more women in the classes now than eight years ago, and the kids dressed a bit more casually.

But the most striking thing was their youth. Maybe it was an illusion, but they looked so uncomplicated and eager, they made him feel like Rip Van Winkle awakening to a strange new world.

Well, he'd get used to it. Fortunately, he'd brushed up on his old textbooks last summer, so he wouldn't have to rely on his eight-year-old memory of freshman year. And surely it wouldn't take long to get used to the kind of academic-speak the professor was using, terms like "site manipulation" and "afunctional aspects of space making."

It sure beat hearing plain old English words like "stuck," "broken" and "overflowing."

The plain fact was that he felt too darned excited to concentrate. But surely that would pass as he settled into life in Cal Poly's College of Environmental Design.

Eric leaned forward and listened intently to the instructor.

"CAN I PEEK YET?" Emma, reclining on a lounge chair, regarded Eric hopefully.

"In a minute." Rapidly, the pencil shaded the side of her face. Shaking his head to clear away the smell of graphite, Eric stood back to appraise his work.

He liked to sketch, although he rarely had time for it anymore. More than that, no photograph could capture the intimacy of this image of Emma, her face softer than usual and her belly large with baby Mark or Kiri, the names they'd decided on.

"I'm not satisfied with it," he said.

Emma swung her legs over the edge and straightened, arising slowly. Beside him, she studied the picture. "You make me look so—sensuous."

"You are sensuous." She'd had no problems for two months, but they hadn't resumed intimate relations. Maybe it was the result of frustration, but Eric found her more beautiful than ever. He couldn't imagine why he'd ever preferred her thin.

"Mommy! Can Kiki stay for dinner?" Otto banged out the back door with his little friend hot on his heels.

"I'm afraid not." Emma shrugged. "Her daddy's picking her up and they're going to a movie tonight."

"Aw, phooey." Otto turned to Kiki. "Come on. Let's go sting those Bad Wasps!"

The two pretend Magic Bees dashed inside again.

"Do they ever just walk?" Eric caught the edginess in his voice and didn't like it, but sometimes the noise and rowdiness frayed his temper. Especially when he wanted to concentrate on Emma.

"Not that I can recall." She laid a hand on his arm. "School's putting pressure on you, isn't it?"

"I'm putting it on myself," Eric said. "I know it's early in the year, but I feel kind of creaky next to those kids. I'm going to have to work extra hard if I'm going to shine."

He put away his sketch, and they sat side by side on lawn chairs. It was a warm September afternoon, the air humming with lawn mowers and, from a radio down the street, mariachi music.

There ought to be a sense of the winter to come, of life's cycle nearing its completion. Eric missed that annual reminder of mortality, which he'd experienced so keenly one autumn as a teenager when he'd visited his grandmother in Buffalo, New York.

Here in Southern California there was only one sunny day after another, sometimes interspersed with clouds or rain or a touch of cold. In winter, the days grew shorter and a little cooler, but that was all.

Oddly, though, these past weeks he'd been all too aware of the passage of time. "What if I'm not that special, Emma?" He hadn't realized until he spoke the words that that was what he feared most. "What if I'm just average?"

"You'd survive." Thank goodness she didn't offer him the kind of meaningless reassurance anyone else might have given. *Of course you won't fail. Don't worry about it.* "But you'd never forgive yourself, would you?"

"I know I have the potential. I just can't let myself get distracted. It's such a different environment—"

Otto and Kiki dashed out the door again, slamming it behind them. "I want apple juice!" Otto said. "Please, please, please!"

"Aren't you old enough to get your own?" Eric hoped he wasn't being too sharp with the boy. "Mom shouldn't have to jump up and down and wait on you, in her condition."

"I don't mind." Emma scooted forward in her chair, a preliminary to the complicated task of rising.

"Sit." He hurried into the kitchen to pour Otto's umpteenth glass of juice.

A short time later, once again settled with Emma, Eric couldn't remember what he'd been about to say. While he was collecting his thoughts, Otto burst outside again.

"Not more juice!" Eric protested before the boy could speak.

Otto lifted his chin defiantly. "Kiki's daddy's at the front door."

"Oh. Thank you, Otto." Emma rolled to her feet, waving away Eric's offer of help, although she leaned gratefully on his arm going up the steps into the house. Eric would have offered Otto an apology, but the boy had already raced back inside.

The man who waited in front stood a few inches shorter than Eric, but he wore an unmistakable air of command. As they shook hands, Eric guessed Sam Frye's age at about thirty-five, but a silver streak in the front of his hair made him look older.

This, he recalled, was the man who spent most of his time in Japan. Eric watched with interest as Kiki ran up to her father and climbed into his arms.

"Whoa." Sam set her down again. "Did you help Otto clean up his toys?"

"That's all right," Emma said.

"No, it's important." Sam frowned at his daughter until she pouted and ran toward Otto's bedroom. "Kids have to learn to help."

"When did you get back in town?" Eric asked as they sat around the living room.

"Last week." Sam twined his fingers together. "We really appreciate your taking Kiki for the afternoon, Emma. I'm only beginning to get to know my son. And getting over my jet lag."

"Suffering from a little culture shock, too?" Emma asked.

"You said it." Sam tilted his head as if listening to some inner voice. "In Japan everything's different, even the way the air feels. Going back and forth is like traveling between worlds."

From the way Emma watched Sam, Eric guessed she yearned to tell him of Josie's unhappiness but didn't want to interfere.

Eric decided to see if he could help. "These separations must be hard on your wife."

"She manages all right, but she gets sloppy with the discipline." Sam started to pull out a cigarette and then, after a glance at Emma, put the pack away. "Sorry. That's one of the things that's different here."

"It must be hard," Eric went on. "Not being around your kids much. And your wife."

"Well, that's just the way it is." Sam stood up as Kiki returned. "All done?"

She nodded, and this time made no attempt to approach him. To his credit, Sam noticed the change and knelt down to her level. "Honey, I didn't mean to push you away. But it's important to behave properly. Now come here."

Reluctantly, Kiki started forward, then chortled with delight as her father swooped her up to sit on his shoulders.

After they were gone, Emma said, "Thanks, Eric. I know you were trying to help."

"I'm turning into a busybody." He wasn't sure what had motivated him to poke his nose into Sam Frye's business, however subtly.

"You're scowling again," Emma said. "How about some dinner? I'm making quiche."

"Great. Thanks." Eric looked at Otto, who was moping near the door, missing his friend. "Let's see. Do you think you'd like to do that, too?" Without further warning, he grabbed the little boy and set him up high for a piggyback ride.

"Wow." Otto bounced lightly. "I could really poke holes in wasps' nests up here!"

So they played Magic Bees through the house until dinner was ready.

THE FOLLOWING DAY, a Monday, Emma and Eric both took off time to go shopping and get ready for the baby.

It was surprising how many things she needed, since she'd saved all of Otto's old equipment. But she'd borrowed and long ago returned his rocking swing, so she needed one of those, and the stroller had become so battered through overuse that she decided to replace it.

As they shopped, Eric kept getting lost in his own thoughts, and Emma began to regret inviting him along. She hadn't meant to bore him, but she needed his help to carry packages and, more than that, she wanted him to be part of the preparations.

Of course, it was understandable that getting ready for a baby meant more to her, but she wished the timing weren't so bad. If only Mark or Kiri could have been born before their father returned to school.

As they loaded the car, Emma tried to imagine what it would be like to find herself in a classroom, trying to compete with younger students. But after so many years as a hairdresser, she couldn't put herself in the shoes of a beginner.

Back at the house, Eric set to work assembling the swing while she fetched old boxes of baby clothing, toys and other items to sort.

She hadn't expected the task to take long, but Emma couldn't help lingering. A baby jumpsuit reminded her of the great-aunt who'd selected it for Otto. A set of nesting plastic boxes with bells in them had been donated by a former neighbor.

Most of all, the items brought back memories of Bill. He'd been so excited about the baby-to-be that one day he'd gone out, all by himself, and purchased a diaper stacker. It was the wrong color, but Emma had hung it proudly. Now, lifting it out of the storage box, she felt tears prickle.

Eric knelt beside her. "Thinking about your husband?"

Emma nodded wordlessly, wondering how he so often managed to read her mind.

"You never talk about him."

"I wouldn't know what to say." She spoke through the lump in her throat. "I miss him, but I don't like to dwell on the past."

"I wish I'd been here." Eric fingered a lacy baby bonnet, one of those impractical gifts that she'd nevertheless cherished. "I wish I'd known Otto from the beginning. I'm sorry I was short with him the other day."

"Kids can be irritating." She hadn't blamed Eric. Sometimes she wanted to yell at Otto herself, but then he would look so crushed, she couldn't bear it. "It doesn't hurt them to be brought up short once in a while. I think they need to learn when their behavior annoys others."

They worked together, sorting out clothes and utensils to be washed, and tentatively Eric broached subjects that puzzled him. "One of the students at school—she must be about nineteen—carries her baby around in a backpack."

"It doesn't cry?" Emma set aside a stack of receiving blankets to be washed.

"No. She claims she's going to tote it all the way through college," Eric said. "I always thought babies were a lot of work."

"Some of them are easy, so I hear," Emma said. "Although not any that I've met. And I think she's forgetting one thing—that baby isn't going to be so little in a few years. Does she think she can take a three-year-old to class?"

Eric chuckled. "I guess she's a bit short on common sense." He held up what looked like a miniature hammock. "What's this?"

"Baby sling." Emma picked some lint off the thick fabric. "I used it for a while with Otto, but he was too independent to carry much."

"Are babies—" Eric hesitated "—I mean, how much of a personality are they born with? Isn't it mostly up to you and me?"

Emma hooted. "I wish! I used to think that, too. Then Otto popped out and issued a list of demands. Talk about knowing his own mind! Of course, the home environment makes a difference, but some personality traits are inborn. In fact, I read a study of identical twins who were raised separately and they even married people with the same names."

Sitting on the floor beside her, he wrapped his arms around his knees. "It still doesn't feel real, Emma. I'm sorry. I know it does to you."

"It didn't before I had one." She wished he would ask more, lots more. Most of the time Eric's involvement with the baby seemed to be concentrated on Emma instead of the child to be. "Are you sure you like the names Mark and Kiri?" They'd been her suggestions, and Eric had readily agreed.

"Well, you didn't like Hermione," he joked. "And you said Alphonse was definitely out."

"You realize that you're going to fall in love." At his startled expression, Emma could see that he hadn't understood. "With your child, silly."

"Oh. I suppose." He shook his head. "Emma, I'm not sure I'm up to this. You're so patient with Otto."

"You'll be fine," she said. "You have to learn to be a father, just like I had to learn to be a mother."

He left that afternoon to attend a mandatory lecture. Their farewell kiss was almost comical; Emma stretched up on tiptoe and Eric had to lean past her extended abdomen.

After he was gone, she lay down on the couch for a much-needed nap, but her brain still buzzed with the day's activities.

She'd assured Eric that he would be fine, but she knew children came second to him, or maybe third, after his career and Emma. That was pretty far down the ladder.

It was a bit late to think about that, she told herself sternly, giving up on the nap and going out to the garage to bring in a music box that played "The Carousel Waltz." Then she sat on the floor and listened to the lilting tune over and over, just as Otto had done when he'd first learned how to wind the music box, and tried to imagine tiny baby fingers poking wonderingly at the painted horse.

VERN AVERY. Now there was a name that didn't ring a bell.

Eric checked the number on the slip of paper again before dialing. Who would have called him from New York?

He glanced at his watch. It was one o'clock on a Friday afternoon, so Mr. Vern Avery should still be in his office, unless he was the type who left early for the weekend. Which was possible, since Eric had no idea who he was, anyway.

"*Science Future Magazine,*" said a female voice with a heavy Brooklyn accent.

He asked for Avery, and was put on hold. Impatiently, Eric listened to a tinny rendition of "Wind Beneath My Wings," mauled by what sounded like a couple of out-of-tune violins and a synthesizer. He would have preferred silence.

Boy, he told himself, are you crabby today.

Well, no wonder. His class assignment was driving him crazy. "Given a flat site in the desert, create a celebration of the sun and water," the instructions read. "The response to the sun must take the form of a mound, while the response to water must take the form of an excavation."

Now what was that all about? He'd expected some realistic architectural challenges, not an assignment to figure out an artistic way to build a sand dune and sink a well.

"Mr. Jameson?" A masculine voice broke into the music. "Vern Avery here. Managing editor of *Science Future Magazine.* Congratulations!"

"Is this..." Eric finally let himself think the unthinkable. "Does this have anything to do with the cities of the future contest?"

"It does," Avery said. "You're the grand-prize winner. I'll be sending you a check, and we'd like you to be guest of honor at our convention in late September. It's being held in Anaheim, near you. We'll have your model enclosed in Plexiglas, and the computer printouts and drawings displayed with it."

"I— Sure." Eric couldn't quite take it in. "I mean— great! Did you get a lot of entries?"

"Seventy-five," said the editor. "Some of them were quite interesting. You'll see—we're going to display some of the finalists at the convention. What we liked about your ideas was that you didn't just focus on buildings. You thought about life-styles and values, how people are going to live."

And that, Eric acknowledged silently, was exactly the advantage that he had over his fellow students. He was older, and what he lacked in youthful ebullience, he made up for in experience. "I'm honored."

"Another thing." The editor cleared his throat. "We have a series of articles coming up, speculating what life will be like in the next century."

"I'll look forward to reading them."

"Good. Because we'd like you to illustrate them. What we're really looking for are cover paintings."

"Cover paintings?" Eric echoed. He had once made a hobby of sketching and painting, and had attended some night-school classes over the years with his mother, who enjoyed painting still lifes. He supposed he was up to the technical requirements, but such an assignment would take a lot of time. "I'm not sure I can handle it. I've started back at architecture school."

"Well, give it some thought," Avery said. "You might find it stimulating. We'll need the first one by the third of January, so that gives you a little while. Your model is impressive, and so are your drawings. No one else thought to show us scenes from everyday life in their city."

Cover illustrations. It was the kind of thing Eric might daydream about as a sideline, but would never have pursued. "You haven't mentioned payment."

"Oh, we can't forget that! For this special series—we'll need four paintings altogether—I think we could make it, say, a thousand apiece?"

Eric barely stopped himself from saying what popped into his mind, which was, *I'd have to fix a lot of toilets for that.* The money would go a long way toward helping Emma and the baby. And the paintings could be worked on late at night or early in the morning, when he had time.

He didn't suppose Emma would be too crazy about the idea. But however old-fashioned it might sound, Eric wanted to be a good provider. And right now his confidence needed the boost that Vern Avery offered.

"I'll do it," he said, and hung up with Avery's repeated congratulations ringing in his ears.

Suddenly the prospect of figuring out how to celebrate the sun with a mound didn't feel so intimidating. Not for a man whose city of the future had been selected as the winner from seventy-five entries.

Chapter Twelve

Emma tossed the gossip magazine aside. "Those columnists haven't even seen it," she said. "They don't know what they're talking about."

Corinne shrugged. "The readers don't know that."

The musical special starring Genevieve and Alyssa, most recently scheduled for September, had been postponed indefinitely by the network's new programming director. Unidentified industry sources were quoted as saying the show had incurable problems.

"Of course, I haven't seen the whole thing, either," Emma admitted, pouring a glass of milk from the trailer's refrigerator. "But I saw most of it while they were taping, and it was terrific."

"Especially their hair?" Corinne teased, and they both chuckled.

Working together in such quarters had established an unlikely friendship. It was a good thing, too, because Emma and Corinne spent a lot of time, like now, waiting around until they were needed.

Like Emma, Corinne had always been fascinated by show business, but her life had taken a different course.

At eighteen, Corinne had left her home in Houston and driven to Hollywood with only a few hundred dollars to her name.

She'd spent the next months working for a temporary help agency and pounding on doors. Finally she'd landed a job in the mailroom at a studio—a plum position for upward mobility—but got laid off when a producer's son wanted her post.

Undeterred, Corinne wangled her way into a talent agency as a file clerk, working her way up to secretary. Unfortunately, good secretaries were hard to find, and she finally realized the head of the agency had no intention of promoting her.

About that time, she'd begun dating a client, one of Alyssa's backup musicians. When the singer decided she needed a personal assistant, Corinne offered her services.

Her goal, she'd told Emma, was to become a producer. She'd helped organize Alyssa's last tour, and was taking an evening course in producing.

Now she crumpled the magazine and tossed it in the trash. "No sense in upsetting Alyssa."

"I'm upset enough for her." Emma closed her eyes as a wave of stomach acid fought its way up her throat, stopping just short of her vocal cords. She groped in her purse for antacid pills, and chewed two of them.

"You think you're upset?" Corinne said. "I want her to become a big enough star to get me assistant producer jobs on her projects. At this rate, who knows?"

"You'll make it." Emma stretched her puffy ankles out in front of her. "You're not going to let yourself get sidetracked."

The younger woman regarded her wistfully. "Sidetracked? No, I don't guess my cat's going to make any major demands. But in a few years I'm going to be thirty, and my biological clock's ticking."

Emma hooted. "Corinne! You're only twenty-five!"

"But you're only three years older than me and you're on your second child—" Corinne stopped as the door to the trailer banged open.

Alyssa stalked in, grumbling as she sometimes did, although there was something odd about her today. She looked irritated, which meant Genevieve had been stealing scenes again, and yet—

Today, the cords in Alyssa's throat didn't bulge and she wasn't tossing her head every thirty seconds. But why would she pretend to be angry if she wasn't?

"Would you believe, Barry's giving a lunch in my mother's honor?" Alyssa snapped. "I suppose he'll expect me to stand up and pay tribute. Well, anyway, it's a command performance. You two better come along."

Emma gazed wistfully at her ankles, which were just beginning to feel better, and swung her feet down. She followed Corinne and Alyssa out of the trailer.

September sunshine baked the parking lot as they crossed it. She'd been doubly foolish, not only to get pregnant but to time it so she'd deliver in the fall. October and November might be pleasant, but September was usually Southern California's hottest month, and this year was no exception.

Even walking the few hundred feet to the building left Emma breathing hard. Her abdominal muscles stretched and twinged at every movement, and her body radiated so much warmth it was a wonder the other two women didn't suffer heat stroke.

At least the building, like the trailer, was air-conditioned. Emma slogged down the corridor, wondering if she could put her feet up in the cafeteria, or even sneak out early. Surely the lunch couldn't last long, with taping scheduled to resume in an hour.

She caught a glimpse of someone around a corner. The woman bore an amazing resemblance to Josie.

Emma smiled to herself. She'd have to tell her friend about it. People were always urging Josie to try an acting career because of her beauty, and now it turned out some look-alike had beaten her to it.

"Just a minute." Alyssa pushed open the door of the ladies' room. "Emma, would you help me? I've got some hair scraggling down in front."

"Sure." Taking out the styling comb and brush she always carried in her purse, Emma came to her employer's rescue.

The hard plastic couch in the rest room looked surprisingly inviting. "Maybe I'll just sit here for a minute," Emma said, after Alyssa's hair had been restored. "You go on ahead."

The singer shifted from one foot to another. "I—I'm afraid my mother will tick me off. You're so good at running interference, Emma. I don't want to blow up again, not in front of Barry."

Emma refrained from mentioning that the producer would love it. Although she respected his desire to promote *Hotel Marango,* she disliked the way he was fostering this mother-daughter feud.

"Well, sure." Suppressing a sigh, she lumbered to her feet and followed Alyssa.

They rounded a corner and paused outside the cafeteria. From inside, Emma could hear voices chattering and dishes clanking. "Is he having this catered?" she asked.

"Let's go see." Not meeting her eyes, Alyssa passed through the door. Puzzled, Emma followed.

The whole cast and crew had assembled informally, perched around the tables, already sampling the centerpiece of boiled seafood and smoked fish. The strange thing, Emma noted, was the pile of gift-wrapped boxes in the center of another table.

Then she saw the actress who looked like Josie, except that it really *was* Josie. Because there was no mistaking Betsy beside her, or—good heavens, Stella Jameson, and—Eric?

"Surprise!" cried Genevieve from the side, a delighted grin enlivening her usually serene face, and more cries of "surprise!" filled the air.

"What—?" Emma turned questioningly to Alyssa.

"We thought you deserved a baby shower," her employer explained.

"I—" Stunned, Emma swayed in place, grateful when Eric took her arm. "Well, you certainly did keep it a secret!"

Eric helped her into a chair and brought her a plate of food. They didn't get to talk, though, because Emma found herself surrounded by friends and members of the cast and crew, each with a story to tell about how they'd sneaked around ordering food and arranging the guest list without her catching on.

What amused her most was how her two different worlds had collided without a ripple. Betsy carried on an animated conversation with a continuity girl, while Stella and Genevieve were comparing their own memories of pregnancy. Alyssa looked somewhat uncomfortable until Josie fell into place beside her, asking questions about her upcoming compact disc.

Eric, his plate filled with the catered food, pulled a chair up next to Emma. "Alone at last," he said.

She rested her head on his shoulder. "This is wonderful. I can't believe they did this."

"Thank Alyssa and Genevieve," he said. "You'd have been proud. They worked together on the whole thing and I didn't see them quarrel once."

"How long has this been going on?" Emma lifted her head. "And how'd you keep me from finding out?"

"About a month," he said. "And I can be very cagey when I want to be."

"I'm learning." A warm glow settled over her, seeing all her friends around, knowing they must truly care to have gone to so much trouble.

The thing about being married, she'd discovered during her time with Bill, was the knowledge that you had months and years ahead of you. That you were committed to each other, and whatever difficulties might arise, it was only a passing phase.

Right now, her heart needed that reassurance with Eric. Somehow, today, she felt a little more as if they were part of a family.

"Hey." Eric touched her arm. "What's going on?"

"I'm overwhelmed," Emma admitted. "This is so— thoughtful."

"Why don't you open the presents?" Alyssa called from the punch table. "Before we all have to get back to work."

"I'll keep track." Practical Betsy whipped out a steno pad and perched nearby.

The wrappings were so beautiful, Emma hated to tear them apart, but the wall clock warned there was less than half an hour left, so she dug in.

She unwrapped enough baby blankets, baby clothes, stuffed animals and books to stock a nursery for triplets, and thanked everyone from the heart, knowing that infants had a way of needing exactly the things you didn't expect them to. She especially appreciated the toys, which Otto would enjoy, too.

The two largest gifts, those from Alyssa and Genevieve, she left for last. They were both huge and roughly the same size. Apparently even the baby shower had become a forum for trying to outdo each other.

Finally Emma tore open Alyssa's present. She glimpsed a curve of dark burnished wood first, then a brightly colored saddle....

"A rocking horse!" And plenty big enough for Otto to ride, Emma saw with delight. Set up on giant springs, it looked hand carved and expensive. "This is wonderful!" Then, catching an enigmatic look on Genevieve's face, Emma hurried to open the second, equally giant gift.

And inside found another, nearly identical rocking horse.

"I don't believe it." As Emma stared from one horse to the other, she could feel the tension in the room as the cast and crew awaited the fireworks. Quickly she added, "This is terrific! Otto and the baby won't have to fight over who gets to ride!"

"Brilliant minds run in the same course," Betsy added diplomatically.

Then Genevieve began to laugh. Soon she was howling with mirth, and even Alyssa had to smile.

"We both must look so silly!" Genevieve chortled. "Trying to buy you the biggest thing we could find!" Then she calmed down. "Actually, Emma, I was remembering a rocking horse I gave Alyssa for her fifth birthday. She rode it every day until it simply wore out."

"That's what I was reminded of!" Alyssa stared at her mother. "I'd forgotten all about it until I was in the toy store."

"You don't know what I went through to get you that horse," her mother said. "I knew you wanted one, and back then, they weren't so easy to find. I had to special order it— I must have spent a week on the phone, making sure it arrived in time."

"I loved it," Alyssa said. "I used to pretend I was Elizabeth Taylor in *National Velvet*."

"Do you remember when I took you for your first riding lesson?" Genevieve seemed to have forgotten everyone else in the room. "You took one look at that horse and screamed."

"He wouldn't stand still." Alyssa giggled. "I wanted my dream horse, not some stomping, snorting thing as big as a building."

For the first time since they'd joined the cast of *Hotel Marango,* the two Loos women sat down together, talking animatedly. Around the room, everyone visibly relaxed.

Until, that is, the producer walked in.

Barry Gray's face started off with a smile and wilted into a frown as he glimpsed his two stars in friendly conversation. Emma saw him question an assistant producer, then shake his head.

She had to bite her lip to keep from speaking up and trying to forestall whatever would come next. Instead, she watched helplessly as Barry composed his expression and walked over to where the two women sat. The room fell silent as people strained to hear.

"We're going to improvise a little change in this afternoon's script," the producer said. "I think it will work better."

The mother and daughter turned toward him warily. "Improvise?" Alyssa sounded on the verge of panic. She handled her lines well with the help of a private acting couch, but Emma knew she lacked formal training.

"That scene where you seduce Jon and win him back," Barry said. "That really lets the tension drop in our viewers' minds."

"But the writers came up with a lovely scene where I scheme to get him back," pointed out Genevieve, whom Emma knew adored having a soliloquy.

"This will work better." Barry's voice took on a false heartiness. "Alyssa, you'll seduce him all right. And then his phone will ring, and it's Genevieve, and he walks out on you."

Alyssa stared at him in disbelief. She'd been agonizing over the seduction scene, Emma knew, and the director had encouraged her to identify with her character completely. Appearing in scanty clothing in front of the crew was going to be difficult enough, and now Alyssa would have to endure a humiliation that, make-believe or not, couldn't help but feel like a slap in the face.

"Now, just a minute," began Genevieve, coming to her daughter's defense.

"That's not all," Barry said. "Genevieve, then you get to seduce him. We'll contrast your sophistication with her naïveté. I think wardrobe could come up with a really knockout black nightgown, and we'll use soft focus, of course. Afterward, you can still perform your soliloquy while he's sleeping. You'll shift from seductress to—pardon my French—first-class bitch. It's the kind of performance people remember at Emmy time."

He'd won her over and he knew it. Genevieve turned to her daughter and shrugged. "I suppose we must go along."

"Go along!" Alyssa growled. "I'd have to break your leg to stop you!"

"There's no point in getting personal." Her mother stood up and brushed off her skirt. "The show comes first, darling. You have to take a more professional attitude."

Alyssa bit back her response. As she turned away, Emma saw the resentment on her face.

She knows she can't win. But why can't she see that it's Barry and not Genevieve who's setting her up?

The party was over, and everyone left in a subdued mood. Josie, Betsy and Stella gave Emma hugs, while Eric and one of the stagehands carried the gifts out to his van.

He came back in to say goodbye. "Try not to worry about them," he said. "They'll survive."

"I can't help it." Emma took two more antacid pills for good measure before abandoning her chair. "I can feel Alyssa's hurt as if it were my own."

"You're too empathetic for your own good." Eric kissed her. "You're a natural mother."

She chuckled. "That I am. This was fun today, until Barry barged in."

"Don't forget about Saturday." He nuzzled her hair.

"Are you kidding? My big chance to see your city of the future?" She knew how much the project had meant to him and how much he wanted to impress her at the convention. "And don't forget about tomorrow night."

"Dinner at Betsy's? Right."

She held his hand and walked him to the exit door, her spirits lifting. The joy of making your dreams come true was sharing them with someone you cared for; Eric knew that as well as she did.

BETSY AND MATT lived in the area of La Habra known as North of the Boulevard. Located above Whittier Boulevard, it lay immediately below the Heights and featured gingerbread-style houses set amid manicured, rolling lawns.

The Bellagos had added a family room and a pool and decorated in dark green and peach. The effect was pleasantly crisp, although the updated decor couldn't disguise the early 1960's style of the house.

"I don't suppose it's very impressive to an architect," Betsy said as she led Eric, Emma and Otto out to the back, where Matt and Roy were playing in the water.

Eric never knew how to respond to comments like that. Although part of his brain couldn't help analyzing any structure he saw, he certainly didn't look down on houses just because they hadn't been designed by Frank Lloyd Wright.

"You've done a good job of decorating," he said carefully.

"A diplomat!" Betsy smiled.

Once they reached the backyard, Emma strapped water wings onto Otto's arms. "Are you going in, too?" she asked Eric.

"Sure." Like Otto, Eric had worn his trunks and brought his dry clothes in a bag, so now he stripped off his T-shirt and dove into the pool.

Cold water broke over him. Keeping a watch out for fellow bathers, he swam several laps before emerging beside Otto. "Want a ride?"

"Sure." Otto boosted himself onto Eric's shoulders, and rode gleefully alongside Roy. The boys began a pretend jousting match.

Matt laughed as he bobbed around the pool beneath his son. Eric wondered why the man disliked the idea of a second child, but unlike Emma he didn't feel right delving into the details of his friends' lives. Besides, he'd barely met Matt, so he didn't suppose they qualified as friends yet.

Soon it was time to dry off, change and enjoy drinks around the barbecue. Eric tried not to think about the work he should be doing tonight. These days his studies dominated his thoughts, even creeping into his dreams. He needed an evening off.

Roy and Otto busied themselves with toy trucks, ignoring the vegetable platter Betsy had set out. The two women sat side by side in patio chairs, talking comfortably. Eric pretended an interest in the barbecue, although he felt like a fraud.

He wasn't used to suburban settings or to attending events as a couple. He wondered how well Matt and Betsy had known Bill, and whether they were silently comparing the two men.

What a crazy thought. Why should he assume they were judging him any more than he was judging their house?

"Betsy tells me you're studying architecture," Matt said. "What kind of work are you interested in? Tract housing? Office buildings?"

It was a question Eric had asked himself many times, and not yet resolved. "I'm fascinated by communities as a whole, from a design standpoint. But there aren't too many opportunities to create a whole city."

"Power." Matt flipped a hamburger expertly. "Sounds like you're into control."

"Am I?" Eric had never viewed his ambitions from that perspective. "Maybe so. What about you? Emma tells me you're on the point of making partner."

The corners of Matt's mouth tightened. "Could be."

"Something wrong?"

His host checked a steak for readiness. "One of our staff members has been making noises about tokenism."

"He thinks you're getting promoted because you're a minority?" It hadn't occurred to Eric before how much tougher any task would be if he had to battle racism, in whatever guise.

"Thinks so, or wants other people to think so." Matt glared at his tongs as if they had committed some personal affront. "It's fighting dirty, and boy, would I like to give him a taste of what it's really like to fight dirty. But I won't. I have my self-respect."

"I take it there's a lot of infighting in law firms. Or yours, anyway," Eric ventured.

"You put a bunch of competitive, loud-mouthed—excuse me, articulate—people in the running for the same promotion, and what you get is office politics like you wouldn't believe." Matt laid four hamburger buns on the grill.

"What's your ultimate goal?" Eric asked. "Start you own firm?"

Matt shook his head. "Judge."

"Talk about power," Eric said.

"You got that right."

By the time they'd finished their meal and started on Betsy's cheesecake, Eric had begun loosening up. He liked these two people, even if he still didn't feel as if he quite belonged here.

Becoming involved with Emma meant entering into her life, including her relationships with friends. Sometimes Eric wished they could move somewhere new, where invisible threads didn't tie them at every step to past events and old memories. Except that in a way it was the memories that had brought them together in the first place.

Between forkfuls of cake, he sneaked a glance at Emma. The flowing pink maternity sundress lent her skin a faint blush, and her body had taken on earth-goddess curves.

It struck him full force, the impact of what he and Emma had created without thinking. It was as if, purely by accident, they'd taken their lives and tossed them into the air, letting the pieces fall in all sorts of unexpected new patterns.

Eric had always thought this year would be marked indelibly by one major event: his return to school. Fate, he reflected, had certainly pulled a fast one on a man who liked to be in control.

ERIC POINTED to the wall clock. "How about that for your focal point?"

"It'll just make me nervous." Emma lifted her head from where she lay on the floor cushions. "That crack in the plaster—I'll take that."

The instructor, making her way between rows of puffing mothers-to-be, stopped to offer advice. "Why don't you pick something you can take along and set up in the delivery room—a photograph, or even a stuffed animal."

"A picture of Otto," Emma agreed. "All right. But for now, the crack will do."

"Ready?" Eric began huffing out loud. He felt a little silly, panting this way, but if the instructor said it would help Emma get through childbirth, he'd do anything.

It was a relief when they took a break, helping themselves to punch and cookies and joining the other expectant parents in the Friday-night course.

Their classmates were a gregarious lot. Several men introduced themselves, shook Eric's hand and stood there beaming at him. Fathers-to-be, and proud of it.

One man talked about adding a family room onto his home and another was already planning ahead to when he could coach Little League.

They seemed so comfortable in their role. Some had older children; others had been married for a number of years, postponing a family until they could afford for their wives to take time off.

That was how Eric had always expected it to be for him, not that he'd given the matter much thought. He'd simply assumed that when the time came, he'd be one of the guys.

Glancing across the refreshment table, he watched Emma converse easily with two other bulging women. Emma was by far the most beautiful woman in the room, he thought, but then he had considered her the most beautiful woman at the baby shower, too, and he doubted the actresses present would have agreed.

There was something warm about Emma—nurturing, that was the word. Being near her made Eric feel more comfortable about the upheavals in his life.

By all rights, they should be attending as husband and wife. A wave of longing rolled over him, to be done with dreaming and struggling. To be married to Emma and earning a good living at a routine job—all right, plumbing. To have time for the children, and not wake up in the middle of the night assailed by concerns over this or that assignment.

Except that, in his heart, Eric would always feel that he had failed if he settled for second best. He couldn't live that way and he knew Emma wouldn't want him to.

The childbirth instructor called them back to work. Eric went gladly, relieved to throw himself into physical activity, even if it meant kneeling on the floor and tilting his pelvis, trying to imagine that he, too, was pregnant.

Chapter Thirteen

t was only half past nine on Saturday morning, Future-Con's official opening time, but hundreds of enthusiasts had arrived at the hotel ahead of time. Emma's first reaction was that Otto would have loved the science-fiction convention, which looked like a grown-up version of Halloween.

As she, Eric and Peter entered the lobby, a group of men and women in *Star Trek* costumes were exiting an elevator. And to one side, three antenna-sprouting aliens clustered around a café table, eating breakfast and reading their programs.

"It's not all this kooky," Peter assured her. "A lot of real scientists are interested in this stuff."

"The display's on the mezzanine level." Eric led his brother and Emma to the escalator. On the way up, she gripped the moving rail tightly, thrown off balance by her seven-months' girth.

"It's the highlight of the convention," Peter informed them. "Did you see the article in the *Times* today? They couldn't stop talking about Eric's piece."

"You exaggerate." Eric grinned as they rode upward. "Isaac Asimov's keynote speech is the highlight, but they did mention my name."

"There." Peter, the tallest, spotted the display as soon as they stepped off the escalator.

At first, Emma could see only thick clumps of people. A Eric and Peter cleared a path, however, she realized th crowds swirled around Plexiglas-covered tables displayin, miniature cities.

A purple ribbon adorned the largest of these, and sh hurried forward to inspect what Eric had created.

He'd meticulously cut and shaped thin white bits of rag board to create a dazzling spectacle of curving roadways an domed buildings. The city of the future, in Eric's vision bubbled in sunlight.

Emma tried to analyze the elements that formed such dazzling whole: the open spaces, the entertainment and ed ucation centers—explained on an accompanying chart—an the office buildings with their own elevated railway stop feeding directly to the residential areas.

Intellectually, she could appreciate what he'd done. Bu even stronger was the impression of beauty and the sam sense of wonder Emma experienced when she saw picture of such real gemlike cities as Venice and Salzburg.

"Where's the hospital?" she asked. When Eric didn't re ply, Emma glanced up and saw that his face had gone chall white.

"N-not—now," he stammered. "I mean, you aren't du for two months."

Emma swallowed a chuckle, which came out as a gasp instead. "I meant in your model!"

For the first time that morning, Eric laughed. "I guess am a little tense, aren't I?"

"A little," Peter drawled.

"The hospital's here." As he pointed, Eric launched int an explanation of the ideas that lay behind his creation "The whole city is circular—offices in the center, and the self-contained rings with shopping malls, medical facilitie and recreation centers encircling the homes...."

People gathered to listen, ask questions and pipe up with their own opinions. Soon they had a lively discussion going.

It was Peter who noticed Emma shifting uncomfortably from foot to foot, and led her to a bench. "He gets carried away," he explained as he waited with her.

"I don't blame him. It's wonderful." Emma watched Eric talk animatedly with a professorial-looking gentleman.

"Wait till you see the cover he's working on for *Science Future*," Peter said. "So far he's only done a rough sketch, but—Emma?"

She wished her face didn't reflect every emotion she felt, because right now the bottom had dropped out. "I— He didn't tell me about any illustrations."

It couldn't be that important, she tried to tell herself. It must have slipped his mind.

"I can't understand that," Peter said. "Maybe he wanted to surprise you. He's hardly talked about anything else since the first article arrived last week. There's going to be four altogether."

He talked on, but the words flew past Emma unheard. *He's hardly talked about anything else—except to me.*

Did Eric think she'd object? She had to admit, she wasn't thrilled about him taking on another obligation right now. How was he ever going to succeed at his studies if he was launching a second career as an illustrator?

The thing that scared her most was the realization that Eric had held a secret back from her, something that mattered to him. Their dreams were the one area of their lives that they shared most deeply, that had brought them together, and now he was holding out on her.

Inside, the baby kicked Emma hard in the ribs.

This pregnancy was hard on her career, too; three days ago she'd reluctantly turned down a regular position styling a TV anchorwoman's hair for the local six o'clock news.

Emma could have worked it around helping Alyssa, but there was no way she could sacrifice additional time with her children.

She couldn't quite sort out her feelings toward Eric right now—dismay that he wasn't sharing his thoughts with her, and also a twinge of resentment that he could forge ahead, leaving her to take on the less glamorous job of maintaining a family.

Yet at the same time, she swelled with pride, watching more and more people approach him with comments and questions. Whatever might be wrong, they could work it out.

DOCTORS HAD a peculiar sense of humor, purposely setting their scales ten pounds high. Or make that fifteen, Emma reflected glumly as the nurse jotted down the number.

"Are we done yet?" Otto asked, making her wonder why she'd decided to pick him up early from preschool so they could spend time together. Doctor visits weren't exactly the ideal setting for fostering parent-child bliss.

She wished Eric could have come, but he'd had to pitch in and help Peter with an overload of emergency calls.

"We still have to see the doctor, honey." Emma checked her watch. They'd only had to wait fifteen minutes, but with Otto nagging her to go home, it might as well have been hours.

"If you'll step into Room B." The nurse accompanied them and took Emma's blood pressure, then presented Otto with a sticker and a sugarless lollipop. He accepted them gravely and settled down at last, savoring the sucker as if it were some rare gourmet treat.

Dr. Meyers entered a minute later, frowning as he studied Emma's folder. She'd had a follow-up ultrasound the previous day.

"Well." He set the chart aside and came to press against Emma's abdomen. "It appears the baby's turned head down. That's good."

"What did the ultrasound show?"

As he measured her bulge with a tape, the doctor said, "The placenta hasn't migrated as we'd hoped. However, it doesn't completely cover the birth canal, either. We'll have to watch things very carefully. You're—let's see—thirty-two weeks. I don't think you need to be confined to bed, but I'd advise you to take things easy."

Emma inhaled deeply. Taping at *Hotel Marango* was in full swing, but at least Alyssa spent her spare time in a recording studio laying down tracks for a new single, so Emma didn't have to work extra hours.

"I can't take off work right now," she said. "But mostly I sit around with my feet up."

"Sounds ideal." The doctor ran through a few questions and seemed satisfied with the answers; to her relief, he didn't chide her about her weight gain.

"Do you have any idea if it's a boy or a girl?" Emma couldn't help asking.

"Sometimes we get a clear indication, but we haven't got one here, and without an amniocentesis, there's no way to be sure," Dr. Meyers said. "If you want my guess, it's probably a girl." He turned to Otto. "How'd you like a baby sister, young man?"

Otto shrugged. The doctor quirked an eyebrow at Emma.

"He refuses to talk about it," she said.

"Getting close. He'll have to deal with it." The doctor patted Otto on the shoulder. "You'll enjoy having a little playmate."

"Yeah, I guess." Otto stared off into the air.

Emma tried to raise the subject again on the way home, but Otto promptly began speculating why his friend Ken got into so much trouble at preschool. Ken, a bright, lively child, was the foster son of one of the school's aides.

"He always sits in the chair," Otto said, referring to the time-out seat.

"Do you sit in the chair?" Emma asked.

"Sometimes."

"Why? What do you get in trouble for?" She started away from a traffic light.

"Oh—talking at storytime." Otto interrupted himself to exclaim over a construction site as they passed. "Can I have a backhoe, Mommy?"

"You mean a big one? You're joking."

"I want one," Otto said, but without the stubborn fury he would have invested into the words six months before. He was getting older, Emma realized with a twinge of regret, before his next words brought her up sharply. "Mommy, is Eric the baby's daddy?"

"Yes." She braced herself to be asked why they weren't married.

Instead, Otto said, "Who's my daddy?"

Obviously he'd forgotten the explanation she'd given him many times. "Your daddy was my husband. His name was Bill and he died because he got very sick."

"Well, who am I going to live with, then?" Otto asked.

"What?" Emma halted the car in front of the house and turned to him in shock. "Live with? Me, of course."

"But you're going to be the baby's mommy." All of a sudden Otto's little face crumpled. "I don't want to go away!"

"You're not going anywhere!" She leaned over and hugged him as fiercely as she could, given the size of her abdomen and the obstacle presented by his booster seat. "Whatever gave you that idea?"

"Because..." His voice broke, then started up again gamely. "Ken says that when his baby was born, his mommy couldn't take care of them both. She said she was the baby's mommy now, and he had to go live with Mrs. Whitaker."

Silently, Emma raged at such cruelty. She'd heard rumors that Ken's family had all sorts of problems, but whatever they were, Emma couldn't imagine treating a child so callously.

"Honey, what happened to Ken was—well, unusual. Lots of mommies have more than one child. Look at Josie. She didn't send Kiki away when Greggie was born, did she?"

"No." Otto thought it over.

"Have you been worrying about this for a long time?" Emma caught his small hands in hers. "I wish you'd told me!"

"I thought maybe I could go live with Stella," Otto said. "Then I could still see you and Eric sometimes."

"Oh, honey." Emma hugged him again, nuzzling his soft cheek. "I would never give you up. Never, never, never! You're my precious little Otto...."

"I love you, Mommy," he said, and curled up in her arms contentedly.

IN THE NEXT TWO WEEKS, the weather veered from a late-September cool spell to an October heat wave. Day after day, temperatures soared above a hundred degrees, and the air conditioning in Emma's car was no match for it. She barely managed to summon the energy at night to play quietly with Otto.

Fortunately, he grew mellower following their revealing conversation. If only, Emma told herself, Alyssa and Genevieve could be so easily pacified.

Barry Gray's improvised idea of double seductions had struck a responsive chord in the tabloids, which took great glee in implying that the soap mirrored real life.

Ford Burgess Leaps Bed To Bed shrieked one headline, beneath which the actor was quoted as saying he "couldn't decide which one he likes best, the mother or the daughter."

Mom's Expertise Puts Alyssa To Shame read another inflammatory stretch of bold type. Even some of the television entertainment shows, usually more responsible in their reporting, speculated on the rumors.

Genevieve took the rumors calmly but Alyssa simmered. Emma wished the older actress would show a bit more sympathy toward her daughter instead of assuming that she, too, could simply dismiss it all as nonsense.

The day matters came to a head started out as a real scorcher. By ten o'clock that morning, Emma's ankles were already swollen. She would have taken off early, but Alyssa was scheduled for a major scene that afternoon.

After the hair touch-up was complete, Corinne dragged Emma along for moral support to watch Alyssa's character, the innocent Janelle, confront her rival Lita Amaro— Genevieve—at a café.

Lights flooded the set and the director called for action. Nervous and vulnerable, Alyssa approached the elegant Lita, who was dining with one of her admirers.

"I need—I need to know what you want with Jon," Alyssa said. The catch in her voice sounded genuine.

"Jon?" Genevieve made a face to her companion, ridiculing the girl before her. "Jon who?"

"That's not the line," Corinne whispered. "It's supposed to be— 'Wouldn't you like to know.' "

Not a major change, but Genevieve ought to realize it would confuse her inexperienced daughter. And it was expensive to reshoot scenes, so Alyssa would have to make the best of it.

"*My* Jon," she replied, and inside, Emma cheered.

At this point, Genevieve was supposed to wave to another table and cut Alyssa dead, but instead the older actress said, "Why don't you just give up? Everyone knows you're no match for me."

The words formed a direct challenge. Worse, as she spoke, Genevieve waved her hors d'oeuvre fork, which held an oyster speared on the end. Unexpectedly, the oyster flew through the air and splatted against Alyssa's cheek.

There was a moment of shocked silence. Genevieve sat staring at her daughter.

Alyssa's shoulders quivered and then straightened. With grim purpose, she lifted a glass of water and tossed it in her mother's face.

Genevieve touched her wilted hair in disbelief, and then, snatching up another glass, heaved it at her daughter.

Corinne gestured wildly to Alyssa. Realizing the cameras were still rolling, the singer wiped the water from her eyes and stalked away.

Emma caught a glimpse of Barry Gray standing to one side, a smug smile creasing his face.

No doubt he would leak print photos of the scene to the tabloids and arrange clips for the TV entertainment shows. By the time the episode aired in a few weeks, he'd score tremendous ratings.

And he'd never care that he might have done irreparable harm to the relationship between a mother and daughter.

Struggling to keep up with Corinne, Emma followed her in Alyssa's wake down a corridor and into the ladies' room.

"Look at me!" Alyssa wailed, examining her wilted image in the mirror. "They actually taped me this way! I'm ashamed to go out in the parking lot looking like this."

"It was a dramatic scene," Corinne offered, trying to run damage control. "People will think you were just acting."

"No, they won't." Alyssa shrugged out of her soaking blouse. "Get me something to wear, will you?"

"Of course. And I'll bring the hair dryer, too, Emma," Corinne said. She opened the door, then stepped back as Genevieve entered.

"Well, well," the actress snapped. "That was quite a display of temper."

Alyssa slammed her hand against the wall, making Emma and Corinne jump. "I guess throwing an oyster in my face doesn't count."

"Accidents will happen. You can't take these things personally." Genevieve nodded to Emma. "My dear, I'll need my hair done right away. I have another scene in an hour."

"She's *my* hairdresser, Mother." Clad only in a slip, Alyssa stalked toward her menacingly.

"By my generosity." Genevieve stood her ground, refusing to be intimidated. "Don't forget, I was the one who found her. And right now, I'm scheduled for a scene."

"She's going to do *my* hair first," Alyssa growled.

"We'll see what Barry has to say about that." Genevieve turned away.

"Oh, yes, run to Barry!" Fury had wiped away any trace of composure. "You take every chance you can to humiliate me. You're jealous, aren't you, Mother? What is it—my singing career? Or the fact that you're not young anymore, and I am?"

Genevieve's rich voice boomed through the ladies' room and out into the hall. "Anyone could be a rock 'n' roll star if they screamed loud enough. Emma, come with me. *Now.*"

Despite the sharp pull on her wrist, Emma hesitated. "Genevieve, I accepted a salary from Alyssa before I knew you were going to join the show...."

"I don't want to hear this kind of rudeness from, of all people, my *hairdresser.*" For the first time, Genevieve's venom was directed at Emma. "Exactly who do you think you are? If it weren't for me, you'd still be bending over a shampoo bowl—"

"That isn't the issue." Emma tried to keep calm. "Why don't you let me ask Alyssa if she can spare me for a while?"

"Oh, go on. Go with her." Without warning, Alyssa's fury, too, turned on Emma. "You don't want to work for me anymore? Fine. There's lots of good hairdressers!"

Emma knew she ought to keep her peace, and that when tempers settled, both women would probably apologize. She knew they didn't mean those insults.

But her ankles hurt so much she could hardly stand, and her abdomen ached and stomach acid was wreaking torture on her esophagus. They'd purposely embarrassed her today in front of Corinne and whoever might be listening in the hall. And she'd had enough.

"Fine," she snapped. "I like and respect both of you, but these past months I've had to stand by and watch you act like two spoiled children quarreling over your toys. Well, I'm not one of those toys. Give me a call when you grow up!"

She stalked out of the room, paused at the trailer to retrieve her belongings and then hurried to her car.

By the time she reached the freeway, her outrage had given way to a lowering cloud of anxiety. What had she gone and done?

Actresses might be allowed their temperaments, but hairdressers weren't. Like bartenders, their role was to listen and soothe. When word spread of Emma's tantrum—as she had no doubt it would, probably with Barry's help—the doors of Hollywood would be closed to her.

She fought against tears. An apology might smooth things over, but Emma didn't think she could manage one. Not unless the two of them showed remorse first. Emma wasn't usually hung up on matters of pride, but she had to draw the line somewhere.

She mulled the matter all the way to her off-ramp, and then something happened that drove it completely out of her mind.

At first it felt like a trickle, then a gush. She must be bleeding again.

Emma refused to give in to panic. She wasn't in pain and she didn't feel weak. It would be faster to drive straight to the hospital than to stop somewhere and wait for an ambulance.

Giving herself the kind of pep talk she'd always reserved for her clients, Emma kept herself on course all the way to the emergency room.

Chapter Fourteen

Afterward Eric could never remember how he got to the hospital, although he must have driven his van, because he found it later in the parking lot. All he could remember was the nurse on the telephone saying he was needed urgently.

The labor and delivery area was full of people in white uniforms rushing around ignoring him. Eric had to ask three of them before someone directed him to the right room.

Emma lay on a hard, narrow bed, hooked up to an array of high-tech equipment that thumped with heartbeats. To Eric's worried eye, Emma looked much too pale, but she smiled as he came in.

"I thought I was bleeding," she said. "My waters broke."

"But you aren't due for six weeks." Eric couldn't help stating the obvious.

"The doctor's on his way," Emma said. "Hold my hand?"

He reached out, and then had to stifle a groan as she gripped him with unexpected strength, her fingernails digging into his skin. "Hey!"

"I—I'm sorry," she gasped. "I had a contraction."

Eric noticed that the paper running across one of the machines showed a hill with a jagged peak. "Is that what it looks like?"

"I guess. I'll tell you what it feels like." Emma closed her eyes as he stroked her forehead. "It feels like your whole body is caught in a vise and you're being squeezed to death by your own muscles."

"Shh." Eric continued his rhythmic stroking. "Try to relax. Remember what the instructor said."

"Oh, no!" Emma stared at him in horror. "My focal point! The photograph—it's at home with my overnight bag."

"We'll have to use something else." Eric dug out his wallet, hoping to find a suitable photograph. Unfortunately, he'd dumped out some aging pictures months ago and filled up his wallet with credit cards, which he had no intention of sticking up on a piece of equipment. Besides, who knew what permanent damage might be done if Emma fixated through labor on the eye-boggling hologram on the front of his MasterCard?

Finally he pried out his black-and-white library card, which featured a picture of a zebra. "How about this?" At Emma's nod, he wedged it into a suitable spot.

She was recovering from a second contraction when Dr. Meyers arrived, still wearing a suit and tie.

"Emma." The doctor came alongside and Eric yielded his place. "I'm a little concerned because of that placenta previa. With the baby being so early, I think we should do a Caesarean section."

Eric's mind couldn't quite absorb what the doctor was saying. Caesarean section—what was that? Some kind of test? Then it hit him—a C-section.

"Is that really necessary?" he heard himself ask. "I've read that doctors perform too many C-sections."

Dr. Meyers didn't take offense. "That's a reasonable concern. Is it necessary? We can't be sure. It's my recommendation at this point, because I don't like to put the baby through more stress than necessary when it's still so small.

And there's always the danger that the placenta will separate prematurely."

"I think it's a good idea." Lying there, tied up to all those wires, Emma looked remarkably self-possessed. "The most important thing is to keep the baby safe."

"Well—okay," Eric said.

After that, things moved very quickly. Before he knew it, Eric was dressed in a cap and gown, holding Emma's hand in the operating room while the doctor drew a tiny head from the incision.

A moment later, someone said, "Congratulations! It's a girl!"

"Her name is Kiri," Emma said happily.

But Eric's mind wasn't on names. He couldn't tear his eyes from the tiny body being worked over by the pediatric team. Was she all right? He'd seen her move— She had to be okay—

A wail pulsed through the air. An almost visible wave of relief ran across the room, or maybe, Eric thought, it was just the sigh of his muscles unknotting themselves.

"Sounds like her lungs are fine," Dr. Meyers said as he stitched up Emma's wound. "She's beautiful."

A nurse laid the well-wrapped baby in Emma's arms. Kiri yawned and started to fuss, then calmed as Emma hummed to her. Eric was debating whether he dared reach down and pick up the baby, when the nurse reclaimed her.

It took another half hour before Emma could be transferred to the recovery room. Chased away by a motherly nurse, Eric wandered to the newborn nursery to check on his daughter.

The pediatrician joined him. "She looks fine," the doctor said. "She weighs—let's see—four pounds ten ounces. That's a good size, and she's well developed. That's why she's not in intensive care. We'll want to keep her a while for observation, but she looks very healthy. Congratulations."

Eric thanked the man automatically. He couldn't think of anything but the tiny baby on the other side of the window.

He double-checked the name tag on the clear plastic box that enclosed her. Kiri Jameson. Emma had even given the baby his name.

An indescribable emotion choked up through his throat, stinging his eyes and making it hard to see the perfect little creature in front of him. The diaper looked enormous, and her skin was so red, and if those tubes were hurting her he was going to break in there and make the nurses take them out.

But she didn't seem to be hurting. In fact, he could swear Kiri was smiling at him. Surely she couldn't really see this far. She was probably dreaming about whatever newborn babies dreamed about—softness, and the way Emma smelled, and how she was going to wrap her daddy right around that minuscule finger.

By comparison, the other babies in the nursery appeared positively enormous. Eric checked out one of Kiri's neighbors and saw that the weight tag read "9 lbs. 2 oz." That wasn't a baby; it was a horse!

Half an hour later, he was still standing there, watching his daughter sleep.

LEANING HEAVILY against Eric, Emma shuffled down the hospital corridor in her bathrobe and slippers. Only two days, and already they had her walking around as much as possible.

This was her first trip all the way to the nursery. She ached to see her baby, who had been placed in the intermediate care room.

"There." Eric pointed through the window. "That little scrapper."

Kiri lay wailing inside her isolette, as the plastic boxes were called. To Emma, she looked tiny.

"That's her hungry cry," Eric explained as a nurse arrived to comfort and feed the baby.

"I should be doing that." Emma's milk hadn't come in yet, and she knew it was important that the baby receive extra nutrition, but she wished she could do more for little Kiri.

On Eric's arm, she made her way to the door and asked a nurse if she could come in. Checking the pediatrician's instructions, the nurse said he preferred that she wait until the following day.

"The baby's temperature has been unstable, and that can be a sign of infection," the nurse said. "We want to keep her as healthy as possible."

"Of course." Emma retreated reluctantly.

She needed to hold Kiri and bond with her. With Otto, Emma had felt a strong rush of maternal protectiveness almost instantly, but this birth was different.

First, there'd been her fears during that heart-stopping drive to the hospital. Then she'd been surrounded by so many people, all those doctors and nurses, that it had felt as if she were merely an observer.

On the walk back to her room, Emma couldn't focus on Eric's excited discussion of their daughter's merits. To her dismay, Emma realized she felt kind of lost. It was such a nebulous feeling that she didn't even know how to describe it to Eric.

Maybe, Emma thought, this was how he felt sometimes, too. Maybe this was why he hadn't told her about the magazine assignment. Actually, later on, he'd begun referring to it as if she already knew, so obviously he hadn't meant to keep it a state secret.

Finally Eric's words penetrated her mental fog. "You'll need someone to take care of you when you come home, so I'll be moving in. Now, don't argue."

"I'm not." Emma sank onto the edge of the bed, glad that her roommate had left this afternoon. "I'd appreciate it. If it won't interfere with your studies."

Eric shrugged. "Who knows? Frankly, some of these assignments don't make a lot of sense. I want to design buildings and communities, not 'interior and exterior forms.' Sometimes I feel like the instructors are trying to turn me into an avante-garde artist instead of an architect."

"At least you haven't told your professors where to get off," Emma reminded him. "Which puts you in better standing with them than I am with Alyssa and Genevieve."

"What about the other people who've been calling you?" Eric prompted.

"I'll get in touch with them." Emma leaned back wearily. "When I'm up to it."

"You need to sleep." He kissed her lightly. "Emma, we'll work things out. And by the way, I hope you don't mind, but I'm picking Otto up at Betsy's tonight. I think he needs to sleep in his own bed, don't you?"

The nurse came in with a pain pill, and Eric slipped out. Emma felt as if she should be more in control of the situation, as if she should be the one setting up arrangements for Otto, but she couldn't muster any energy. She drifted off to sleep, still thinking she was awake.

When she woke up at 2:00 a.m. not only her incision but also her breasts hurt. To her touch, they felt rock hard. She rang for the nurse, who showed up with another pain pill.

"My milk's in," Emma said.

"I'll bring you a pump," the nurse promised, and disappeared.

When she didn't come back right away, Emma tried to go to sleep, but, perversely, her mind wouldn't stop buzzing. Finally she swung out of bed, put on her robe, and set out down the hall.

The bright lights of the hospital gave Emma a sense of timelessness, as if there were no day or night. She could hear other new mothers talking sleepily to their babies, and realized the infants must have been brought in for the early-morning feeding.

Sure enough, when she reached the nursery, it was almost empty. There were only a few new arrivals and Kiri, wide-awake and wailing lustfully.

Emma shuffled to the door. The night nurse paused in filling out her reports.

"My milk came in." Emma showed her identity bracelet. "Can I have my baby?"

"You scrub over there." The nurse provided her with a clean gown and cap and directed her to a sink, where Emma followed the instructions required of intermediate-care parents.

Then the nurse found a private corner for her behind a screen and placed tiny Kiri in Emma's arms.

Emma wasn't sure what to do. With Otto, she'd held him near her breast, and he'd latched on, tucking down to business like a pro. Kiri, however, was small and disorganized. Emma couldn't seem to get all the parts properly supported and hold the baby in the right position.

When she finally managed it, Kiri gave a few hearty sucks and stopped.

"Too hard for you?" Emma asked.

Two bright eyes peered up at her. Preemie or not, Kiri was alert.

"You like being up in the middle of the night, don't you?" Emma asked. "I can see we're going to have a lot of fun."

Kiri opened her rosebud mouth and then closed it again with what Emma imagined to be a contented sigh. She was an exquisite baby, much prettier than most, Emma decided. And smarter too, of course.

The nurse poked her head around the screen. "I though[l] you might need this." She held out a thin, tube-shaped bo[t]tle of formula.

"Thanks." Emma cradled Kiri in one arm and manip[u]lated the bottle until the baby was sucking steadily. Tomo[r]row, she decided she'd try that pump, and get her baby on[ ]breast milk.

She wanted nothing but the best for her daughter.

ALTHOUGH SHE WAS GLAD to leave the hospital four day[s] later, Emma wished Kiri could have come home. But th[e] doctor wanted to keep her for observation until she bega[n] gaining weight steadily. Still, the next week passed quick[ly] as she spent extra time with Otto.

On the drive to the hospital the day they hoped Kiri woul[d] be released, Eric told her that his second project had r[e]ceived only a modestly positive critique.

"I *know* I can do better," Eric said as he steered into th[e] parking structure. "But I have some kind of block. I kee[p] resisting what the professors want me to do."

"You're just not used to being back in a classroom." A[l]though her incision was healing well, a speed bump se[nt] twinges through Emma's lower abdomen.

"I know. It's all these abstractions," Eric agreed. "I'[m] supposed to gain an understanding of the interior nature [of] nonsolid forms. As if anyone would hire me to design [a] functioning raindrop!"

Emma hoped his concerns weren't getting in the way [of] enjoying these precious early days of Kiri's life. So far she'[d] managed to keep from getting upset by the fact that sh[e] hadn't heard from Genevieve or Alyssa. Only Corinne ha[d] sent a baby gift and a note of congratulations.

Thoughts of her professional dilemma flew out the wi[n]dow as soon as she saw the pediatrician making his round[s] at the nursery.

"Mr. and Mrs. Jameson?" Although they'd told him they weren't married, the doctor kept forgetting. "We ran a test last night on Kiri's breathing. She had a couple of minor episodes of apnea, not breathing for a few seconds. Nothing to worry about, but I'd recommend we send her home on a monitor."

"A monitor?" Eric frowned. "Hasn't she had enough needles stuck in her?"

The pediatrician smiled. "Fortunately, the monitor isn't that complicated, and it isn't painful. I've asked the home-health coordinator to show you how it works and give you some instructions in CPR. I believe she's available now."

CPR? Emma's heartbeat speeded up as she followed a nurse to the conference room. It had never occurred to her that Kiri might be in any long-term danger, since she'd been so healthy this far. There hadn't been an infection, and her temperature had stabilized enough for her to be transferred to a regular bassinet.

"Hi, I'm Sally." The coordinator was a heavyset woman with a kind face who probably had kids of her own. "Most parents find the idea of a monitor scary, but just think of it as a precaution. Like a smoke alarm. You can rest easy, knowing that if anything did go wrong, you'd be awakened in time to help."

Eric eyed her dubiously. "Don't they ever have false alarms?"

"Yes, often." Sally displayed an electronic box resembling a tape deck. "Sometimes a contact pulls loose, and it makes a long continuous bleep that signals equipment failure. If she stops breathing, you'll hear an intermittent 'beep-beep-beep.' Of course, most of the time she'll be breathing again on her own by the time you reach her."

"What happens when we suffer a heart attack from hearing the beeper go off?" Eric grumbled.

"We haven't lost a parent yet." Sally showed them ho to turn the monitor on and off, how to recharge the batte and, using a doll, how to attach the contact points with belt that wrapped across the baby's chest and fastened wit Velcro.

"We'll practice on Kiri in a minute," she said. "But firs you need to know CPR."

Emma couldn't imagine actually performing cardiopu monary resuscitation on Kiri, but in a way it reassured he to learn how. Eric mastered the technique quickly, a though he had to restrain himself from pressing too hard o the doll's chest.

The last thing they did was to fasten the belt on the daughter, which proved a lot harder than doing it with doll. Kiri puffed out her stomach while they were attachin it, then let the air out. The belt flopped and the equipmer bleeped, making Emma jump.

"Now you know what it sounds like," Sally said. "Try again."

"It's like saddling a tiny horse," Eric said as he tigh ened the belt, ignoring the baby's squeak of protest.

Emma found it hard to be firm with such a small infan but she persevered.

"Be sure to keep the belt on any time she's asleep, unle: you're holding her," Sally reminded them. "When she awake, it's not necessary."

The pediatrician reappeared. "The good news," he saic "is that we're releasing your daughter today."

Excitement prickled along Emma's arms. What sh wanted to do was to snatch Kiri out of the bassinet and tak off with her, but there were papers to sign, and then a vo unteer had to wheel the baby to the entrance while Eri pulled the car around.

Getting her into the baby seat turned out to be a hercu lean task with the monitor belt on, but finally they mar aged. Emma kept twisting around in her seat, unable to take her eyes off Kiri.

"I can't believe it," she said. "She's really ours."

"I wish she didn't need that contraption." Eric slowed for merging traffic. "Still—I'm glad, too."

They swung by Otto's preschool to pick him up. He showed them his latest painting and pretended a disinterest in the baby, but kept sneaking peeks at her. Once Emma saw him poke a finger into the baby's curled hand and grin when Kiri gripped him.

At home, Eric fixed hot dogs for supper while Emma got the baby settled. Afterward she spent some time alone with Kiri, feeding her expressed milk in a bottle because she was still too little to nurse well. Finally Kiri went to sleep.

A check revealed that Otto was playing with his toy fire station. She found Eric in the dining room, where he'd set up a study center in one corner.

He scarcely noticed when she entered. Emma moved alongside and saw that he was inking in the details of an oddly shaped space station.

"It'll have to be blown up, of course," Eric said. "I'll be doing a full oil painting. The article has some interesting concepts. Look at that form—kind of an iron cross. Here's where the crew will live...."

He went on explaining, although Emma found it hard to follow. She tired easily since her surgery, and her thoughts kept flying to Kiri and the monitor, half expecting it to sound at any moment.

She loved the excitement on Eric's face as he talked about his illustration, but it troubled her, too. So far, he hadn't shown any of the same enthusiasm for his architecture studies.

Still, that would come. Every job involved its apprenticeship.

The glow of the chandelier refracted in his eyes like tiny sparks. In the strange shadows that it cast, she could imagine him much older, a man with whom she'd spent twenty years but who would never cease to challenge and attract her. That was the thing about falling in love, Emma knew: she now cared as deeply for his happiness as for her own.

She stood there listening and nodding and asking questions, trying to give him the support he needed. She would be here for him while he found his way, while they both found their way side by side.

Chapter Fifteen

A week before Thanksgiving the weather turned cool, and Emma wasn't sure she'd be able to take six-week-old Kiri to the Saturday outings she and Otto had recently resumed. Fortunately, the day warmed up by noon, and they arrived at Burger King on time.

As she unhooked Kiri from the monitor and laid her gently in the carriage, Emma reflected how quickly she'd adapted to the piece of infernal equipment, as Eric referred to it. There'd been a number of alarms but no emergencies; the beep itself probably startled Kiri into taking a breath.

"Mommy, they have Magic Bee toys!" Otto hopped up and down excitedly. The prizes that came with the kids' meals were one of the prime attractions of the fast-food restaurant.

"Hey!" Betsy waved from her car, where she was helping Roy out of his booster seat. "How's the little tyke?"

"Still breathing," Emma joked.

"Smiling at you yet?"

Emma pushed the carriage up the walk. "She smiles a lot but she doesn't look me in the eye. The doctor says because she was early, it'll probably be a few more weeks."

"At least she's healthy." Betsy examined the baby. "Her hair's growing."

"Thank goodness." The nurses had shaved Kiri's temples when they attached the hospital monitoring equipment, and Emma couldn't wait for the bald places to grow out.

They found Josie at the playground, half finished with her food. "The kids couldn't wait," she explained.

At sixteen months, Greggie chased his sister around the play area, clambering onto the merry-go-round by himself. He'd changed dramatically this past year, Emma thought. It was hard to imagine Kiri going through the same transition, but of course she would.

The conversation touched on Kiri's latest checkup, and then Betsy said, "Well, I have some news."

The other women spoke simultaneously, as if by prearrangement, "You're pregnant."

Betsy gave them a look that was half amused and half disappointed. "You mean you can tell?"

"No, of course not," Josie said. "What else could it be?"

"You're beaming from ear to ear," Emma pointed out. "Come on, tell us. When are you due? What did Matt say?"

"I'm only a month along," Betsy said. "And Matt, well, after we had our conversation, I guess he saw that making room for his family isn't going to destroy his career. If it slows him down a little, so what?"

"I read once that nobody ever said on their deathbed, 'Gee, I wish I'd spent more time at the office,'" Josie said.

"Speaking of which, have you heard anything from Genevieve or Alyssa?" Betsy turned to Emma.

She shook her head. "After Thanksgiving, I'm going to call some of the people who contacted me earlier and see what I can scare up."

They discussed their plans for the holiday. Throughout the conversation, Josie seemed more nostalgic than usual.

"You act as if this were your last Thanksgiving," Emma commented as her friend finished bemoaning the fact that a favorite cousin couldn't attend the family get-together.

"Oh." Josie bit her lip, checked on the kids, and then said, "I've been meaning to tell you guys something."

"Uh-oh," Betsy said.

"You can't *both* have big news," Emma protested.

"Sam and I..." Josie started to rise as Greggie tumbled off the merry-go-round, but sank back when he picked himself up and set off toward the climbing platform. "We've decided we need to be together as a family."

"Oh, Lord," Betsy said. "You're not moving to the land of samurai and geishas!"

"I *won't* wear a kimono," Josie said. "And Sam promised we'll make regular trips to Hong Kong and Australia. Now, come on, guys, don't tell me you're not jealous!"

"Positively green," Betsy said.

"I'm pleased for you." Emma touched Josie's hand. "We'll miss you."

"You mean you're not going to be here for this baby?" Betsy pretended to glare. "When are you moving, anyway?"

"Next month." Josie sighed. "You wouldn't believe the packing I've got to do. And organizing what goes into storage, what to ship. We're not going to stay forever, but it feels like it."

They enjoyed the rest of the afternoon together, although they all felt somewhat nostalgic, too.

"It's scary, isn't it?" Emma asked the others as they got ready to leave. "You want something so much, but when it comes you see that it means giving up other things."

"I've become spoiled, having a four-year-old," Betsy admitted. "Sometimes I wonder if I'm crazy, going back to diapers and night feedings. But I know I'm going to love it!"

"I can't begin to imagine what my life's going to be like," Josie agreed. "But at least we'll all be together."

"And you won't stay there forever," Emma pointed out.

"Not more than a year or two," Josie said. "We want the kids to go to school here. So don't worry—the Saturday morning gang will ride again!"

THE JAMESONS CELEBRATED Thanksgiving in the old-fashioned way, inviting family and close friends. Stella's younger sister, Leanne, who was divorced, brought her five-year-old son, Grant. He and Otto dug into their toys and soon were racing through the family room, waving toy drills and shouting, "Bang bang!"

"You refuse to buy them the guns, and what good does it do?" observed Leanne wryly, depositing a fruit salad on the kitchen counter.

"They'll shoot each other with sticks, anything they find," agreed Stella's co-worker, a rotund lady with the unlikely nickname of Babe. She had brought an orange-curried rice dish that smelled heavenly.

Emma balanced Kiri in her arms, wishing she knew how to break through to Eric's grandparents. His grandmother, Frances, sneaked longing glances at the baby but her husband, Norton, pointedly ignored Emma.

In a way, she couldn't blame him. When he was young, out-of-wedlock babies were hushed up and hidden away, and their mothers given the cold shoulder. Besides, Norton was Harlan Jameson's father, and Eric had warned her about his grandfather's rigidity. "He holds everyone up to the highest possible standards, and he has no tolerance for failure."

A retired civil engineer, Norton had been president of most of La Habra's service clubs at one time or another. He still served as honorary grand marshal of the annual Corn Festival Parade.

Now, Emma turned, startled, at a touch on the shoulder. It was Stella. "Could I hold her?"

"Of course." Emma shifted the baby into Stella's arms.

Eric's mother gazed lovingly down into the tiny face, as if she'd forgotten all about the holiday and her guests. "She's so alert. Don't you think so?"

"Oh, yes." Actually, Emma, making a tremendous effort to be objective, had to admit that her daughter wasn't particularly advanced for the age of seven weeks. But then, if she'd reached her due date, Kiri would actually be about a week old, so Emma supposed she might be advanced, after all.

"Hey!" Peter called. "The doohickey's popped up in the turkey. Does that mean it's done?"

Reluctantly, Stella handed the baby to her sister. "Isn't she beautiful, Leanne?"

"She certainly is." Clucking, Leanne settled into a chair with her great-niece.

Emma checked on Otto and found him playing hide-and-seek with Grant in the family room. There was no sign of Eric, who'd emerged briefly to greet her and then retreated to his room. With design review coming up next week, he couldn't let himself relax for one day.

Emma pitched in to help Stella, carrying dishes to the dining room table, setting out silverware and filling the water glasses. The soft counterpoint of voices soothed her, taking her back to Thanksgivings at her own grandparents' home.

She had missed having relatives around. Being an only child and losing her parents young had left a gap in Emma's life that friends could only partly fill. She felt as if, in Stella, she'd found what she was missing.

They'd spent several hours together the previous day, shopping for Kiri's room. As her gift, Stella wanted to present them with a baby comforter and decorations but needed to make sure they would blend with what Emma already had.

They'd wheeled the baby between stores, getting to know each other as they shopped. They were pleased to find that they both liked old-fashioned prints and ruffles, and they also shared a passion for the chocolate-chip cookies that sold for outrageous prices in the mall.

"Dinner's ready!" Stella called. "Where's Eric? We need him to carve."

"Busy," muttered Norton as he selected a seat at the table. "A busy man." He looked pointedly at Kiri, whose infant seat had been given a place of honor on a side table.

Emma didn't know how to respond to what was obviously meant as a dig, and was grateful for the distraction as the two boys ran up demanding to be fed.

Eric emerged apologetically from his room, but Emma could see his thoughts lingered with his assignment. He'd worked so hard these past weeks; she hoped it would pay off.

After making short work of the turkey, Eric served Otto and his nephew, then took a seat beside Emma. They joined the others in giving thanks.

"There's nothing like Turkey Day!" Babe proclaimed as everyone set to eating. "Leanne, I want your recipe for that cranberry sauce. And this stuffing! Stella, what is that flavor?"

"Well, I don't know." Eric's mother glowed beneath the praise. "It's got all sorts of things in it...."

Their words blurred in Emma's mind into a warm sense of contentment. The significance of the day transcended the food and even the company. Yes, she was thankful for her blessings, which shone like the vibrancy of dawn against the dark moments she was leaving behind.

Throughout the meal, Norton ate in silence. Once she caught Eric giving his grandfather a suspicious look, but the old man behaved himself.

Until, that is, Leanne complimented Peter on how well he was doing as the new head of J&J Plumbing.

"I figured it's my turn to make a living around here," Peter responded modestly.

"I'll say it's your turn." Norton's needling tone didn't appear to be directed at Peter, however. "Your turn to go to college. Some people don't like to give others a chance."

Beside her, she felt Eric stiffen. Through Norton's tones, Eric must have read the disapproval of his father. Within families, people knew how to push each other's sensitive buttons, and Norton was doing exactly that.

It was Stella who responded. "If you mean Eric, he urged Peter to go."

"I hate school." Peter made a face. The easygoing son, he'd apparently escaped the intense ambition that had defined his father's life.

"Norton," Frances warned.

The old man pushed his plate aside. "Nobody asked my opinion, but I'll give it. That young man ought to be supporting his child, not fooling around with studies he's too old for. He's a good plumber and that's something to be proud of."

The muscles stood out in Eric's jaw. Emma could feel him reining in a sharp retort.

She knew it wasn't her place to speak, but she wanted to. "I should think you'd respect Eric for what he's doing, Mr. Jameson. After earning a living for his family all these years, he's going back to better himself, and that isn't easy."

She feared the old man would turn his acid tongue on her, but instead he said, "I like a woman who stands by her man. I don't blame you for this whole mess. It's a man's responsibility to make it legal."

"He offered," Emma said. "We're not ready."

"Look ready enough to me." Norton eyed the baby. "Kiri. What kind of name is that? What's wrong with Mary or Elizabeth?"

Emma exhaled slowly and felt the tension ease around the table. Apparently Norton Jameson had said all he intended to say to Eric, and was now blustering for the sake of blustering.

"I like the name," Frances announced. "It's like that opera singer, Kiri Te Kanawa."

"Well, I don't know what kind of name that is, either," Norton grumbled. "What are the rest of you still eating turkey for? I saw a pumpkin pie in there. Am I going to have to eat it by myself?"

"No," Otto piped up from where he sat messing his green beans into his mashed potatoes. "I want three pieces!"

"I want four pieces," said Grant.

"I want five pieces!" cried Otto.

"You're not getting any unless you finish your vegetables," Emma told him.

"Thank goodness somebody has some sense around here," said Norton.

Later, when the others lay semi-comatose in the living room and Eric had retreated to his studies, Emma helped Stella clean up the kitchen.

"I'm sorry about Norton," Stella said as she put the food away. "He has old-fashioned ideas."

"Doesn't bother me." Emma scraped a plate and rinsed it. "But Eric—"

"Eric feels these things so deeply." Stella sighed. "Peter's my happy child. Eric's the worrier. He takes the weight of the world on his shoulders."

"I wish I could help." Emma attacked an encrusted pot with a scrub brush. "I wanted to encourage him and instead I've added to his pressures."

Stella stopped her work and looked Emma straight in the eye. "Don't you ever regret what's happened! I love that baby. You've brought me something I didn't expect to have for years and years, maybe ever. To heck with Norton Jameson if he doesn't approve."

The older woman's fierceness caught Emma by surprise. She realized what perhaps should have been obvious before, that since birth Kiri had joined the short list of people Stella lived for.

"Eric's lucky," Emma said softly. "So is Kiri, to have you for a grandmother."

"I don't know what I am to you, at least not technically." Stella snapped the lid on a plastic container. "But I'm family. You remember that. You're one of mine now, Emma."

"You bet I am," Emma said, and caught Stella up in a hug. It took a moment for the other woman to respond, and then they were clutching each other like long-lost friends.

"Oh, dear," Stella said, quickly wiping away a tear. "I don't know what I'm getting so weepy for."

"Pure happiness," Emma said. "You deserve it."

One more thing to give thanks for. One more very special thing.

WHY SOME FIEND had set aside the last week of November for design review, Eric would never understand. Underneath all the holiday festivities had run an undercurrent of anxiety.

Now he set his model out on one of the worktables in the studio, tinkering with the tiny pieces that had been dislodged in transport. He tried not to concern himself with the other students' work, but he couldn't help it. Some of them looked not only sophisticated but entertaining, as if they'd been playing instead of struggling the way he had.

The final assignment of the quarter had been another of those nebulous tasks that he had a hard time taking seriously. The first part, abstract design, required him to select three objects and connect them in two different ways, either by penetrating, grasping, colliding, wrapping, articulating or layering.

The second part, architectural design, called for him to take one horizontal and one vertical cut in his project and develop these into a series of rooms suggesting anticipation, transition, gathering and solitude.

He desperately wanted to rearrange his thinking, so he'd spent long hours studying the work of famous architects and sample projects displayed by the second-year architecture coordinator, as his instructor was called. He'd based his final selection on the shapes of children's toys, wrapping them together in a way suggestive of Christmas presents.

Building the models had taken an incredible amount of time. Sometimes Eric wondered whether Emma wished he would move out. He'd turned her dining room table into a display area, and only rarely found a few hours for Otto or Kiri.

His daughter was changing so rapidly. Almost two months old—was that possible? She made cooing noises like a small bird. Eric enjoyed playing with her; he didn't even mind changing her diaper. He just wished he had more time.

"Hey," one of his classmates called from the doorway. "They're coming."

Reluctantly Eric followed the others out into the courtyard, making way for the coordinator, Joseph Haymes, and half a dozen critics who were to help him evaluate the models.

The other students gathered in small knots. He found himself standing next to another older student, a woman in her late thirties who he knew had teenage children.

"I like your Christmas presents," she said. "They remind me of when the kids were little."

"Thanks." But her faint praise didn't make him feel any better. He wanted to be brilliant and original, the way his city of the future had been.

It felt like hours before the critics finally left and he was able to collect his project. Eric knew he ought to leave, but he couldn't bring himself to go yet.

He waited until he saw Haymes head toward the adjacent building where the instructors had their offices. Eager for feedback, Eric followed.

Haymes was pouring himself a cup of coffee when Eric entered. The office, although modern and of a reasonable size, was so cluttered with files and models that it seemed claustrophobic. Or maybe that impression was the result of nerves.

"You want to know your grade?" Haymes said. "I'm going to be hard on you, Jameson. You're getting a C for the quarter."

Eric gripped the back of a chair. He'd never gotten anything below a B in his life. He knew that in his other, general education classes he would probably average close to an A, but this was the only course that mattered.

"Why?" he asked in a choked voice.

Haymes' mouth twitched sympathetically. "You've done all your work, completed every assignment, turned in your sketchbook. But you haven't learned the fundamental lesson we were trying to teach."

"You—" Eric couldn't believe the judgment was this harsh. "You don't think I'm cut out for this field?"

"I didn't say that. As a matter of fact, you've asked some interesting questions this term. I suspect you'll make an excellent architect." Haymes gestured him into a chair. "Look, Jameson, the point of these exercises was to stimulate your creativity. You take the whole thing too seri-

'ously. You've been trying so hard to be brilliant that you haven't had any fun.''

"Fun?" Eric echoed.

"There'll be a lot of years ahead to design three-bedroom houses or gas stations or whatever area you go into," Haymes said. "Along the way, you're likely to forget that design is supposed to be visual and exciting. We've been trying to open you up."

Eric felt foolish. The coordinator was right. He *had* been more concerned with impressing his professors than with developing his insights.

"Like a lot of returning students, you've had to deal with the real world," Haymes went on. "This is college—it's supposed to be a special place. Not everything has to be practical. Not at this level."

Eric took a deep breath. "So you think I could bring my grade up next semester?"

"Probably quite easily," Haymes said. "Our next projects will be more to your liking. But remember, Eric, you've got a long haul ahead of you. You need to relax and enjoy the trip."

"Thanks." Eric stood up. "Thanks for being honest."

He walked out into the patchy November afternoon, wondering why the simplest things were sometimes the hardest to see.

"I'M NOT SURE WHAT I have to do," Eric said the next morning. "Maybe I need to take some time off. To travel and get in touch with myself and see things fresh. I don't know, Emma. I feel kind of stupid, to have been pushing myself so hard in the wrong direction."

She sat on the sofa with Kiri in her lap. It had been a difficult morning. She'd called Susan Salonica, only to be told the actress was out of town. True or not, she couldn't be sure. Next, Emma had placed a call to the TV anchor-woman, but another hairdresser had been hired.

One by one, she'd run down her list of names and numbers. No one needed her services. A few promised to call back another time, but she wasn't holding her breath.

One of the gossip columnists had got hold of the blowup and made it a juicy item in her column. "What mother-daughter feud finally got so out of hand it brought a dressing-down from their mutual hairstylist?..." Not exactly headline material, but enough to put Emma's career in the deep freeze.

And now Eric—he couldn't seriously be thinking about dropping out, could he?

"You aren't going to give up, are you?" she said.

He ran his fingers through his already rumpled hair. "No, of course not. I just wish I could have last semester back and do it right."

"Maybe getting a C was just what you needed," she ventured. "To make you see things from a new angle."

He shot her a surprised look. "You're not disappointed in me?"

"Who is going to care, when you're a distinguished architect, that you didn't knock your professors dead with your very first project?"

"Me," Eric admitted. "But I get a little carried away sometimes." The baby yawned in his face. "Looks like nap time."

Emma took her daughter to the bedroom, nursed her and laid her down to sleep in the bassinet. When she came back, she found Eric at his workstation, concentrating on the illustration in which he invested so much of his time.

She folded her arms, watching him from across the room without interrupting.

Neither one of them was a quitter. They hadn't come this far only to give up their dreams because of a few obstacles.

Emma slipped onto the sofa and leaned her head against a pillow.

She didn't know how, but she was going to get her career back. And the sooner the better.

Chapter Sixteen

The whole month of December, Eric felt as if he'd jumped onto a treadmill and couldn't pause long enough to figure out how to jump off again.

The deadline for his illustration was moved up by two weeks due to a change in printers. When he finally shipped it off to New York, he barely had time to take a deep breath before buckling down to his studies.

This quarter, at least, the assignments focused on subjects that made sense to him. His current undertaking involved designing a small motel in the desert, taking into account problems of environment and topography.

It was his chance to redeem himself. Determined to bring his grade up to a B or better by the end of the year, Eric brought his full concentration to the task.

He came up for air barely long enough to help Emma haul in a Christmas tree, then returned to work. Vaguely, he knew a precious time in their lives was approaching: Kiri's first Christmas.

But he didn't dare stop. He was going to prove to Joseph Haymes and anyone else who cared to notice that he was the best architect in his class. Already, now that more practical considerations and calculations were required, Eric had become one of the students off whom others bounced their ideas and problems. He relished the position, and couldn't take a chance on falling behind due to holiday inattention.

The weather turned cold the day before Christmas. Cold for Southern California, anyway, with a nippy reminder that only a few hours away in the mountains, snow was transforming the landscape into a fairyland.

Eric hadn't meant to wait until the last minute, but shopping was an activity that always got pushed to the end of his list. Now, taking a quick break from his studies, he hurried to the Brea Mall to pick up gifts.

One step inside and he forgot, for a moment, that he really did intend to stay only a few minutes.

It wasn't just the glittering green-and-gold decorations, or the jingling sounds that seemed to emanate from midair. Or even the faint aroma of pine wafting from a seasonal Christmas store.

There was something different about the people. They smiled more than usual; peered dreamily into shop windows; licked chocolate from their fingers with the eagerness of little children.

Children danced excitedly around their mothers; shopping bags gave tantalizing glimpses of brightly colored packages; and at the center of the mall, Santa Claus ho-ho-hoed merrily as he teased small tikes into telling him their fondest wishes.

Eric could almost have sworn the mall had been transported to some other time, a Victorian era when people treasured the small things of life and weren't in such a hurry to touch the future. He felt his heartbeat slow and his breathing come more easily. There was plenty of time to browse and consider, to poke through scented candles he had no intention of buying but loved to sniff, to pick up a stunning, elaborately costumed doll that reminded him he now had a precious little girl of his own.

Reluctantly, he forced himself to narrow his choices. He stopped at Sears to buy Peter some coveted carpentry tools, then selected a soft, fleecy robe for his mother. Although Kiri was too young to understand about the holiday, he couldn't resist adding a big-eyed panda bear to the collection.

In one toy store after another, Eric gazed longingly at expensive train sets from Germany and battery-operated cars that could zip a child up and down the sidewalk in style. Far beyond his budget, but not beyond a little boy's dreams.

Remembering how, recently, Otto had begun spending hours at the kitchen table drawing and coloring, Eric selected a set of washable marking pens, watercolors, crayons, construction paper and thick drawing paper. He added some holiday stencils and a package of stickers, and had the assortment gift wrapped.

Emma. Gazing into the windows of chic jewelry stores, Eric knew he couldn't afford anything worthy of her. In a luxury department store, he fingered a six-hundred-dollar black cocktail dress, imagining how stunning she would look in it, and reluctantly passed it up.

What he'd really like to give her was another chance at her career. Eric didn't doubt that it would come in its own time; Emma had special talents, and he was sure they wouldn't go unappreciated for long. But although she hadn't said much about it, he knew the subject troubled her, and he wished he could whip out a credit card and purchase a solution.

On his way to the escalator, Eric walked by the lingerie department. He hesitated, spotting a mannequin resplendent in a lacy lavender nightgown trimmed with tiny bows.

He'd never purchased anything so intimate for a woman. Not that he thought Emma would take offense, and yet— somehow, a gift like that presumed a great deal.

It would look beautiful on her. Emma loved delicate, exquisite things, and the color would bring out the glow in her cheeks.

Best of all, Eric could imagine how enticing it would feel to run his hands over all that lace and to feel the softness beneath. He and Emma hadn't resumed relations yet; the C-section required a long recovery, and then Emma had been tired from the demands of two children.

But now Kiri was sleeping through the night. And these past few days, immersed in his books, Eric had caught a few questioning glances from Emma. The time had come.

Feeling a bit like a guilty schoolboy and half expecting the salesgirl to scold him, he purchased the nightgown in Emma's size and had it gift wrapped in white-on-white lace paper with a lavender ribbon.

Emma had suggested they open gifts tonight, since they'd be going to his mother's in the morning. Eric decided to hide the package until the children were asleep. After all, once one special treat was unwrapped, he hoped it would be time to unwrap another.

AFTER THEIR DINNER of ham and scalloped potatoes, Emma let Eric clean up while she got out her cookie cutters and began mixing dough. Otto climbed up on a stepstool and did his best to help, which mostly consisted of poking his fingers into the batter and then licking them.

"Can Kiri eat cookies?" he asked.

"She's still too little." Emma smiled. Otto had become attached to the baby, even asking that she be laid on a blanket next to him on the floor while he watched *Sesame Street*. The brother and sister would lie there side by side, cheerfully observing the antics of Big Bird.

"Next Christmas," Otto said, and helped himself to another chocolate chip.

While the cookies were baking, Emma got out Otto's presents. He'd been snooping around looking for them all week, but she'd tucked them into a corner of the garage, which was off-limits.

From her stepmother came a turquoise jogging suit decorated with a rocket ship. Otto, who had yet to develop any sense of modesty, shed his jeans and sweatshirt in the middle of the living room and put on his new clothes.

Next he tore into Emma's gift, a giant bucket of Lego pieces that he'd been coveting. Gleefully, Otto began scattering them on the floor.

"Now hold on," Eric said. "We aren't done."

Otto gazed around expectantly. "Where is it?"

Eric disappeared into the bedroom, returning with a box covered with multicolored animals and a big silver bow. "From me."

Otto held the present for a minute, just staring at the pretty decorations. "Where did you get it?" he said.

"Brea Mall."

"Why?" Although Otto didn't ask as many questions as he once had, he still seemed possessed of an insatiable curiosity—and at the oddest times, Emma reflected.

"Because I love you." Eric knelt and drew the boy into a hug.

"I love you, too," Otto said. Then he added, "Do you love Kiri?"

"Of course." Eric reached over to stroke the baby's cheek. She cooed softly in her infant seat.

Some of the tension of the past few months flowed out of Emma. Tonight she felt as if the four of them were truly becoming a family, as if Eric was finally letting himself be drawn into their circle.

The ripping of paper drew her attention back as Otto pulled out an assortment of drawing supplies. "Wow!" he said. "Mommy, can I draw?"

She was about to agree when the oven timer sounded "Wouldn't you rather have a cookie first?" she asked.

"Yeah!" Otto darted ahead of her into the kitchen, and danced from foot to foot as she retrieved the cookie sheet with its tantalizing burden.

The three of them attacked the cookies, savoring the still gooey centers. Emma poured glasses of milk, and then settled down to nurse the baby.

She was just finishing when the doorbell rang. "Trick or treat?" asked Otto, who still hadn't recovered from the Halloween wonder of going door-to-door and being handed all the candy he could eat.

"I'll get it." Eric hurried out. She heard him open the door, followed by laughter and cries of "Merry Christmas."

When she went to investigate, she found Betsy, Matt and Roy, all bundled up in their coats and carrying songbooks. When they spotted her, Betsy nudged Matt and they burst into a harmonious rendition of "God Rest Ye Merry Gentlemen."

"Want to go caroling?" Roy demanded of Otto.

"Sure!" he said. "What's caroling?"

He found out a few minutes later. Eric carried Kiri nestled into a backpack, while Emma bundled Otto into a heavy jacket.

Out they went, into the clear starry night. The old neighborhood, with its towering palms and overgrown camellia bushes, had been built in the 1920s. The houses featured old-fashioned porches and tonight, with Christmas lights winking, Emma walked with a sense of timelessness through the crisp air.

They went from door to door, singing "Come All Ye Faithful" and "Silent Night" and all their other favorites. At each house, people would come to the door—sometimes an elderly couple, or a family with a happy cluster of chil-

dren, or parents with teenagers. Everywhere, faces softened and eyes glowed, and the little group of carolers were
offered more hot chocolate and cookies than they could
consume.

"This is fun!" Otto declared as they headed home. "I like
this better than Halloween!"

"Let's do this all the time," Roy said.

Betsy laughed. "Next year."

"Next year!" the boys agreed, clearly having no idea how
much time would have to pass before then.

Emma checked Eric's reaction, but he was occupied with
shifting the backpack, making sure Kiri was comfortable.
He'd clearly been enjoying the evening. She just hoped that
for once he wouldn't bury himself in his books as soon as
they got home.

After good-nights were said and Otto and Kiri were snug
in their beds, Emma finished putting away the cookies and
picking up the wrapping paper. Then she went into the bedroom and retrieved the package she'd hidden there.

"Merry Christmas," she told Eric and watched as he
pulled out the emerald-green cashmere sweater.

"This is beautiful." He slipped it over his shirt. "Perfect
fit." Then he handed her a delicately wrapped package, so
lovely that Emma hated to tear the paper. "Well, go on."

She took it, suddenly shy, and lifted away the paper carefully at the ends. From the box inside, she drew a luxurious
lavender peignoir.

"Your turn." His mouth quirked as he indicated she
should put it on.

Emma disappeared into the bedroom. When she came
out, Eric had dimmed the lights and closed the curtains. On
the coffee table sat two glasses of white wine.

"It's been a long time," Emma murmured.

When he didn't answer, she realized he was staring at her.
She could feel his gaze tracing the deep V of the neckline,

the revealing plunge of lace, the silky fabric clinging to he
hips.

Excitement burned inside her. This was her man, he
friend and lover. After so long an abstinence, tonight fel
like the first time all over again.

He drew her down onto the couch. They toasted eac
other with quick sips of wine, and then his mouth, stil
tasting of the drink, came down gently on hers. His hand
found her shoulders, the swell of her breasts, the sensitive
nipples.

Emma gasped with the all-but-forgotten pleasure. He
body flowed against his, helping to undress him, to pull hin
close. How naturally they fit together, how explosively they
explored each other, how eagerly they moved, urging eacl
other on.

The glory of the Christmas tree dimmed before the radiance of their union. Emma felt as if she could fly, as if the
world were moving with them, shifting into new and enticing patterns.

They rocketed into fulfillment together and then lay in a
tangle on the couch, not needing to speak, simply treasur-
ing the joy of being together.

Later, falling asleep in bed, Emma noted hazily that Eric
was getting up again. Going back to his studies.

He didn't really need to work that hard, she thought, but
pride filled her. He was doing it not only for himself but
because he wanted the best for his family, and she understood.

Because she wanted the best for him, too.

THE DAY AFTER CHRISTMAS was traditionally the second
busiest of the year, beaten only by the day after Thanksgiving. Shoppers jammed the stores seeking marked-down
bargains, wrapping paper and cards for the next year, re-
duced-price toys and clothes. And then of course came the

exchanges, the loving gifts that didn't quite fit or turned out to be the wrong color.

Busy as she was running the exchange desk at the store where she worked, happy memories of the previous day played through Stella's mind like a movie. Who would have believed that she'd have grandchildren this year?

Kiri was priceless beyond words, a perfect little doll, although by next Christmas she'd probably be toddling her way around the house wreaking merry havoc in her wake. And Otto, for all his fierce independence, had a tender streak that reminded Stella of her own boys at that age.

She loved every minute of Christmas—the shopping, the cooking, the decorating. These last years, with the boys grown and Harlan gone, she'd spent most of her energy creating Christmas treats for foster children.

This year, she'd done that, as well, but she'd had the special privilege of hosting her own little family again. There was nothing like children in the house to chase away the shadows.

"I'm afraid I just wouldn't wear these," a matronly woman confessed, turning in a set of black lace bra and panties.

"Would you like an exchange or a refund?" Stella asked, and soon moved on to the next person in line.

It was almost time for lunch when she looked up to see a handsome man of about her age, sharply dressed in a gray suit. He was holding out a pair of gaudy fake-ruby cuff links.

"My niece means well, but these aren't quite my style," he said, and then paused, staring. "Stella! Is that you?"

"Gary!" Gary Bertram and his wife, Jenny, had been close friends of Stella and Harlan's for a time, but after Harlan's death they'd drifted about. "How are you? How's Jenny?"

"We've been divorced about three years," Gary admitted. "She decided with the kids grown she wanted to do all the things she'd never done, and unfortunately that included living alone. How about catching a bite to eat?"

"Great timing. I was just about to go!"

A minute later, Stella's lunch replacement slipped into place behind the cash register. She joined Gary in a stroll to the food area.

He was a bit shorter than Harlan but with a strong masculine build that indicated he kept in shape even now in his fifth decade. The best thing was the way Gary kept turning toward Stella, brushing her elbow, pointing things out to her, making her feel special.

As they walked, she sketched in her life during these past years, how her boys had grown and of course the arrival of grandchildren.

Gary shook his head wistfully as they sat down with their sandwich plates. "That's been my one regret—that we never had kids."

"You'd have been a good father."

"I don't know. I worked all the time," he admitted. "But I've always thought I'd make a wonderful grandfather."

They reminisced—about a trip the four of them had taken to Mexico, about the members of a bridge club that they'd once joined, about a surprise birthday party they'd given for a mutual friend.

Stella was surprised how easily the words flowed between them. Before, she and Jenny had paired off while the two men talked business or politics.

Now she noticed how attentive Gary was, how easily he smiled, how his hair had silvered rather than grayed. His features, once a bit softer than Harlan's had sharpened with age, giving him a more sophisticated air.

"I love to travel," he said. "Fortunately, my investments have done well. But it's not much fun traveling alone. Do you go places much?"

"I'm afraid I spend most of my time working," Stella said.

"Maybe we could do something about that." Before she could decide what to say, Gary added, "Would you have dinner with me tonight? Think you could take two meals in a row in my company?"

"I'd love to," she said.

Later, back at the store, Stella realized this would be the first real date she'd had since Harlan died. Oh, she'd joined a square dance club for a while and made friends there, but nothing romantic had developed.

Not that she expected anything romantic to develop now. Not at her age; not to a grandmother.

So why did she keep wondering which dress to wear tonight, and whether Gary would like her favorite perfume, and if they might go dancing after dinner?

It must be that girlish quirk inside her heart that simply wouldn't let go. As if the years hadn't happened, and she were young again.

Now why on earth should she be feeling that way?

Chapter Seventeen

The night before New Year's Eve, Eric glanced up from his station in the dining room to where Emma and Otto sat at the kitchen table playing Disney Lotto. In her infant seat, the baby alternated between a puzzled pucker and sudden trills of laughter as she watched.

Already she resembled her mother. Beautiful.

Eric rested on his elbows, studying Emma as she helped Otto match Donald Duck pieces. Even when he got frustrated, she stayed calm, reassuring him that he could make the matches himself.

When Kiri fussed, Emma sang to her. The baby quieted immediately.

This past week, Emma had started back at the salon. She worked so hard, and yet she never complained. He knew that he, too, worked hard, but he couldn't help feeling she was easing his way just as she smoothed things over for the children.

On Christmas, when they'd made love, he'd felt once again the warmth and openness that he cherished so much. But he couldn't help suspecting that Emma held things back sometimes, meaning to protect him from her worries or the simple irritations that children could bring.

In a way he missed their old relationship—the fearlessness, the ability to talk about their deepest hopes and desires. But that had been before either of them had much to lose. Now that they needed each other so much, maybe they were afraid to take the risk of leveling. Or maybe he simply didn't want to acknowledge how much Emma was giving up for his sake.

But things wouldn't stay that way, Eric told himself. Vern Avery's glowing appreciation of his painting had helped restore his confidence, and so had the more practical assignments this quarter. In a few years, Eric would be able to support Emma while she found another Hollywood connection.

Telling himself that he would make all the sacrifices up to her, Eric bent over his studies of desert heat and flash floods.

By the time he lifted his head again, he noticed with a start that it was nearly eleven o'clock. The children had gone to bed, and Emma lay curled on the couch in front of the TV.

Then he realized that he was listening to an energy-charged duet by Alyssa and Genevieve of "A Boy Like That" from *West Side Story*.

The special! And it must be nearly over. Guiltily, he remembered Emma mentioning that it was finally going to air on December 30. He'd intended to pour some champagne and watch with her.

Quietly, Eric stood up and moved toward Emma, whose attention was riveted on the screen.

Her eyes followed every movement, her mouth pursing and then curving into a smile. Unconsciously, she touched her hair as if fluffing up Alyssa's, or maybe Genevieve's.

Through the speaker, the voices surged into an emotional counterpoint that raised shivers down Eric's spine. Why had there been any controversy about this TV special? It was terrific.

Then he looked at Emma again, and saw that she was crying.

Tears ran unchecked down her cheeks. She chewed on he lower lip as she gazed longingly at the screen. Eric could fee how much she missed her friends and her work.

Damn those two women and their egos! Damn that pro ducer, and the gossip columnist.

The song ended. Emma lifted the remote control an clicked the set off. "I'm sorry." She turned toward hir apologetically. "I don't know what got into me."

"I do." Eric brushed a tear from her cheek. "And I'm th one who's sorry."

"This has nothing to do with you. I'm the one who los my temper." Emma leaned back, closing her eyes.

"Don't shut me out," Eric said.

"I'm not." Emma sighed and cuddled closer. "I've got s many things to be thankful for. A lot more, really, tha Alyssa or Genevieve."

"We both do." He cradled her in his arms. "But I wan you to have everything. Everything you could possibly want."

She smiled, and he saw the tears were gone. "It's good fo us to have a few things left to hope for, to work toward. I life were perfect, we'd get awfully bored."

"I'd like to try it anyway," Eric said, and they bot chuckled.

EMMA LAY AWAKE long after Eric's breathing had mel lowed into a steady flow.

Somewhere tonight, Alyssa or Genevieve had thrown party. They would have invited their friends and their en tourages, catered the whole event and displayed the broad cast on the biggest screens technology could offer.

She should have been there, sitting with Corinne and Amalie, cheering and celebrating. She should have been par of the excitement, the planning for new achievements. In stead, she was left wondering who had fixed their hair fo the occasion and whether the stylists had botched Genevieve's color touch-up or given Alyssa too much curl.

Gradually, Emma's thoughts clouded over and she dozed. In her dream, she sat in the audience listening to Alyssa sing. Every time Emma tried to call to her, Alyssa's voice would crescendo and drown her out. It got louder and louder. Too loud, too shrill....

The next thing she knew, Emma was sitting bolt upright with her heart pounding, hearing the scream of Kiri's monitor.

Before rational thought could intervene, Emma leaped out of bed and raced through the house. It had been weeks since the beeper had gone off. The pediatrician had even suggested taking Kiri off entirely in another week. Oh, God, what if...

She pounded through the doorway and halted in confusion. In the dark, she made out a tangle of shapes in Kiri's crib, and saw with alarm that the side rail had been dropped.

"What...?" Emma flicked on the light.

Otto sat up, blinking. "Turn it off, Mommy!"

Only then did she realize that the harsh, unvarying bleep meant an equipment failure, not a breathing problem. With a sigh, Emma switched off the monitor. "What are you doing here?"

Even as she questioned Otto, she reached into the crib and scooped up a wide-awake Kiri, who issued a happy coo and stuck her finger into her mother's mouth. For the second time that night, tears brimmed in Emma's eyes—this time from relief.

"You said you were tired," Otto replied.

"I did?" Then Emma recalled snapping at him earlier in the day, and apologizing that she was on edge because Kiri had woken her up the previous night. "But—"

"I'm taking care of her tonight," Otto announced. "Only I can't hear her from my room."

"So you decided to move in with her?" Emma fought a smile, knowing Otto wanted to be taken seriously. "You were going to sleep with her?"

His head bobbed vigorously. "Only I got caught in all the wires. Can you plug her back in, Mommy?"

"You were trying to help me." Emma leaned against the crib and gathered both her children close. "You sweetheart. Otto, you don't have to do that."

Her son yawned. "Well, you can take over now." Having done his duty—by his own lights, at least—Otto swung down to the ground and ambled toward his bedroom.

Standing in the doorway, Eric rumpled the boy's hair as Otto passed. "Everything all right?"

"Under control," Emma said.

She felt as if she should add something, but the moment passed. Eric went back to bed, and after a few minutes Emma reattached Kiri's monitor and nursed the baby to sleep.

Pausing in Otto's room, she noted the soft snore issuing from beneath his favorite Snoopy blanket. What a good-hearted little boy she was raising, she thought.

Bemused, she made her way back to the bedroom.

Eric lay quietly beneath the covers, but she didn't think he'd fallen asleep yet. Slipping into place, Emma considered cuddling up to him but decided against it. They were both tired.

As she closed her eyes, she felt him shift restlessly. She wished she could reach out and smooth the tension away. Eric worried far too much about his studies. Couldn't he see that he was doing fine, that he didn't have to get the very best grade in the class on every project?

But she understood. Stella and Eric both had told her enough about Harlan Jameson for her to understand that even perfection was only temporarily good enough for him. Behind his father's praise, Eric had once told her, had always lain the implication, *Well, thank goodness you didn't screw up this time.*

Emma could feel the demons driving Eric, the same ones that had kept his father working long hours when he should have been with his family. The demons that had driven Harlan Jameson until he died.

There had to be a way to pull Eric from their grasp. One day very soon, she was going to find it.

ERIC AWOKE with the sense that he'd overslept, but when he checked the clock, it was only seven.

Then he realized what was wrong. Kiri usually woke them by six, sometimes as early as five.

Beside him, only Emma's hair was visible as she burrowed into her pillow. He decided to let her sleep.

Eric pulled on his robe and hurried down the hall to Kiri's room. Surprised to hear the music box playing on her crib mobile, he opened the door.

There stood Otto on a footstool, waggling a teddy bear as Kiri chuckled and waved her hands and feet. "She likes Homer Bear," Otto said. "Can I give him to her?"

"Sure. I mean, if it's all right with your mommy." It must have been all right in Otto's mind, because he promptly nestled the bear next to its new owner. "Have you had breakfast?"

"No." Otto plopped off the stool. "Can I have cookies?"

"Not very nutritious." Eric knew he ought to do something with the baby, but he wasn't sure where to start. How did Emma manage to be so organized in the morning?

"You need to change her diaper," Otto pointed out.

"Oh. Right." Feeling foolish that a four-year-old knew more than he did, Eric unhooked Kiri's monitor and laid her on the changing table. He supposed he ought to put on fresh clothes, too, but pulling thin tubes of fabric onto those squirmy limbs had to be a major project. He decided to leave it for an expert.

It took three tries, but he finally got the diaper taped securely. The next challenge turned out to be fastening Kiri into her infant seat. Her feet kept getting entangled with the safety belt, and finally he fitted her into it, grateful for the flexibility of infants.

Now what did Otto eat for breakfast? "Oatmeal?" Eric asked tentatively, hoping the answer would be no, which it was. "Toast? Cereal?"

"How about strawberries?" Otto opened the refrigerator and peered inside.

"In December? Sorry." Eric looked over his shoulder. "Yogurt?"

Otto lifted down a plastic container of leftover macaroni and cheese. "I'll take this."

He didn't see how it could hurt. "I'll zap that in the microwave." Eric reached to take it from Otto, but the boy hung on.

"I want it cold!" Otto said.

"Cold?"

"Can I have a fork?"

"Sure." Eric pushed in Otto's chair for him. "You want something to drink?"

When he finally had the boy settled and was about to fix himself some toast, Kiri began fussing. "What's wrong with her?" By this time, Eric openly acknowledged Otto's superior insight.

"She's hungry," the boy said between mouthfuls of macaroni.

"Well, what does she eat?" Eric hoped it wasn't oatmeal. He had no idea how to cook it.

"Milk," Otto said. "Mom keeps some in the freezer for the sitter."

With the boy's help, Eric managed to warm up a bottle of breast milk in a pan of hot water—you weren't supposed to microwave it, Otto informed him—and fed it to Kiri.

Emma still hadn't awakened by the time he finished his own breakfast. Fortunately, the baby was yawning, so he put her down for a nap and helped Otto dress.

"I could watch cartoons," Otto said.

Eric supposed that would be all right. He wanted to shower and then hit the books before Kiri woke up. He intended to let Emma sleep; she wasn't working today, and he knew she needed the rest.

In the living room, Otto stopped in front of the Christmas tree. Eric noticed that the needles looked brittle beneath the tinsel and glittering balls; he'd have to bundle it for the trash collector in a day or so.

"Did you see the bird?" Otto pointed to a tiny, hand-wrought cardinal, a splash of red among the dark green branches.

"Beautiful," Eric responded automatically.

"There's blue ones, too." Otto indicated a jay perched cockily beside a glass ornament. "I helped put them in."

"It's a splendid Christmas tree," Eric said, beginning to share the boy's enthusiasm.

"Yes, it is." Otto nodded sagely. "And we will keep it forever."

Eric wanted to agree with him. It *was* a beautiful tree and it ought never, never to be stripped of its glory and trussed up like some dead thing to be carted off in a refuse truck. He wanted to stand here and drink it in, as Otto was doing, to wallow in the now.

A dizziness seized him, as if all his blood cells had collided with each other in midartery and begun swirling around randomly. Into his mind popped the incongruous image of a shopping mall map with a red arrow marked You

Are Here, only the arrow hung over his head pointing downward.

Here and now. This moment, this place. Really, what else was there? What was life but one "here and now" strung onto another?

As long as he could remember, Eric had lived in the future and for the future. He remembered very little of the past eight years because so little of it had actually existed for him.

The only joy he had experienced had come on those rare occasions when he forgot about tomorrow and became an active part of the life going on around him. That had mostly occurred, he realized, through Emma's influence.

Living in the future had done even more than rob him of pleasure and peace of mind. It had cheated him of the creativity with which he should have approached last quarter's assignments. If he hadn't been so focused on his goals, he would have let himself go. He could have had fun with his schoolwork. And, ironically, he probably would have earned a better grade.

Eric's mouth twisted wryly. Already his thoughts had returned to his obsession with getting ahead. Why was he worrying about his studies when right in front of him stood an absolutely glorious Christmas tree, and a little boy to make him appreciate it?

We will keep it forever. Not in adult terms, perhaps, but if Eric didn't think about the future, if he pushed aside unimportant adult concerns, if he stood here long enough— well, maybe those birds would flock into the air, and the tiny elf embedded in one of the ornaments would begin hammering at his workbench and the air would twinkle with magic. Maybe time would stand still.

Yes, they would keep the tree forever. And when forever ended, well, that would be time enough to tell it goodbye.

How long he stood there, Eric had no idea. Then Otto aid, "I'm missing my cartoons," and at the same time, omeone punched the doorbell imperiously, three times.

"Who the heck...?" Eric said. Tearing himself reluc- antly away from the tree, he opened the door.

"I want to see Emma. And I want to see her now," said Jenevieve, and stepped over the sill.

Chapter Eighteen

Emma would never have believed she could get dressed so quickly. There was barely time to run a brush through her hair and dab on a bit of lipstick. She knew how Genevieve hated to wait.

The doorbell had awakened her, and then the sound of her former client's voice had brought her fully to her senses. What on earth was the imperious actress doing here?

"Genevieve." Smoothing down her skirt, Emma hurried out. "What can I do for you?"

The actress, dramatically wrapped in a cloak and hood, drew herself up as if to make a pronouncement.

"Really, the question is what *should* you have done for me." Genevieve held a copy of the morning's *Los Angeles Times*, open to a page inside the View section.

It was an article on last night's party to celebrate the broadcasting of the special. In a circle of other stars stood Genevieve and Alyssa.

Even in the black-and-white photo, Emma could see there was something wrong with Genevieve's hair. It frizzed around her face as if she'd been given a bad perm.

"Oh, dear," Emma said, and eyed the hood. "Is it really that bad?"

"Worse." Genevieve dropped the cloth to reveal the hideous truth. Some stylist had not only frizzed the life out of

t, he or she had cut it badly. The classic upsweep was ru-
ned; wisps stuck out every which way. "He said he wanted
o be creative, and to give me a new look. And I'm such a
.ucker, I fell for it."

"I'm so sorry." Emma bit her lip sympathetically. Even
hough Genevieve's own rudeness had cost her Emma's
.ervices, she certainly hadn't deserved to look this awful on
.er big night.

"Alyssa should be here any minute. When I told her I was
:oming, well, she decided to join me. I think the plan is to
.ssue a joint apology. But I did get here first."

"Would you like some coffee?" Eric offered.

"Hot chocolate?" Otto piped up. "We have orange soda,
.oo."

"Just tea, thank you." Genevieve glanced around. "Now
vhere is that splendid little baby?"

"Just waking up," Emma said, hearing familiar squeak-
ng noises from the direction of the nursery. Genevieve fol-
owed and watched intently as Emma changed the baby into
. clean sleeper. "Want to hold her?"

"I'd kill for the chance."

Emma handed over the baby. "This is Kiri."

"My goodness." Genevieve sank into the rocking chair,
:radling the infant. "She's so alert!"

"They're born with a personality, aren't they?" Emma
:elaxed in the doorway, letting her daughter work her own
:harm on the crusty actress.

"Alyssa certainly was." Genevieve ran a finger lightly
>ver the baby's cheek. "She would never hold still. Always
.nto everything. Well, not this early, I suppose. But soon."

"You love her, don't you?" Emma said.

"Alyssa? Well, of course. But that doesn't mean I have
to like her." Genevieve never took her eyes off Kiri. "Do
you suppose I'll ever have a grandchild?"

"If you do, are you going to fight over how to raise it?" Emma teased.

Genevieve lifted her head as if to argue, then made a wr face. "Probably. We fight over everything else, don't we But we do love each other. I guess we both have a hard tim showing it."

Eric appeared from the kitchen and set a cup of tea nex to Genevieve. "We're glad to see you. Emma and I loved th special."

"It did turn out well, didn't it?" Genevieve took a sip o tea, then returned her attention to the baby. "I'm sorry was rude to you, Emma. I hate to admit it, but we deserve your tongue-lashing. We let Barry push us into creating media circus. And then we took our bad tempers out o you."

"And I'm sorry I snapped at you, especially in front o other people," Emma said. "I was tired and my ankles hur and I couldn't take any more."

"I don't blame you." Genevieve shook her head. "We were awful. Both of us. Me especially. I'm more mature and I really have no excuse. But I've paid for it. You don't know what I've been through these past months. My hair ha looked like a rat's nest and now—well, it's ruined."

"Oh, I could do a few things," Emma said. "Condition it, give it a bit of shape. But it'll take a while to grow out."

"I'd like that," the actress said. "Yes, I really would."

The doorbell rang.

"Alyssa," said Genevieve.

Emma answered it herself. There on her doorstep stood America's number one pop singer. She hadn't bothered to wear a hat and Emma could see plainly what hadn't shown up in the picture, that although the cut was tolerable, Alyssa's tresses had taken on a decidedly orange cast.

"My mother hasn't signed you up for an exclusive contract or anything, has she?" Alyssa asked.

"Happy New Year," Emma said.

The singer blushed. "I'm sorry. It was such a long drive, and I'm so mad at myself, and I just feel really stupid. Can I come in?"

"Oh, please." Emma stood aside.

Otto glanced over from his cartoons. "Hi," he said. "Are you Raggedy Ann?"

"Oh!" Alyssa clapped her hands over her head.

"Otto isn't strong on tact." Emma led her through the kitchen to the nursery.

"Don't worry. The commentator on *Hollywood Nightly* already beat him to it. Said I looked as if a bird had made a nest in my hair and then bled all over it." Alyssa paused at the sight of her mother sitting in the rocking chair, crooning to Kiri. "Is this her? This precious little thing?"

Soon mother and daughter were perched side by side, both crammed into the same rocking chair, sharing the baby between them. Genevieve's interest wasn't surprising, but Alyssa's fascination caught Emma off guard.

"I'd *love* to have a baby," Alyssa sighed, happily wiping away a few drops of milk that dribbled out of Kiri's mouth.

"You would?" Genevieve said.

"And you know, Sam says—"

"Who's Sam?"

"I'm going out with him tonight. Mother! You know— the real estate broker."

"The normal one? The one who actually stands up when I walk into the room? I thought he was your lawyer."

"Mother!"

Emma and Eric exchanged smiles.

"You were about to tell us what Sam says," Genevieve prodded. "Something about babies."

"He says I'd make a terrific mother," Alyssa explained. "He really likes kids. He's involved in Big Brothers, and you can see it on his face, when we see a baby carriage on one of our walks—''

"You go for walks?" Genevieve said. "With Sam? I'm impressed."

"I'm not weird *all* the time!" Reluctantly, Alyssa surrendered the baby and stood up. "Anyway, I was wondering if Emma would forgive me and do something with this hideous mop. I mean, it is New Year's Eve—''

"You're not the only one with plans," Genevieve chided. "Some of my friends are giving a party—''

"Come on, both of you." Emma reclaimed Kiri and handed her to Eric. "If you don't mind making an appearance in an ordinary beauty salon, I'll get you both fixed up right now."

"Would you?" Alyssa cried. "Oh, Emma. I'll never say a harsh word to you again! I promise!"

"I'll let you go first." Genevieve eased her way out of the rocking chair. "On condition that you make me a grandmother before I get too old to enjoy it."

"Tonight?" Alyssa teased.

"I rather intended for you to get married first."

"Oh, *that,*" her daughter said. "How old-fashioned. But we might."

Emma turned hesitantly to Eric. "Would you mind—''

"I'll take the kids to the park." He shifted Kiri comfortably in his arms. "A nice walk, lunch at wherever Otto picks—it'll be fun."

"You're sure?" she said.

"I'm sure."

"You're a good man," Genevieve said. "Happy New Year, Eric."

"You're both going to look stunning tonight," he answered, and went to lure Otto away from the cartoons.

ERIC COULDN'T understand why Emma was apologizing. "What for?"

"For dumping the kids on you like that." She gazed at him over a row of half-empty Chinese food cartons spread across the kitchen table. Otto had already downed his egg rolls and retreated to play in his room, and Kiri was sleeping. "I needed the time, and I just took it."

"Well, of course you needed it. Genevieve and Alyssa showing up like that was a blessing. Do you think I'd begrudge you the chance to get back on track?" Eric demanded.

"But I really didn't leave you much choice—"

"Like I've been doing?" he pointed out. "I don't recall ever asking your permission to study all evening."

"That's different." Emma discarded a hot pepper and nibbled at the kung pao chicken.

"Why? Because I'm a man?"

"Well—"

"Or because we're not married?" He rested his elbows on the kitchen table.

"No—"

"Why is it any different, Emma?"

"Because you weren't expecting it," she said.

The Tiffany lamp patched her face with colored light, giving the bones a fragile look. The house sat quietly tonight, although from down the street came the premature snap of firecrackers.

"Another year gone by," Eric said.

"It's been a special year." She set her fork down.

"Will you marry me?" To his surprise, he found it difficult to breathe as he awaited her answer.

"Why?"

"Why?" he repeated in surprise. "So—so you can dump the kids on me more often."

"Eric, your studies—" Her fingers brushed his hand. "
don't want to hold you back."

"I read a saying once that didn't mean much to me, n
back then," Eric said. "It was, 'Life is what happens whi
you're making other plans.' Life is something I stumble
into this past year, Emma. My self-worth has always d
pended on accomplishments other people could admire.
didn't understand what it meant to win a child's trust, or
be able to change a diaper competently. I even remembere
the right way to warm Kiri's bottle without Otto remindi
me."

Emma's fingers closed around his. "It's wonderful. B
that's no substitute for your dream."

"I don't want substitutes." His thoughts took shape as I
voiced them. "But I've discovered that somewhere along tl
line, I added another dream to my repertoire. I want to sha
my life with the woman I love, and I want to watch my chi
dren grow up. It isn't a secondary dream, Emma—it in
fuses everything else with meaning."

"And your studies?" Her lower lip quivered. How lor
had she ached to hear these words?

"I'm going to take them as they come." Eric searched fe
the right words. "I can't grab hold of the future. I can
twist it around and make it happen the way I want. I'm go
ing to try to live in the here and now, Emma. That doesn
mean I've given anything up, only that . . . I'm not in such
hurry to get there."

"I know." Emma ducked her head so wisps of hair traile
along his arm. The tantalizing softness stirred a masculir
quickening. "I was so glad to see Genevieve and Alyssa to
day and yet—the funny part is, I felt a little sad. I'm goir
to be busy busy busy from now on. It's been so nice, hav
ing time to spend at home—I'll miss that."

"We'll work it out. I love you, Emma."

"I love you, too," she whispered, letting him draw her onto his lap. "Eric, I've been afraid to care too much. I didn't want to hold you back. All this time, I've tried to arrange my life so I wouldn't need you. But I can't help it."

"I don't want you to help it." He pulled her tightly against him. "Need me as much as you like. I plan to stay here for a long, long time. Does forever sound like long enough?"

"Almost," she said.

Their kiss had only begun when Otto pattered into the kitchen, and they pulled apart. "Juice," he announced, smacking a bottle onto the table.

"You're too old for a bottle." Emma, still resting in Eric's lap, picked it up and clicked her tongue. "This is Kiri's!"

"She's not using it," Otto offered.

"Give it to me, please." She stood up and reached out, but the boy backed away.

Before the disagreement escalated, Eric said, "Otto, I have an idea." He knelt and rummaged through a cabinet. "I know I saw it—ah." He pulled out a canteen with a straw stuck through its lid. A birthday gift, it was inscribed with the name Otto in bright red letters. "How about this? It's even got your name on it."

"Oh, I like that," Otto said. "I always drink my juice in that."

"Always, starting from now?" Eric filled it, carefully diluting the juice half and half with water as Emma did. "When that's finished, it's bedtime, buster."

"Okay, Daddy." Otto retreated, sipping as he walked.

"He never called me Daddy before." Eric repressed the urge to run after the boy and shower him with hugs. He had a feeling Otto wouldn't appreciate his sentimentality.

"You've earned it," Emma said. "And the answer to your question is yes, Eric. Of course I'll marry you."

As they kissed—slowly, lingeringly and without inter
ruption—he could hardly remember the first time he'd sa
with her in this kitchen, nearly a year ago. It had been onl
a room, then, a stage setting. Now he knew the contents o
most of the drawers, could identify the scent of the ai
freshener, even remembered which glass was Otto's favor
ite.

In a funny way, his relationship with Emma was like that
too. He'd come to know her this past year, at her best an
worst, pregnant and worried, elated and glowing. He knew
her strengths and weaknesses, and he wanted to be the on
she turned to in sadness and in joy. Forever.

AFTER OTTO FELL ASLEEP, they took their glasses o
champagne and the half-full bottle to bed, toasting eacl
other by the flickering light of a candle on the headboard
Outside, the "pop-pop" of firecrackers intensified.

"Didn't the ancient Chinese believe they frightened de
mons away?" Emma mused, feeling the languid tingle of the
champagne percolate through her veins.

"Maybe I should have tried them on my own persona
demons." Eric slipped an arm beneath the pillows and
around her shoulders, drawing her closer. "But you managed to rout them all by yourself."

She spilled a few drops of champagne on her nightgown,
but Emma didn't mind. Tonight the bubbles in her drink
soared to her brain and the length of her body prickled with
Eric's nearness. She didn't want any more champagne or
any more words.

"Let's celebrate," she whispered, setting her glass aside
and leaning over for an exploratory kiss.

When their lips parted again, his mouth trailed down to
Emma's breasts and stomach. Her body responded to his
caresses with the same intensity as the first time they made

love, but there was something deeper now than all those
months ago.

Then, a new Emma had broken through to the surface,
wild and passionate, experiencing lovemaking as if for the
first time. Fire had danced and feinted, sending up sparks,
flaring and crackling as it kindled green wood.

Now, as she buried her face in Eric's neck and let her instinctive movements arouse them both, they ignited a blaze
that roared steadfastly, richly woven with textures of scar-
let and gold. The bonfire built with seasoned wood snapped
and smoked less dramatically, but would warm them the rest
of their days.

As they lay quietly afterward, like embers still hot to the
touch, Emma heard a chorus of shouts from the house next
door. "Happy New Year!" over and over again, voices
overlapping and mingled with laughter.

"Happy New Year," Eric murmured, and kissed her
neck.

From a distance came a blurred TV rendition of "Auld
Lang Syne." Snatches of memory flooded Emma's mind: a
New Year's Eve when she was a child, watching her mother
string balloons around the living room for a party; the restaurant where she and Bill had gone dancing every year; her
first New Year's alone with Otto, returning from Betsy's
home to her own quiet, dark house.

Eric touched her cheek. "Tears? Why, Emma?"

"Remembering," she said.

"Look forward." Then he smiled. "But not too far forward."

"Not past breakfast," she promised, and snuggled close
as he poured a second round of champagne.

PENNY JORDAN

Sins and infidelities...
Dreams and obsessions...
Shattering secrets
unfold in...

THE HIDDEN YEARS

SAGE — stunning, sensual and
vibrant, she spent a lifetime
distancing herself from a past too
painful to confront... the mother
who seemed to hold her at bay,
the father who resented her and
the heartache of unfulfilled love.
To the world, Sage was
independent and invulnerable—
but it was a mask she cultivated to
hide a desperation she herself
couldn't quite understand...
until an unforeseen turn of events
drew her into the discovery of the
hidden years, finally allowing
Sage to open her heart to a
passion denied for so long.

The Hidden Years—a compelling novel of truth and passion
that will unlock the heart and soul of every woman.

AVAILABLE IN OCTOBER!
Watch for your opportunity to complete your Penny Jordan set.
POWER PLAY and SILVER will also be available in October.

This October, Harlequin offers you a second
two-in-one collection of romances

A SPECIAL
SOMETHING

THE FOREVER
INSTINCT

by the award-winning author,

Barbara Delinsky

Now, two of Barbara Delinsky's most loved books are
available together in this special edition that new and
longtime fans will want to add to their bookshelves.

Let Barbara Delinsky double your reading pleasure with
her memorable love stories, A SPECIAL SOMETHING and
THE FOREVER INSTINCT.

Available wherever Harlequin books are sold. TWO-D

MILLION DOLLAR JACKPOT
SWEEPSTAKES RULES & REGULATIONS
NO PURCHASE NECESSARY TO ENTER OR RECEIVE A PRIZE

1. Alternate means of entry: Print your name and address on a 3" ×5" piece of plain paper and send to the appropriate address below.

In the U.S.	In Canada
MILLION DOLLAR JACKPOT	MILLION DOLLAR JACKPOT
P.O. Box 1867	P.O. Box 609
3010 Walden Avenue	Fort Erie, Ontario
Buffalo, NY 14269-1867	L2A 5X3

2. To enter the Sweepstakes and join the Reader Service, check off the "YES" box on your Sweepstakes Entry Form and return. If you do not wish to join the Reader Service but wish to enter the Sweepstakes only, check off the "NO" box on your Sweepstakes Entry Form. To qualify for the Extra Bonus prize, scratch off the silver on your Lucky Keys. If the registration numbers match, you are eligible for the Extra Bonus Prize offering. Incomplete entries are ineligible. Torstar Corp. and its affiliates are not responsible for mutilated or unreadable entries or inadvertent printing errors. Mechanically reproduced entries are null and void.

3. Whether you take advantage of this offer or not, on or about April 30, 1992, at the offices of D.L. Blair, Inc., Blair, NE, your sweepstakes numbers will be compared against the list of winning numbers generated at random by the computer. However, prizes will only be awarded to individuals who have entered the Sweepstakes. In the event that all prizes are not claimed, a random drawing will be held from all qualified entries received from March 30, 1990 to March 31, 1992, to award all unclaimed prizes. All cash prizes (Grand to Sixth) will be mailed to winners and are payable by check in U.S. funds. Seventh Prize will be shipped to winners via third-class mail. These prizes are in addition to any free, surprise or mystery gifts that might be offered. Versions of this Sweepstakes with different prizes of approximate equal value may appear at retail outlets or in other mailings by Torstar Corp. and its affiliates.

4. PRIZES: (1) *Grand Prize $1,000,000.00 Annuity; (1) First Prize $25,000.00; (1) Second Prize $10,000.00; (5) Third Prize $5,000.00; (10) Fourth Prize $1,000.00; (100) Fifth Prize $250.00; (2,500) Sixth Prize $10.00; (6,000) **Seventh Prize $12.95 ARV.

   *This presentation offers a Grand Prize of a $1,000,000.00 annuity. Winner will receive $33,333.33 a year for 30 years without interest totalling $1,000,000.00.

   **Seventh Prize: A fully illustrated hardcover book, published by Torstar Corp. Approximate Retail Value of the book is $12.95.

   Entrants may cancel the Reader Service at any time without cost or obligation (see details in Center Insert Card).

5. Extra Bonus! This presentation offers an Extra Bonus Prize valued at $33,000.00 to be awarded in a random drawing from all qualified entries received by March 31, 1992. No purchase necessary to enter or receive a prize. To qualify, see instructions in Center Insert Card. Winner will have the choice of any of the merchandise offered or a $33,000.00 check payable in U.S. funds. All other published rules and regulations apply.

6. This Sweepstakes is being conducted under the supervision of D.L. Blair, Inc. By entering the Sweepstakes, each entrant accepts and agrees to be bound by these rules and the decisions of the judges, which shall be final and binding. Odds of winning the random drawing are dependent upon the number of entries received. Taxes, if any, are the sole responsibility of the winners. Prizes are nontransferable. All entries must be received at the address on the detachable Business Reply Card and must be postmarked no later than 12:00 MIDNIGHT on March 31, 1992. The drawing for all unclaimed Sweepstakes prizes and for the Extra Bonus Prize will take place on May 30, 1992, at 12:00 NOON at the offices of D.L. Blair, Inc., Blair, NE.

7. This offer is open to residents of the U.S., United Kingdom, France and Canada, 18 years or older, except employees and immediate family members of Torstar Corp., its affiliates, subsidiaries and all other agencies, entities and persons connected with the use, marketing or conduct of this Sweepstakes. All Federal, State, Provincial, Municipal and local laws apply. Void wherever prohibited or restricted by law. Any litigation within the Province of Quebec respecting the conduct and awarding of a prize in this publicity contest must be submitted to the Régie des Loteries et Courses du Québec.

8. Winners will be notified by mail and may be required to execute an affidavit of eligibility and release, which must be returned within 14 days after notification or an alternate winner may be selected. Canadian winners will be required to correctly answer an arithmetical, skill-testing question administered by mail, which must be returned within a limited time. Winners consent to the use of their name, photograph and/or likeness for advertising and publicity in conjunction with this and similar promotions without additional compensation.

9. For a list of our major prize winners, send a stamped, self-addressed envelope to: MILLION DOLLAR WINNERS LIST, P.O. Box 4510, Blair, NE 68009. Winners Lists will be supplied after the May 30, 1992 drawing date.

Offer limited to one per household.

LTY-H891

HARLEQUIN®
OFFICIAL SWEEPSTAKES
RULES

NO PURCHASE NECESSARY

1. To enter, complete an Official Entry Form or 3"× 5" index card by hand-printing, in plain block letters, your complete name, address, phone number and age, and mailing it to: Harlequin Fashion A Whole New You Sweepstakes, P.O. Box 621, Fort Erie, Ontario L2A 5X3.

   No responsibility is assumed for lost, late or misdirected mail. Entries must be sent separately with first class postage affixed, and be received no later than December 31, 1991 for eligibility.

2. Winners will be selected by D.L. Blair, Inc., an independent judging organization whose decisions are final, in random drawings to be held on January 30, 1992 in Blair, NE at 10:00 a.m. from among all eligible entries received.

3. The prizes to be awarded and their approximate retail values are as follows: Grand Prize — A brand-new Mercury Sable LS plus a trip for two (2) to Paris, including round-trip air transportation, six (6) nights hotel accommodation, a $1,400 meal/spending money stipend and $2,000 cash toward a new fashion wardrobe (approximate value: $28,000) or $15,000 cash; two (2) Second Prizes — A trip to Paris, including round-trip air transportation, six (6) nights hotel accommodation, a $1,400 meal/spending money stipend and $2,000 cash toward a new fashion wardrobe (approximate value: $11,000) or $5,000 cash; three (3) Third Prizes — $2,000 cash toward a new fashion wardrobe. All prizes are valued in U.S. currency. Travel award air transportation is from the commercial airport nearest winner's home. Travel is subject to space and accommodation availability, and must be completed by June 30, 1993. Sweepstakes offer is open to residents of the U.S. and Canada who are 21 years of age or older as of December 31, 1991, except residents of Puerto Rico, employees and immediate family members of Torstar Corp., its affiliates, subsidiaries, and all agencies, entities and persons connected with the use, marketing, or conduct of this sweepstakes. All federal, state, provincial, municipal and local laws apply. Offer void wherever prohibited by law. Taxes and/or duties, applicable registration and licensing fees, are the sole responsibility of the winners. Any litigation within the province of Quebec respecting the conduct and awarding of a prize may be submitted to the Régie des loteries et courses du Québec. All prizes will be awarded; winners will be notified by mail. No substitution of prizes is permitted.

4. Potential winners must sign and return any required Affidavit of Eligibility/Release of Liability within 30 days of notification. In the event of noncompliance within this time period, the prize may be awarded to an alternate winner. Any prize or prize notification returned as undeliverable may result in the awarding of that prize to an alternate winner. By acceptance of their prize, winners consent to use of their names, photographs or their likenesses for purposes of advertising, trade and promotion on behalf of Torstar Corp. without further compensation. Canadian winners must correctly answer a time-limited arithmetical question in order to be awarded a prize.

5. For a list of winners (available after 3/31/92), send a separate stamped, self-addressed envelope to: Harlequin Fashion A Whole New You Sweepstakes, P.O. Box 4694, Blair, NE 68009.

PREMIUM OFFER TERMS
To receive your gift, complete the Offer Certificate according to directions. Be certain to enclose the required number of "Fashion A Whole New You" proofs of product purchase (which are found on the last page of every specially marked "Fashion A Whole New You" Harlequin or Silhouette romance novel). Requests must be received no later than December 31, 1991. Limit: four (4) gifts per name, family, group, organization or address. Items depicted are for illustrative purposes only and may not be exactly as shown. Please allow 6 to 8 weeks for receipt of order. Offer good while quantities of gifts last. In the event an ordered gift is no longer available, you will receive a free, previously unpublished Harlequin or Silhouette book for every proof of purchase you have submitted with your request, plus a refund of the postage and handling charge you have included. Offer good in the U.S. and Canada only.   HOFC-SWPR

HARLEQUIN® OFFICIAL SWEEPSTAKES ENTRY FORM

4-FCARS-2

Complete and return this Entry Form immediately – the more entries you submit, the better your chances of winning!

- Entries must be received by **December 31, 1991.**
- A Random draw will take place on **January 30, 1992.**
- No purchase necessary.

Yes, I want to win a FASHION A WHOLE NEW YOU Classic and Romantic prize from Harlequin:

Name _____ Telephone _____ Age _____

Address _____

City _____ Province _____ Postal Code _____

Return Entries to: **Harlequin FASHION A WHOLE NEW YOU,**
P.O. Box 621, Fort Erie, Ontario L2A 5X3   © 1991 Harlequin Enterprises Limited

PREMIUM OFFER

To receive your free gift, send us the required number of proofs-of-purchase from any specially marked FASHION A WHOLE NEW YOU Harlequin or Silhouette Book with the Offer Certificate properly completed, plus a check or money order (do not send cash) to cover postage and handling payable to Harlequin FASHION A WHOLE NEW YOU Offer. We will send you the specified gift.

OFFER CERTIFICATE

Item	A. ROMANTIC COLLECTOR'S DOLL	B. CLASSIC PICTURE FRAME
	(Suggested Retail Price $60.00)	(Suggested Retail Price $25.00)
# of proofs-of-purchase	18	12
Postage and Handling	$4.00	$3.45
Check one	☐	☐

Name _____

Address _____

City _____ Province _____ Postal Code _____

Mail this certificate, designated number of proofs-of-purchase and check or money order for postage and handling to: **Harlequin FASHION A WHOLE NEW YOU Gift Offer,** P.O. Box 622, Fort Erie, Ontario L2A 5X3. Requests must be received by December 31, 1991.

ONE PROOF-OF-PURCHASE

4-FWCAR-2

To collect your fabulous free gift you must include the necessary number of proofs-of-purchase with a properly completed Offer Certificate.

© 1991 Harlequin Enterprises Limited

See previous page for details.